# A VERY SCOTTISH SCANDAL

## ANYA LONDON

# Chapter 1

*Hayes Icefall loathed Edinburgh.*

He despised the incessant rain and the stinging wind and the tourists who seemed to have tripled since his last, bitter visit.

Mostly he hated the memories.

The cab dropped him off at the George. He had no reservation at the historic hotel. Then again, he didn't plan to stay. Every square inch of this damn street set his skin crawling.

Stepping into the pelting rain, he glanced across George Street, where the Dome had been fully strung out for Christmas. It was barely mid-November.

The restaurant, its columns wrapped in thick ribbons of glittering lights, its balconies filled with Christmas trees and its windows decked with ribbon-topped wreaths, burned too bright for a random Wednesday.

The energy-guzzling light show boiled his eyeballs in their sockets, but it sliced through the dark, dreary evening and made it hard to look anywhere else.

He'd found the decorations charming once. The Dome had been lit up for the holidays too when he had proposed there all those years ago. Its glimmering ornaments had mocked him after Liselle turned him down.

Yanking the collar of his wool coat higher around

his throat, he spun away from the eye-cutting brightness of the restaurant and toward his quarry's hotel.

The rain and the wind whipped at him as he made his way toward the doorman.

He despised this weather.

*It fucking can't get any colder.*

And then it began to hail.

With a curse, he bounced through the door the kilt-wearing doorman had swung open for him.

Marching toward the correct wing, he ignored the concierge and the check-in desk and the staff's friendly greetings. He knew where he was going. Had no need for pleasantries. Taking the elevator to the seventh floor, he exited into a carpeted corridor. Three doors later, he reached his destination.

Curling his wind-numbed fingers into a fist, he knocked.

The TV inside went silent.

Clearly, the occupant didn't want visitors.

He knocked again. "Joy. It's me. Open the damn door."

The quiet stretched from three slow seconds to four, five…

Keeping his voice low, he continued. "I don't have all night. I know you're in there."

Her footsteps cut through the silence.

The scrape of a chair being dragged from the door made his fists clench. She had barricaded herself inside. He'd been correct. Someone had frightened her, and that someone would pay.

Joy undid the two locks and wedged the door open a mere inch. Her eye—the color of good Scottish whiskey and the only one he could see through the crack—narrowed. "What the hell are you doing here?"

Three years later, and she still made his heart thump wildly in his chest. A good reminder to stay the fuck away from her. "Let me in."

"Not on your life."

Joy Campbell continued to impress him. Even scared, she stood her ground.

But he didn't have all night—he had people to see. "I'm not having this conversation out in the hall."

"I'm not having any conversation with you, period," she grumbled, but she jerked the door open the rest of the way. "I told you I never wanted to see you again and you thought hunting me down was a good idea?"

Her hair had been tossed up in a messy knot, the dark tendrils falling around her pale face. The oversized, red plaid pajamas she wore hid most of her skin, but exposed enough of her throat for him to detect the bruises.

He reached for her. "He do this to you?"

When her breath caught and she sprang away, he froze. Fuck. He'd scared her. Snagging his hand back, he made himself stand still.

"Why are you here?" she pressed again.

"Your sister called me."

At the mention of Evie, Joy shook her head. "Don't two babies under two keep her occupied enough?"

But the explanation worked. With a sigh as deep as Loch Ness, she stepped back and let him inside.

Moving past her, he drew in the subtle scent of her— of sunlight and salt-kissed ocean air. That fragrance had haunted him for months after he'd walked away.

His eyes swept over the room: the unmade king-sized bed, the neatly stacked snacks on the nightstand, an electric kettle and cup of tea on the round table by the window. She'd clearly settled in for the night. "Your friends called her when you didn't show up at Heathrow."

Guilt flickered across her pale features. "I wasn't… ready to return Stateside yet."

"And disappearing was the way to go?"

"I didn't disappear." She shut the door. "I just… left London and didn't tell anyone."

He studied her rigid back. Tried not to remember the teasing trail of freckles sprinkled along her spine. He'd kissed those freckles long ago. "That doesn't sound like you."

Releasing the handle, she whirled on him. "Well, you don't know me, do you?"

There, she was wrong. He'd memorized her background when he'd needed access to her connection three years ago—and had kept close tabs on her since.

Ignoring her question, he asked one of his own. "Why Edinburgh?"

"How did you even find me?"

At this rate, they would be interrogating each other all night. He didn't have the time.

"You weren't hard to track down." He took in the shadows beneath her eyes, the worry lines etched deep between her brows. "Figured I'd come see in person what happened."

The fact that Edinburgh made him physically ill and he'd boarded the first flight anyway, he kept to himself.

She threw her arms out wide. "Well, as you can see, I'm fine. I wasn't ready to go back yet. Decided to see Scotland."

The telltale flush stealing up her discolored neck said otherwise.

"We both know that's a lie. He left those bruises on you."

Striding to the teakettle, she topped off the already brimming cup next to it. "Would you believe I fell?"

"No."

Lifting her cup and saucer, she took a sip of the steaming liquid.

He studied the marks along the delicate span of her throat. "Ryder Lewis did that."

The porcelain rattled in her hands before she slammed the set down, sloshing hot liquid across the table. "*How do you even know his name?* You had no right to pry—"

"Your ex shows up in London the day before you run to Scotland? I took a guess."

Retreating from the mess on the table, she readjusted the collar of her pajama top as though it would help conceal the bruises. "He is taking our breakup hard."

A sorry understatement. Hayes closed the distance between them in two strides. "He fucking choked you."

"He grabbed me. I kneed him. He'll be walking with a limp for weeks."

"He won't be walking at all after I find him," he muttered, lifting her dripping cup of tea and taking a gulp. The hot liquid burned its way to his stomach, but didn't quell the rage that seized him.

Moving to the bed, she straightened the covers. "He thinks I'm the reason he got fired—that I turned him in. I didn't even know he was stealing drugs from the hospital. The administrator only told me after he was let go. And yet he blames me. But I handled it."

"*Handled* it? You ran to fucking Scotland."

She raised a brow at his tone before tidying the pillows against the headboard. Her voice, when she responded, was much too amiable. "I like Scotland."

The exaggeratedly calm pitch made him itch to shake her. He shoved his hands deep into his coat pockets instead. "You never filed for a restraining order."

She glanced at him over her shoulder. "He's going through a lot."

Hayes hadn't battled his way through the Windy City to hear her make excuses for her ex. He held her gaze, daring her to disagree. "Drug addicts are unpredictable."

With one final tug on the edge of the duvet, she stepped back from the bed. "I don't need a restraining order. We just needed some space."

Was she delusional or scared? Most likely both. "He found you on your vacation in London."

Pacing to the window, she drew back the drapery and peered into the darkness beyond. "And now I'm in Edinburgh. He'll chill out, settle down. It's fine. I'm fine. One more week off, and I'll return to my residency."

The question had to be asked. "He hurt you when you were together?"

Releasing the curtain, she fixed him with clear, somber eyes. "No. I'd never have stayed if he did. Being fired changed him."

Hayes tempered his voice. "He spooked you."

"He surprised me."

He didn't buy it. But he knew she'd never admit weakness. He hadn't seen her in three years, but this bruised, bundled creature was a far cry from the Joy he remembered.

That Joy had shimmered with barely contained energy. From the moment they met at their siblings' wedding, he'd been consumed by the need to draw her close and taste the radiance in her smile. But now, wrapped in thick flannel, her skin pale as ice, she looked terrified. Even if she refused to admit it.

First thing tomorrow, he'd deal with Ryder.

But not tonight.

Tonight, he had a deal to close.

Her phone chirped on the table, and the screen lit up with her sister's face. He didn't mind Evie, but why his brother married her the second time around was beyond Hayes. They *seemed* happy, but how long could that last? He'd never seen Jackson more depressed than he was after their initial breakup. Why would he subject himself to the possibility of a repeat?

Lifting her phone to stop its incessant caterwauling, he extended it to her. "Tell Evie you're fine."

Guilt muddied her amber gaze before her eyelashes swept downward. "I should have called her earlier. She sent me a thousand texts." Careful not to touch him, she snatched her phone from his grip and answered the video call.

When his sister-in-law's face popped up on the screen and flooded with relief at seeing Joy, he took several steps away and texted the Blairs.

Tonight, their farm would be his.

"Thank God you're okay," Evie breathed on the other end of the video call. "What happened? Where'd you go?"

While waiting for the Blairs to respond to his message, he slanted a peek at Joy. Despite the tension knotting her slim frame, she smiled into the screen. The fake cheer on her face didn't fool him. He doubted it fooled Evie.

"I just needed another week away," she told her sister, sinking into a chair at the tea-splattered table. "Just me alone. The breakup, the residency, just… everything. I needed a pause. I'm fine. Hayes found me."

"I owe you big, Hayes," Evie called out to him.

"No, you don't." He didn't like favors, one way or the other.

Somewhere near Evie, a baby started to cry. He

heard his half-brother's voice assure his wife he'd get him. Poor bastard.

"How are the kids?" asked Joy, changing the subject.

"They want their aunt back, but I get it, you need time away. Just… stay in touch, okay? I had a hundred calls from Mom and Dad when they couldn't reach you either."

Joy winced. "I'm sorry. I didn't think. I'll call them right now."

Another child began to cry. Jackson and Evie's eldest, Elodie, all of two.

Evie called out to her daughter that she'd be right there, then redirected her attention back to Joy. "I have to go. I'm glad you're safe. Call Mom and Dad. And Hayes"—Joy pivoted the phone so that he could see Evie on the screen—"*thank you.*"

He didn't do gratitude. "Go. Your kid's squeals are blowing my eardrums."

She grinned. "Love you both. See you guys soon."

Joy ended the call. "I should call my parents." She turned the phone in her hands. "Thanks for stopping by. I'll see you in the States."

Refusing to be dismissed, he sank to the edge of her just-made bed just as the Blairs texted.

Disappointment weighed in his gut as he read their apologetic message. They had to return to the farm tonight, but would swing by the George to see him in the next half hour.

He'd spent days honing his argument against their absurd stipulation for the Highlander Honey Farm's next owner—an argument he couldn't deliver over a brief hello down in the lobby.

He rattled off a quick reply and returned his attention to Joy. "Call your parents. Then we'll go eat downstairs."

It's not like he could leave her up here, terrified and alone.

Her stubborn chin lifted. He'd never forgotten the dimple there… had skimmed his lips over the hollow just before the first time he'd kissed her.

"I already ate."

Forcing the memory aside, he checked his phone again. "I haven't."

She planted her hands on her hips, fingers digging into her hip bones in unmistakable frustration. "That's not my problem."

"Fine. Sit there while I eat." He didn't care what she did, so long as she was within his line of sight while he spoke to the Blairs.

"Go away, Hayes."

Forcing her to do something was the equivalent of herding an uncooperative clowder of cats. He might have found it amusing at any other time. But not now. Not with the only place that ever felt like home hanging in the balance.

His gaze flicked to his watch. "I don't have all night."

He knew he fucked up the moment he said the words. Joy didn't take to directives.

Marching to the door, she swung it open and waved a dramatic hand toward the corridor. "Well then, don't let me stop you. You've overstayed your welcome anyway."

He wasn't about to waste time on an argument. "It's just dinner, Joy."

"You think I'd eat with you like nothing ever happened? Are you delusional? Don't make me call hotel security."

He knew of one way to get her to leave her room. "Fine. We'll have the food brought here. Make it a nice and… cozy evening."

Predictably, the thought repulsed her. She scrunched up her nose. "If you want to wear that food in your lap."

"I'd like you in my lap."

Her glare could have refrozen the polar ice caps. "The only thing you like in your lap is your stacks of cash. Goodbye, Hayes."

He settled more comfortably on the bed. "Come closer and I'll prove to you otherwise."

"You're an asshole." But she shut the door. "If I go downstairs with you, will you leave me alone afterward?"

With Ryder Lewis prowling after her? Not a chance in hell. "I'd be more amenable to discussing it after dinner."

Her eyes narrowed. "Fine. But eat *fast*. We'll go after I call my parents."

He kept his face carefully blank. If she detected even a hint of satisfaction there, she would never budge, and the Blairs were already en route.

One chance to convince them to lift their ridiculous mandate, and the farm would be his.

# Chapter 2

Even while speaking to her parents on video, even detesting Hayes with every fiber of her being, Joy Campbell couldn't keep her eyes from straying to him.

Tall, broad shouldered, with a military-straight posture, impossible blue eyes, and closely cropped dark hair, he was every girl's wet dream.

She'd never admit it, but she'd almost wept with relief at hearing his voice through her hotel door. Had almost leaped into his arms when she saw him. Thankfully she'd remembered in time that he was a selfish liar. The memory of their last time together—the way he'd walked out—still stung.

He was nothing but a pretty predator—best admired from afar.

Why was he in Edinburgh?

How did he find her?

What made Evie call *him* of all people?

Then again, her sister didn't know what had happened between them, what he'd done.

And given his connections, if anyone needed finding, Hayes was always everyone's first call.

She should have anticipated that, but she hadn't been thinking straight. When Ryder had showed up at her London hotel on her last night there, she freaked. How could she keep her flight back to San Diego? He knew exactly where she lived—had gone there and pumped soap into her goldfish tank after she'd broken it off.

Instead, she went to Scotland—he'd have no way of finding her here. Maybe he'd simmer down by the time her vacation ended.

She should have told Evie. Or her parents.

Then they wouldn't have sicced Hayes on her.

The bastard. How dare he waltz into her hotel room as though that night never happened? She'd been on her knees with his dick in her mouth and *he walked away*. Joy didn't know why she found *that* the most contemptuous part of what he'd done to her, but she did.

Mentally shaking past embarrassment from her system, she refocused her attention on the video call. After assuring her parents that she was fine and about to have dinner with Hayes, she ended the FaceTime and strode to the closet.

"I'll be ready in five." The sooner she got dinner over with, the sooner he'd leave her alone.

He remained seated as she pulled jeans and a lavender sweater off the hangers. Despite the heat blasting inside the hotel room, he had kept his long coat on. Funny, she never thought of him as being easily chilled.

His voice dropped to a velvet invitation. "Come here and I'll give you a hand."

*The ass!* Had he forgotten how he'd played her three years ago? She'd been halfway in love with him when she'd learned the truth. He'd performed the role of boyfriend, but he never wanted her—just access to one of her connections. Once he'd landed that meeting, he moved on.

"You lost your *hand* privileges a long time ago."

Not giving him the opportunity to offer a lewd retort, she stomped to the bathroom—and slammed the door shut.

When she reemerged two minutes later, fully dressed, he met her at the threshold. His gaze traveled the length of her. She tried to ignore his perusal, but unbidden heat sparked low in her belly regardless.

"I love speed in a woman."

Smug son of a bitch.

Striding past him, she pulled on her thigh-high boots. "Is that why you go through your girlfriends so fast?"

His cool smile taunted her. "I've yet to find one to hold my interest."

Declining to continue the conversation, she retrieved her purse from the row of wall hooks and preceded him into the hall.

They rode the elevator in silence.

Stepped into the lobby that way too.

Hayes had always been taciturn. A man comfortable with silence.

She detested it. If silence stretched even for a few seconds, Joy sought to fill it. Their wordless walk to the hotel restaurant had gored her, but she kept her mouth shut. They hadn't spoken in years, and she wasn't about to gab now. If Hayes wanted to remain mute, let him. She would too. She hadn't wanted to join him for dinner anyway.

She'd tried eating at the restaurant earlier that evening, hoping the din of the packed diners would make her feel less scared and alone, but was told they were booked solid until next week.

Yet the maître d' greeted Hayes by name and

showed them to a secluded table in the crowded restaurant, pulling out her chair and helping with her napkin. After Hayes shrugged out of his charcoal coat, the maître d' took it with him and left them alone at the candlelit table.

Hayes snapped open the leather-bound menu, acting like she wasn't there.

What delightful company. If anyone looked their way, they'd think she was on the most awkward date ever.

Joy eyed the crowded restaurant. Hayes must have bribed someone to get a table this fast. "How'd you get reservations?"

As he readjusted in his seat, the skin around his eyes tightened with… pain? Discomfort? The rare flash of vulnerability passed quickly. Had she imagined it?

The impervious Hayes slipped back into place. "I don't need reservations."

How could she have once found his arrogance charming? He was an asshole. She'd been too blinded by his broad shoulders and six-foot-plus frame to see it before.

"Why are you even in Scotland?"

Disregarding her question, he waved over the waiter and rattled off a meat dish before glancing at her. "You want the cauliflower steak or the salmon?"

Surprised that he remembered she wasn't much of a meat eater, she pried open her own menu and considered her options. "The cauliflower please," she told the waiter. "And the mashed potatoes."

After Hayes added a bottle of red to the order, the waiter poured their water and slid away.

She studied the expensive-looking suit that hugged

Hayes's strong shoulders and the tie that must have cost as much as her monthly salary. "Did your detour here interrupt something?"

"No," he clipped out, but the rigid set of his jaw said otherwise.

"Then why are you dressed up?"

He surveyed his suit with detachment, as though she was overreacting to his everyday wardrobe. "Had somewhere to be."

Except she knew him—he opted for comfortable and obscenely expensive casuals. Outside of weddings, she'd only seen him in a suit once—at the gala that had ended them.

"A date?" *Ugh, nice going, Joy. Why did you have to ask* that? She reached for a glass of water to hide her burning face.

Hayes disregarded her sudden awkwardness. Maybe he didn't notice. "Business meeting."

"In Scotland?" She didn't know why that surprised her. Hayes tended to flit about from place to place.

"Back in the States."

*The States?* The suit screamed expensive, but even bespoke tailoring couldn't survive an international flight without wrinkling. Now that she looked closer, she noticed the creases that spoke to hours of wear.

"You run out of clothes or something? Who flies in a suit?"

He picked up his phone, checking for messages before setting it back down on the pristine white tablecloth. "Didn't have time to change."

That made no sense… unless…

"Wait. You went to the airport straight from your meeting? Why?"

His eyes swept across the restaurant before meeting hers. "Jackson and Evie asked me to check up on you. Flights to the UK don't leave every hour. I was late. My assistant packed for me so I could go to the airport directly."

"Oh." *That*, she hadn't expected. He'd rushed to Scotland to make sure she was okay. If he hadn't shattered her heart three years ago, she might have found it sweet.

Hayes shifted in his chair, and there it was again— that flicker of pain. She *hadn't* imagined it. What had caused it? Was Mr. Centimillionaire stiff from slumming the long haul in coach? Unlikely. He'd never settle for anything less than a private first-class cabin. No, he'd injured himself… but how and when?

Before she could ask him, the waiter brought their wine and poured a tasting. Hayes indicated that Joy should try it.

"I don't really know wine that well," she said with an apologetic smile to the waiter.

Hayes cut in before the waiter could answer. "If you like it, we'll drink it."

She liked it. Knowing Hayes, it probably cost more than her rent. The waiter filled their glasses and left the bottle on the table.

Instead of reaching for his glass, he studied her, his mental gears working loud enough for her to almost hear them. She was about to ask him what his problem was, but he spoke first. "You going to hide in your room the entire week?"

*Who the hell does he think he is?* "I'm not hiding."

His brow lifted in challenge. "You had barricaded yourself inside with a chair."

"A precaution. I'm a single girl alone in a very large hotel. Never know if perverts are stalking the hallways."

Although his phone on the table stayed silent—Hayes didn't do noise—the screen lit up with an incoming text.

Dragging the device closer, Hayes read the message.

When he lifted his head, his stormy eyes pinned hers. "Stay here. Don't leave. I'll be back in five." Rising, he circled to her side of the table and leaned close enough for her pulse to stutter. "I repeat. Don't move from this table."

Without waiting for a response, he slipped out of the restaurant into the adjoining hotel lobby.

He really was odd…

A good quarter hour passed, and he hadn't returned. Another handful of minutes clattered by.

Joy checked her watch again. Where did he go? Craning her neck, she attempted to see through the exit that connected to the lobby, but the angle made it impossible.

Their dishes arrived—his meat, her cauliflower—and still Hayes hadn't returned.

The waiter topped off her wine glass, asked about her companion.

"He'll be back in a few," she assured him, though her annoyance grew.

*First, he drags me out of my hotel room and my cozies, and now he leaves me to dine alone? Where the hell can he be?*

Twisting to look for him yet again and still finding no sign of him, she made her decision.

"I'll be back in two minutes," she told the hovering waiter. "Watch our table for a minute?"

Taking her purse, she set off to find Hayes.

Who did he think he was? Just because he thought

himself king of the world didn't mean he could treat her like crap. Her time mattered too. She wasn't about to let him waste it.

He wasn't hard to spot in the lobby. Not only did he tower over most of the people there, he also filled out his suit sinfully well. Not that it mattered. She wasn't looking.

Broad shoulders hunched over, he spoke to a shorter man and an even shorter woman around her parents' age, both in warm coats.

The man was beginning to bald, but a thick white beard framed his ruddy face. He had his arm caped around the petite woman next to him and gazed down at her with unmistakable adoration. His beautiful companion had swept her blonde hair back in a bun. As she spoke, she emphasized her sentences with wide gestures.

Hayes listened, but his usual swagger had fled. Body rigid with unexpected tension, he said something to the couple, but even his lips were drained of color.

Who were these people and how had they managed to shatter his unflappable demeanor? Maybe she could learn a lesson or two.

Disinclined to interrupt despite her curiosity, she turned back for the restaurant.

"There's Joy."

The woman's voice reached her across the lobby. How did she know her name?

The voice grew louder. "Joy, don't run away! Come say hello. We've been hogging Hayes for far too long."

Joy paused, unsure whether to acknowledge the comment.

"Joy," Hayes called out before she could deliberate further, a thread of irascibility in his tone. "Come meet my friends."

*Friends? He has friends in Scotland? He has friends anywhere?*

Turning, she met Hayes's eyes that simmered with warning.

Approaching them was the last thing she wanted to do, but dashing away now would be rude, and her parents had raised her with manners. Unclenching her jaw, she made herself cross to Hayes and his companions.

When she reached them, she smiled brightly and extended her hand. But before either one of the pair could shake it, Hayes wrapped his arm around her waist and pulled her into his side. She yelped in surprise.

*What in the world?*

She stopped herself from stomping on his foot and leaping away.

"Joy." Hayes tightened his grip around her waist in an unmistakable threat. "This is Callan and Maisie Blair. Cal, Maisie, this is Joy. My wife."

# Chapter 3

His *what*?

Before she could call out Hayes's lie, Cal grabbed her hand—the one she still held awkwardly extended—and enveloped it in a sandpapery grasp. "Pleased to meet you, Joy. Hayes was just telling us how he's in town with his new wife—showed off your picture. Shame we missed you both earlier, but we were with our nephew all day and now we've got to drive back. Glad we can have a chat."

*What new wife?*

Maisie's rosy cheeks lifted as her smile widened. "It's brilliant to meet the woman who finally got this one to settle down. And Hayes said you two eloped? How romantic, though I do wish we could have seen our Hayes get married—bet your folks feel the same way."

*The bastard.*

He was using her for another one of his schemes…

Did it never stop with him?

Was *this* why he came to Scotland?

She strained away from him, ready to claw her way out of his hold.

Yet when she glanced into Hayes's eyes, the rage in her faltered. She'd seen annoyance there before, arrogance, flirtatiousness, but never once this undercurrent of helplessness.

It came and went before she could, now that she'd

recognized it, chew on it, but it had been there, and she had noticed.

Unsure of how to proceed, but refusing to allow any part of him to touch any part of her, she stepped away from Hayes. "A pleasure to meet you both. I didn't mean to interrupt. Our food arrived, so I came to see where Hayes went."

"You should head back." Hayes kept his tone casual, as though the Blairs had interrupted an easy dinner and not a battle about to be waged. "I'll be right there. Cal and Maisie were kind enough to swing by our hotel before their drive back home."

"We couldn't miss your husband on our brief trip to Edinburgh," explained Maisie. "It's been far too long."

She had to tell them he was lying—that he wanted something from them—but how? The silent despair she'd seen in Hayes's gaze had paralyzed her.

Hating herself for playing along even for a moment, Joy plastered on a bright smile she hoped looked authentic and tried to extricate herself from the situation. "I'll leave you to it, then. Have a nice evening."

Maybe if she stepped away for a bit, she could untangle her thoughts and find the right words to tell them the truth.

Maisie waved off her goodbye as gently as one would a ladybug. "No, no, stay a minute. We're almost done. We were just inviting your husband and you to join us on our farm in the Highlands starting Friday. Our nephew, Gene, is in town with his new wife. They're also keen on the farm. Since it's Cal's birthday on Wednesday, we thought why not gather all our favorite folk and celebrate?"

"You can have a look at our operations, meet the other prospective buyers, see what we've done with your husband's barn," Cal added.

*What operations? What buyers? What barn?*

Joy waited for Hayes to decline.

"We'd love to join you," he offered instead.

Like a fool, she waited for the *but*. It never came.

*He isn't serious.*

"It's settled then." Maisie beamed. "We'll see you the day after next. I can't wait to get to know you better, Joy. Hayes has been like a second son to us, and we already feel like we've gained a new daughter-in-law."

*What did Hayes do?*

Unsure of what to say, Joy smiled until her jaw hurt.

"Thanks for stopping by." Hayes heartily embraced Cal and Maisie.

Was she in some sort of nightmare? Maybe she was still asleep in her room, and Hayes and the Blairs were only figments of her imagination? Because the Hayes she knew didn't willingly hug people.

Reaching for her own wrist, she pinched the skin. *Ow.* That hurt. Definitely not a bad dream.

"What a coincidence you've met Gene's wife before." Maisie winked at Hayes. "You'll have to tell us more about her later."

"Never thought Gene would go for an older lassie," Cal said next to her.

Maisie shrugged. "She's not that much older—she's thirty-six. Hayes's age."

"Gene's only twenty-five," her husband pointed out.

As the Blairs left the hotel, Joy offered a weak goodbye and a wave, confusion and disbelief swirling.

Hayes had lied to the people who considered him a son and now was dragging her, his supposed wife, to the Highlands the day after tomorrow?

She wouldn't get trapped in his manipulations.

She'd learned her lesson the last time. Her participation had been inadvertent then. She would be an accomplice now.

No way in hell would she go along with it.

If only she'd told the Blairs the truth right away.

She and Hayes weren't married.

They could barely stand each other.

Hayes turned for the restaurant. "I'm hungry. My steak's cold by now."

Joy had two choices: stand in the lobby and gape, or follow him. With an exasperated rumble, she followed.

***

Hayes focused on breathing. Four counts in… eight counts out. It didn't help.

Cal and Maisie's casual mention of Gene's bride had blindsided him. For a man who anticipated market shifts three steps ahead, he hadn't expected this.

That conniving bitch had married the Blairs' nephew.

Their nephew, who'd never shown interest in the farm before, but now intended to buy it.

Hayes could smell Liselle's scheming from a mile away. She'd lurked around him like a chronic illness for years. Today, she struck, coming for his sanctuary—and the people he held most dear.

He'd burn the farm to the ground himself before he'd let her have as much as an acre of what the Blairs had built. He'd never let anyone hurt them. Even if it meant lying to protect them.

Reaching their table, he pulled out Joy's chair with unsteady hands before taking his own across from her.

How quickly the evening had turned.

He should have told Cal and Maisie that the woman who'd married their nephew was the same one who'd left him for dead in Edinburgh. But the words hadn't come to him in time.

How had she heard about the farm sale anyway? Where the fuck had she dug up Gene?

As soon as the Blairs mentioned her name, his mapped-out argument against the Blairs' stipulation went out the window.

Instead, somehow, he invented a nonexistent spouse.

He focused his attention on the woman across from him. The woman he'd introduced as his wife, who now vibrated in her chair, arms crossed and teeth bared.

He could make her excuses and go to the farm solo—except he wasn't about to let her prance around Scotland while her deranged ex hunted for her.

No, she'd go with him. Play the role of good little wife until Highlander Honey belonged to him.

Good thing he knew exactly how to get her to cooperate.

# Chapter 4

"What the hell was that?" demanded Joy, nearly convulsing with anger. "Why did you tell them we're married?"

His gaze remained locked on hers, but the seething rage she'd glimpsed just seconds earlier dissipated, replaced by a cool resolve. What was he up to now?

"The Blairs are selling their bee farm, Highlander Honey." He picked up his steak knife. "They'll only consider selling to a married couple, one intent on holding on to the farm for several generations."

Hayes Icefall hadn't changed.

"*So, you lied to them?*" The question thundered through the restaurant.

The couple next to them—not even bothering to play it cool—looked at her with rapt curiosity.

Counting out three beats, she waited for them to return to their own conversation and moderated her voice. "You used me to lie to someone again?"

Not a twitch of remorse flashed across his too-handsome face. "If I were single, I'd be out of the running."

"You are single," she pointed out, her hands clenching around the edge of the tablecloth-covered table between them.

He slid his knife into the steak, sliced off a thick sliver. "I'll get married. Eventually. Maybe. Doesn't matter." Slipping the chunk into his mouth, he barely chewed before swallowing. "I want their farm."

"I'm not pretending to be married to you. They seem like a nice couple. I won't lie to them."

The tension in his body eased, and he reached for his wine with loose-limbed swagger. "Not a problem. We'll pack you up, get you on the first flight to Evie and Jackson's, and I'll go alone."

She stabbed into her cauliflower. "I'm not leaving Edinburgh until my vacation is over, and I won't bring my crazy ex to Evie and Jackson's. They have two babies—they've got enough problems."

The annoyance radiating from him hit her stronger than the heat from the nearby fireplace. She could almost hear him grit his teeth.

"I'm not leaving you to deal with Ryder alone." He forked another piece of steak into his mouth.

Her own frustration crested. How dare he dictate to her as though she were a child, unable to make her own decisions?

"Ryder isn't here," she pointed out, pleased that her voice remained steady when all she wanted to do was scream at a pitch that would shatter the panes of historic glass around them.

His hand on the steak knife tightened. "You were easy enough to track down."

"Not everyone has your resources. How *do* you find out so much so fast?"

His shrug was dismissive. "Pays to know people."

She leaned across the table to emphasize her point. "Ryder is my problem. Not yours."

He set down his silverware. "He became my problem when he laid his hands on you. If you don't want to go to Jackson and Evie's, you're coming with me to the Blairs' farm."

Even as she sank back against her chair, she held his gaze, willing him to blink first. "No, I'm not."

Mimicking the angle of her body, he sat back against his chair, too, and considered her across the table. "I'll pay you."

"I'm not for sale."

The asshole looked like he didn't believe her. He sliced off another thick piece of meat. "Evie paid for your medical school. You feel you owe her. You've been taking extra shifts to earn additional money so you can save up, pay her back. I'll pay her back on your behalf— for six days of your time."

She should have been offended, but the offer amused her. Hayes really did think he could purchase anyone. "You can't buy me, Hayes. I'll pay her back from the money I myself will earn. I don't need cash from you. And she doesn't expect it anyways, so it's not like there's a deadline."

The refusal appeared to surprise him. Did not a lot of people turn down his bribes?

She could see him recalculating.

"I donate to a lot of hospitals and medical facilities." He swirled the red wine in its glass. "When you're done with your residency next year, I could make introductions to the hospital of your dreams."

"I'll get hired at the hospital of my dreams on my own merit, so no, thanks. You're on your own here. I won't lie to that nice couple for you."

Finally, he took a sip of the blood-red liquid. "What about the Delices?"

# Chapter 5

*How does he know about the Delices?*

How far did his connections reach?

She'd been moonlighting in the NICU and had gotten to know the Delices well through her shifts. Their baby had been born much too premature, and needed very complicated, very expensive surgeries.

Her heart ached for them. But she hadn't shared anything about the Delices and their baby with anyone outside of her immediate friends' group.

With a trembling hand, she took a gulp of her own wine. "What about them?"

Blatant triumph inched up the corner of his mouth. "Their kid has been in the NICU for weeks. They've got no insurance. The bills are piling up. Their GoFundMe won't knock out a fraction of it. I'll cover the entirety of their hospital bills."

The bastard had learned her weakness and intended to exploit it.

She set down the wine before he could notice her discomposure. "Just like that?"

His white teeth gleamed. He knew he had her. "If you cooperate. The kid will need at least another heart surgery, and probably more procedures moving forward, more medicine. They are hourly workers—they already took too much time off, and they got two kids at home. Their other bills are snowballing. I'll cover it all. Whatever they need. A few days of your time, and you'll change the Delices' lives."

Hayes really would be changing their lives…

If she lied to the Blairs and went along with his plan to buy their farm under false pretenses.

It was an impossible choice.

No longer hungry, she pushed away her food. "How do you know so much about my life?"

His shoulders rose and fell in casual disregard. "I make it a point to keep an eye on people."

"I really, really hate you."

If feelings could kill, he'd be dropping dead to the ground right now, but not even a muscle twitched in his beautiful face.

Her feelings about him clearly meant squat to him. His only passion in life was raking in more money, more properties, more *things*.

Hayes had made his gazillion-dollar fortune years ago, when a major Department of Defense contractor acquired his company for something insane, like a hundred million dollars, with the stipulation that he stay on a while. She deduced his covert network of sources came from his time there.

More recently, just before he launched the Auclair-Icefall Hospitality Group with Jackson, he'd sold his startup, Poinsettia, to a digital health company for a chunk of change too.

What would he do with a honey farm, anyway?

He'd never fill the empty abyss inside him, no matter how many properties he acquired. Taking heart in the fact that he'd never be happy, she let the ridiculous idea of accepting his offer take root.

As much as she wanted to rail and insult and storm away, the Delices needed help. Less than a week of her time, and she'd be able to make a transformative difference.

She suspected that Hayes knew she'd never be able to turn down his offer. The bastard all but gloated from across the table.

Why did Evie have to marry his brother? If she hadn't, then Joy would have never met Hayes and her life would have been much simpler. And yet their paths had become forever intertwined because of their siblings.

They'd done an effective job of avoiding each other at family gatherings so far, but how could she bear to see him at her niece or nephew's future birthdays and act as though he'd never coerced her into lying? Every time she'd lay eyes on him from now on, she'd always remember that he had used her not once, but twice.

Straightening her back, she lifted her chin for more height. "Only until Wednesday, and that's it. And then I never want you near me again. Not at any of the holiday gatherings, or the kids' parties. Nowhere."

The counteroffer didn't appear to faze him. He tilted his head in assent. "Pretend to be my wife until Wednesday, and then you'll never see me again."

That deal she could take. "All right. But you cover the Delices' bills upfront."

Lifting his wine, he studied her over the rim of the glass. "You don't trust me to keep my word?"

"All you've ever done is lie to me." Appetite gone for good, she stood. "I'll see you on Friday."

He rose to his feet. "Like hell. I'm with you until we leave for the farm."

"I'd rather Ryder find me than be anywhere near you." Grabbing her purse, she hightailed it out of the restaurant, dodging a slow-moving waiter carrying a trayful of drinks.

To her annoyance, Hayes caught up to her before she reached the lobby. His warm breath washed over the shell of her ear as he leaned close.

"Like it or not, I'm not letting Ryder put his hands on you again."

She whirled on him, stabbed a finger into his unyielding chest. "What you're doing is so much worse. You're making me lie to a couple who doesn't deserve it."

Snatching her hand back, she fought not to remember what his pecs had felt like under her fingertips, back when she'd thought he actually liked her.

His brows drew together. "I know the Blairs well. I would never do anything to hurt either one of them. No one will care for their farm better than me. I'd never destroy their legacy, but another buyer might."

More lies. It never ended with him. "You don't know anything about apiculture."

Not even a shadow of concern crossed his features. "How hard could it be?"

It was like arguing with a stubborn five-year-old. "You'll move to Scotland to become a beekeeper?"

"I'll keep on their staff. Operations will continue as normal."

"Why do you want their farm so badly?" she asked, genuinely curious now. It seemed so far-fetched for him.

His mask of impassivity splintered open long enough for her to glimpse the helplessness from earlier in his shadowed eyes. It mixed with another emotion she couldn't name. Before she could pinpoint the exact sentiment, the walls came back up. He was hiding something—but what?

"I like the honey," he offered in a tone of practiced indifference.

Shaking her head, she resumed her path out of the restaurant. "I don't believe you."

Like a respiratory illness, he followed. "The Blairs and I go way back."

"And yet you're still betraying their trust."

"Requiring that the new owner have a family is ludicrous."

They passed through the crowded lobby and stepped into the hallway that would take them to their elevator bank.

At the elevator, Joy studied the cream-colored carpet before forcing herself to meet his gaze. "I hate you for making me do this."

His eyes remained cool, unaffected, like the deepest reaches of the Pacific. "I know. But by Wednesday, I'll have my farm, the Delices will have all the resources at their disposal to make their child healthy, and you and I can deal with Ryder and never see each other again."

"Stay away from me until we leave for the farm then."

He pressed the elevator call button. "You know I can't do that. Evie asked me to keep you safe."

"I'm going sightseeing tomorrow. No one will bother me in a crowded city full of people. You crawl back to whatever cave you emerged from until Friday. And use tomorrow to pay the Delices' hospital bills."

"I'll cover their bills tonight. But until Ryder is found, consider me your personal bodyguard."

*Personal bodyguard?* He'd lied and used her three years ago—and was now doing so again. She needed a personal bodyguard to shield her *from him.*

The man was like a dog with a bone, though. Now that Evie had sent him to watch her, he wouldn't back down. Arguing about it in the lobby would do no good. Arguing about it in the hotel room would do no good either. Hayes was stubborn and goal-oriented. He'd stick to her like a shadow—she'd never get him to change his mind.

She *could* drag him with her to see Edinburgh tomorrow. Not that she was scared to go alone. She wasn't. But if Ryder had tracked her to Scotland, he might accost her again. She'd escaped his chokehold last time. Had gotten him good in the balls. But what if he intended to do worse this time around? Hayes was big and scary. It might not be a bad idea to keep him around while she explored.

Besides, he'd told her once before how much he hated Edinburgh. It would serve him right to be forced to spend some time here.

"Fine. But we go to see Edinburgh Castle and the Royal Mile. And the Witches' Well. And we sample whiskey. *And* we see Victoria Street, and whatever else I want to do while here."

"You want to play tourist?"

The dread on his face made her inwardly grin. "Yes."

He considered her. "Fine. You can have a day in Edinburgh, before we go on to the Highlands on Friday."

The elevator doors pinged open, and a gaggle of guests filed out. Only when Hayes followed her into the now-empty elevator did she realize his intention.

"Uh-uh. You're not coming up with me," she told him, crossing her arms for emphasis.

He reached around her and selected her floor. "You

have a stalker who trailed you to the UK. I'm spending the night."

"I've got one bed."

"Didn't bother you before."

"You're an asshole. Get your own room, or sleep in the lobby." When the doors opened and Hayes trailed her into the hall, she almost screamed. "The only stalker I have right now is you."

"I promised your sister I'd bring you back home safe and sound. I intend to do just that. I'll sleep on the floor."

It's not like she'd let him cuddle up with her. "Where's your luggage?"

"Airline sent it to the wrong place. Should be delivered here shortly."

"Hope it's lost forever," she noted pettily.

As they reached her hotel room, she searched her purse for her keycard.

Before she could tag the key to the sensor, Hayes took it from her. "That night of the fundraiser? I wanted to stay."

*He just had to go there, didn't he?* Couldn't they just pretend that night never happened?

She made herself face him. "And yet you didn't."

"You'd have despised me much more if I did." Using her keycard, he unlocked the door and held it open for her, following her inside.

"You used me to get to the keynote speaker. When you met him, you no longer needed me."

The heavy door shut with a decisive click, sequestering her in a room with the man who broke her heart.

Hayes's hands flexed at his sides. "I can still feel the weight of your breasts in my palms, the heat of your mouth around my—"

"Shut up," she groaned, kicking off her boots. "I don't ever want to think about that. You walked away. I'm going to shower. You can make your bed on the floor. In that corner. As far away from me as possible."

"Joy, wait—"

"*Enough, Hayes*. Just. Enough. You used me before, and you're doing so again. Only now you've made me an accomplice, making me no better than you." Turning on her heel, she went to shower—since the bathroom was the only hideaway she had left.

Running the water to let it heat, she stared at herself in the bathroom mirror. Frustration had knotted her brows together. She forced herself to relax her forehead. Hayes had caused her enough grief—she wouldn't let him give her wrinkles to boot.

Lying was wrong; she knew that. Her father was a pastor, after all. The idea of lying to Cal and Maisie, who both seemed so genuine and kind, ate away at her as she shed her clothes.

Stepping into the shower, she let the water drum over her aching temples.

Deceit stood against everything she believed in, yet a few days of pretending to be Hayes's wife would give the Delices' baby a fighting chance.

But she wouldn't let him manipulate the Blairs into selling him their farm. He never stipulated the actual acquisition of the bee farm in their arrangement anyway. Her deal with Hayes only extended to their pretend marriage. She could work with that.

It was time to use Hayes just like he was using her. Get the Delices their funds and make sure the farm went to the person who deserved it most.

Feeling calmer, she emerged from the steam-filled

bathroom in her pajamas—which she'd wisely left there when changing earlier—and spotted Hayes's immaculate makeshift pallet arranged between her bed and the window. He must have made it out of the spare sheets, blanket, and pillow from the closet, because he hadn't borrowed anything off her own king-sized bed. She wanted to kick the resourceful sleeping arrangement.

He sat at her table and worked off his iPad.

Ignoring him as best she could, she hung up her jeans and sweater in the closet.

"You're the only person I know besides me who hangs up their jeans," he said without glancing up from his tablet.

She didn't bother to respond. Skirting around him, she flipped on the electric kettle. While she waited for the water to boil, she spied the remote on the table. Lifting it, she flipped on the television for some background noise.

*Tap, tap, tap.*

She yelped. The remote dropped from her hands and clattered to the floor, the battery compartment splitting open. Batteries flew one way, the compartment cover the other. Kneeling, she hunted out the two AAs that rolled under the bed.

"I'm never this jumpy," she grumbled, shoving the batteries into the compartment they'd escaped.

Hayes was too close, too fast. She had to bite her tongue not to yelp again. *Ryder's fault.* She focused her attention on the batteries so he wouldn't see how on edge she was after all.

He scooped up the cover from the floor, handing it to her. "Understandable. He killed your fish."

*Where had he learned that?* She hadn't even told Evie.

Standing, she snapped the cover back in place and tossed the remote to her bed. "Is there anything you don't know?"

He ignored the question, making his way to the door and swinging it open. Although his looming presence in the doorway blocked her from seeing their visitor, Hayes eventually shifted enough out of the way to reveal the hotel attendant who brought up his suitcase. Taking the luggage, Hayes handed over several bills as tip and the attendant left.

Only then did he face her. A petty part of her wished his suitcase had never been found. But this was Hayes. People moved mountains for him.

"How did you know about the goldfish?" she demanded, refusing to let him move past the topic.

Leaving his luggage where it was, he stalked back to his seat at the table. "You don't spook easily. I looked into what he had done back in California to make you leave your friends and run as soon as you saw him again."

"I didn't run. I extended my vacation."

He raised a dubious brow, but didn't argue.

"And I never told anyone about the fish… well, except for my best friend."

Inconsolable after seeing their poor, dead bodies, she'd called Stacy, sobbing so violently she couldn't string together a coherent sentence.

"She was worried about you."

He wouldn't have…

The realization that he most certainly *would* squeezed out any lingering warmth from her shower. *"You found Stacy?"*

Focused on his iPad once more, he didn't bother to look up. "I called her."

Stacy was too pregnant to join her for the UK trip, but she lived in Seattle and even Evie didn't have her contact information. "How did you get her number?"

He gave her a pointed look, but didn't elaborate.

"I'm beginning to think I have two stalkers—and I've let one into my hotel room."

"You loved your goldfish," he said matter-of-factly.

She'd raised those fish for years—they were more than pets to her.

*"Did you tell Evie?"*

Setting aside his tablet, he stood. "Of course not. She'd flip out and insist on coming with me to find you. And she'd have dragged the baby." The last sentence was punctuated with an exaggerated shudder.

An international flight next to a screaming infant would have served him right.

"Get out of my room, Hayes."

He stretched, and she fought hard not to stare at the flex of muscle—distinct even under all his layers. "It's our room now. Going to grab a shower."

She eyed his luggage. The one his assistant had packed. "Why'd you bring such a large suitcase? You don't seem like a wait-at-the-carousel type."

He kneeled next to his bag. "Extra layers."

Before she could ask a follow-up, he withdrew a toiletries case and immaculately folded flannel pajamas and disappeared into the bathroom. Dismissing her.

Asshole.

The kettle boiled, and Joy made herself a cup of tea. Maybe the chamomile would soothe her nerves. Taking the steaming liquid with her, she perched on top of her bed and set the cup on the nightstand.

She should have told Evie she was staying in the UK

longer. Then Evie wouldn't have sent her guard dog of a brother-in-law after her. Her very grating brother-in-law. Sure, he was attractive. But she preferred her eye candy to not be a pathological liar.

As she sipped her tea, she tried to ignore the sounds of Hayes showering through the bathroom wall. But her traitorous brain visualized him there regardless—steam curling around his wide shoulders, rivulets coursing down the soapy ridges of his abdomen.

To give herself a fighting chance, she grabbed the remote, picked a random television station, and cranked up the volume. But when the water in the shower shut off, her imagination won yet again, and she pictured him in all his naked glory, skimming a towel across his damp skin. She shook her head and tried to focus on the TV.

Soon enough, the bathroom door snicked open.

*Don't be naked. Don't be naked. Don't be naked.*

She wouldn't have been able to resist ogling his bare torso. Instead, he emerged, along with a cloud of warm steam, clad in flannel pajamas and a thick hotel robe over them. Was the man not burning up?

The doctor in her kicked in. "Are you getting sick? It's a good seventy-five degrees in here. Aren't you sweating?"

He shrugged, securing the belt. "Don't like the wet cold out there. Has a way of weaving itself into you."

Her fingers twitched to untie the belt he just knotted. *Great.* She was about to spend the night with a man she couldn't stand, and even then she wanted to see him naked. He must have some magic pheromones—the kind that wiped a girl's memory right out.

*Stop staring.*

Reaching for her tea, she took a sip as she fought for

something smart to say. Well, at least for *something* to say. "It hailed earlier."

He eased himself down to his makeshift bed. "I know."

Settling against her headboard, she tried to pay attention to the TV. It gave her immeasurable pleasure to hear him trying—and failing—to get comfortable on the hard floor. While turning, he inhaled sharply.

*Ignore him.*

He cursed.

She spared him a look. He moved to lie on his back, pajamas, robe, and all. How was he not combusting?

Resettling, he poked at his hip, then smacked his fist against it a couple of times.

She eyed the movement. "You okay?"

"Old injury."

How old? A dozen questions tickled her tongue, but she kept her trap shut.

The TV blathered on. She tried to focus on the screen and not on the man on the floor next to her. He lay on his back and even though his eyes were closed, he was far from relaxed.

Her patience ran out. "You look uncomfortable."

He didn't bother to open even one eye. "The lights, the TV. It's overstimulating. Trying to tune it out."

She shut off the television. "We should sleep anyway."

Climbing off the bed, she double-checked the door had been locked and bolted. For an entire minute, she debated moving the chair back to barricade the entryway, but decided against it. Hayes now occupied her room and, as irritated as she was by her reaction to him, he'd keep the boogeyman out.

Flipping the lights off, she felt her way through the darkness to her bed and crawled under the cool covers.

Hayes groaned as he shifted in—Joy presumed—a struggle to get comfortable.

Rising on one elbow, she attempted to make out his stiff form through the shadows. "You sure you wouldn't rather get your own room?"

He grunted.

She slid deeper under the duvet. It was going to be a long night.

# Chapter 6

Flooded with pain, he jerked awake on the cold, hard ground, just as he had after the ambush.

Where the fuck was he?

*Please,* please *don't let me be back on that empty stretch of road where I was left to die.* His heart slammed against his rib cage as he braced for the pain.

It never came…

*Not an abandoned road,* he reminded himself; *a hotel room.*

It took him several ragged breaths to orient himself. Finally, the violent drumming in his chest eased. He despised this fucking city. Couldn't escape the memories even in sleep.

Flipping to his side, he gritted his teeth against the burn in his hip and checked his watch. Five sharp. *Figures.* He never slept past that.

His gaze moved to the window, where the curtains had been drawn so tightly closed against the still-dark sky that they appeared sealed.

Joy slept soundly in her bed just feet away.

In the shadows, he lay still and listened, comforted by the gentle rhythm of her breathing, the glide of warm skin against crisp, cotton sheets. He let the sounds wash over him and soothe his aching body.

On a soft moan, she turned and snuggled deeper into her duvet, then flipped over again. Even asleep, Joy remained in constant motion, as if staying static was beyond her.

He longed to be the lucky recipient of all that barely contained energy. To cover her with his body, slide deep, take her until the sun broke across the horizon.

But that wasn't their deal.

Six days of having her as his wife, and they'd never see each other again.

Fighting the urge to go to her, he sat up—

Agony slashed through him. Biting back a groan, he curled his hand over his hip in an instinctive, protective gesture. Dots swam behind his eyes, and he pounded at the hip bone as he'd learned to do, until his muscles unclenched and the pain waned.

As the burn of tears retreated, he eased off the floor and hobbled over to the nearby chair. Pulling his iPad from the table to his lap, he dove into his mounting emails.

Joy stirred just as the sun rose behind the curtains. She slept as he'd expected her to—and she woke that way too. With a soft mumble, she stretched, flipped to her stomach, and cuddled her pillow closer under her cheek.

Hayes stilled, watching.

Her dark lashes fluttered, and she opened her eyes, coming fully awake in the span of several blinks. Not realizing she was being observed, she peeked over the edge of the mattress toward the spot where she'd expected to find him.

"Morning." His murmur cut through the darkness.

Clearly startled, she jumped at the greeting, her hand flying to her chest as she gasped. She reached for the bedside lamp and soft light flooded the room. The top buttons of her pajamas had come undone, revealing a tantalizing glimpse of full, bare breast… and the bruises marring her neck.

*The asshole who left them will never touch her again.*

Realizing he'd gripped his tablet with enough force to snap it in two, he relaxed his hold, finger by finger.

The remnants of sleep left her eyes, and she blinked at him as if trying to remember why he was in her room—and what he'd talked her into doing.

He knew when the picture cleared in her brain. Her brows drew together in revitalized anger, and she snapped back the duvet.

"I was hoping seeing you yesterday was nothing but a nightmare." Swinging her legs over the bed, she walked over to the window and drew back the curtains. Though the sun had risen, the heavy clouds gathering overhead absorbed the light, allowing only depressing gray to trickle through.

Flinging open the windows, she let in the soggy, cold air.

Joy was a morning person, she'd once told him, because she loved the promise of dawn.

To him, dawn brought nothing but pain. The chill that swept in punctured the layers of clothes he'd bound himself in and set his teeth to chatter.

Rising, he circumvented her and pulled the windows closed.

Joy raised an inquisitive brow but didn't question him outright. "I have a busy day ahead of me." She walked to the closet and pulled clothing items off the hangers. "You can stay here."

The pain in his hip screamed for him to opt out. He ignored it. "Not a chance."

Outside, the heavy clouds coalesced, thickened, threatening the city with impending rain. Up in their hotel room, tucked away on the seventh floor of the George, with its upgraded heat and insulated windows, warmth lulled. The idea of voluntarily stepping out in the rain that was sure to come any minute twisted his hip more.

Yet he wasn't about to let Joy traipse around Edinburgh unescorted.

Even in the early morning, the city below came alive. Lights went on in nearby houses; cars gathered at a red light. Several unlucky bastards marched wherever they needed to go, bundled against the icy wind.

Joy would drag him out into the cold too. The filaments in his muscles cramped at the thought.

He despised being here. It didn't matter. The pain would be worth it once the farm was his.

Despite her unmistakable annoyance with him, Joy all but pirouetted to the bathroom to change. Clearly, the anticipation of sightseeing outweighed his presence.

A handful of minutes later, the door swung open and she emerged in a cropped green sweater that came just above the band of her jeans, revealing a tantalizing sliver of flat tummy… and holy God, a belly button piercing.

The pearl-capped navel ring winked at him. She hadn't had *that* the last time he saw her… did she?

If he removed her sweater, what other surprises would he uncover?

She must have sensed his interest because she made a face and walked over to her boots, tugging the thigh-high, whiskey-brown leather over her tight jeans.

Fuck, she didn't play fair.

Straightening, she met his gaze and raised an expectant brow.

He had been too busy eye-fucking her to move.

Rising, he grabbed his own jeans. Willed the blood to leave his groin.

With a dramatic flair, she settled on the edge of the bed, crossing her legs as she watched him. "We don't have all day, Icefall."

"You pierce anything else?"

The question didn't appear to catch her off guard. Her cheeks dimpled. "You'll never find out."

Shedding out of his robe and pajama bottoms, he pulled on his jeans before taking a deliberate step toward her. "Wanna bet?"

"Yes. Winner gets out of going to the farm."

The pearl in her piercing called to him. He turned for the bathroom before he did something stupid, like lean down and taste it.

When he emerged, he found her where he'd left her—on the bed, legs swinging. But she hopped to her feet when she saw him.

She'd tamed her dark hair into a thick braid; it fell over one shoulder and begged for him to come closer and tug.

His gaze drifted to her neck. She must have covered her bruises with makeup, but the knowledge that they were there made him simmer with rage.

"Ready?" She regarded him with wary eyes.

He measured the storm clouds outside. As if only waiting for him to look, they split open and gallons of rain crashed to the ground. Fuck, she expected them to go out in *this*?

The storm didn't seem to faze her. She snagged her

pink puffer jacket off its wall hook. "Breakfast first. Then sightseeing."

Grabbing his own coat, he waved her ahead of him into the corridor and admired her ass all the way to the elevator.

In the breakfast parlor, the host showed them to their table. After the waiter brought over a pot of black tea for her and coffee for him, Joy bounced to the buffet and piled her plate high with a disjointed assortment of breakfast items while he portioned off eggs and ham to his own plate.

Done with their buffet selections, they settled across from each other at the small table by the window while rain pounded the streets outside.

He eyed the eggs, vegetarian haggis, smoked haddock, baked beans, and tomatoes on her plate. "An adventurous assortment."

She sliced into the haggis, sampled a bite. "When in Scotland…"

Tearing his gaze away from her, he took a sip of his coffee and cut into his eggs and ham.

They finished the breakfast in silence, but the downpour outside forced them to linger.

With a bright smile for the waiter, Joy requested another pot of tea. When he brought it, she filled her cup before reaching for the croissant she'd smothered in jam and butter. Humming, she took a generous bite, closing her eyes in unmistakable bliss as she chewed and swallowed.

A droplet of strawberry jam caught at the top of her cupid's bow. The thought of licking it off her lips made his dick jump. Looking away, he topped off his coffee from the silver carafe on the table and let the scalding burn distract him.

Yes, he wanted to fuck Joy. What breathing male wouldn't? She was beautiful and magnetic—and best kept an arm's length away.

The sharp ache twisting his hip reminded him of the last woman he'd let get too close. The experience had left him in a cast, despondent, and—when he fell for her again—almost robbed of everything he'd built.

He'd misread the signs with Liselle. He'd thought she loved him, too. He had been wrong, and he never intended to repeat the experience.

His sister-in-law had once asked him if he ever got lonely. He'd take an occasional pang of loneliness in exchange for peace and quiet and a heart that wasn't shattering into jagged little pieces.

The rain slowed, then stopped by the time Joy finished her tea.

Glancing at the change of weather outside the windows, she flew to her feet and reached for the puffer jacket she'd draped across the back of her chair. "Let's go before the rain starts up again."

As she skipped out of the hotel, he grabbed an umbrella from the stand by the door and followed, burrowing deeper into his coat. The icy fist of Scotland gripped him and squeezed yet again, and despite the layers of wool and cashmere, he couldn't get warm.

Although the rain had stopped, clouds persisted overhead, taunting him.

When he failed to suppress a shiver, she turned her whole body to look at him and her mouth opened—then closed. Whatever question she'd intended to ask, she kept to herself. For all of ten seconds.

On a sigh, as though annoyed with herself for even bothering, she said, "You seem chilly. Do you want to go put on another layer? Or maybe grab a hot coffee?"

He shrugged off her concern. "I'm fine. Hate this weather."

"I love fall. The leaves change colors, and the sky gets so blue—well, not now, obviously, but when it's a clear day—and the air turns all fresh and crisp." She sucked in a deep breath, releasing it with a throaty hum of pleasure that bound his body. "Makes you want to go home, cuddle up with a good book, and warm up by the fire."

He followed the tempting rise of her breasts beneath her jacket. "You like being outdoors in this weather because it makes you want to go indoors?"

Tilting her head, she thought about it, then grinned. "Yes. Makes me feel all cozy. And then when you're indoors, you look out at the cold and feel good about being inside, all warm. That's why I love places that have four seasons. Then you appreciate each and every one."

Her face glowed in the silver morning light. He wanted to draw her to him and taste her smile. Instead, he shoved his hands deeper into his pockets. "Coffee isn't a bad idea."

They stopped at a nearby café and he grabbed a large cup of joe to go, chugging the scalding liquid even though he knew it would do little to help.

To get to Edinburgh Castle, they walked along the edge of Princes Street Gardens, its trees bursting with golds, reds, and oranges.

"It's so beautiful," singsonged Joy. "I haven't seen fall in *so long*."

She almost twirled away down a leaf-strewn path, but he snagged her elbow. "Castle's that way."

"Fine," she acquiesced after a longing look at the autumnal trail. "But let's come back here later."

Not a chance. The leaves had been gold and red, too,

the day he'd been left for dead. Walking through a park was the last thing he intended to do on a stormy, fall day.

As they strolled up the steep incline to their destination, he slanted her a glance. "When you pay off your self-imposed debt to Evie, will you move somewhere that has all seasons?"

Joy shrugged. "Maybe someday. She worked so hard, covered my bills so selflessly. I plan on giving every cent back to her, though she doesn't expect it. Even then, I'll never, ever be able to repay her for what she sacrificed for me. She and Jackson have their hands full, so I'll stay in San Diego as long as it takes to help them."

"Residency doesn't give you much time for baby-sitting."

"I make the time. Because it matters. It's the least I can do."

Hayes recognized loyalty and sibling affection. Evie and Joy's parents weren't wealthy, and when Evie started to make a good living, she'd wanted to help out her sister. Now, Joy was returning the favor.

He pushed back anyway. "Your parents are a half hour away from her and are always willing to babysit."

"I know, but it's not enough. I have to be close, to give back in any way I can. Evie has done so much for me and our parents. I want to make sure she feels supported too."

Hayes understood needing to repay debts too well.

When they reached the Royal Mile, they followed the ancient street to Edinburgh Castle.

"I want to see the Witches' Well," said Joy. "And I need a picture."

"I should have known you'd be an overzealous tourist."

She gave him an annoyed look. "I haven't been back

here in years, Hayes. And Scotland means a lot to me. When I was growing up, we didn't have much money— can't take many international trips on a young pastor's salary. But one day our parents surprised us with a trip through Scotland."

"How old were you?"

"Maybe around ten? My parents honeymooned here and returned with us kids. Scotland was the only international trip we ever took. Now that I'm here, I want to retrace our steps—relive that excitement, that wonder. It's something I fear I'm losing as I get older."

"Yes," he teased. "Your ripe, old age of twenty-eight is making you jaded."

"Bet you were born jaded," she shot back. "I think the Witches' Well is that way."

The wall-mounted, cast-iron fountain, filled with a smattering of flowers, wasn't hard to find. They studied the small monument dedicated to the accused witches who had been burned at the stake in Edinburgh. Hayes wasn't impressed, but Joy took several pictures and oohed over the details in the ironwork.

"You want a photo for Evie and your parents?" he asked despite himself.

Eagerness widened her eyes. "Yes, please."

After Edinburgh Castle, she gamboled toward colorful Victoria Street. He kept up despite his aching hip.

Seeing the row of shops painted a vivid orange, blue, pink, and mint green made her gasp in unmistakable delight.

"Did you know this inspired Diagon Alley in Harry Potter?" she asked as they walked along the cobblestone street.

"Never read it."

It had yet to rain again since morning, but the cold gathered and curled around him, drilling deep into his throbbing hip bone. He ground his teeth, but kept going.

Somehow, she must have noticed, because she gave him a concerned look. "You could use a hot chocolate."

Her focus on him grated. "Is your plan to ply me with hot liquids?"

"Yes. It's cold but not that cold." Stepping into him, she laid her palm across his forehead. "You're not running a fever, but you seem to have chills."

The sudden move surprised him. Her palm, tantalizingly soft and warm, lingered on his skin. He steeled every muscle to not lean into her touch.

*You've misread signals before. Ignore it. It means nothing.*

Breath bated, he waited for her to pull her hand away, to step back and give him space not scented with her. When she did, he drew in a full breath and cursed himself for missing even the fleeting contact.

He didn't know how she spotted the chocolate shop, but she was already halfway across the street to it. Following her into the boutique chocolatier, he left a safe distance between them in the short order line.

If she noticed, she didn't say anything, studying the menu of cocoa options with more attention than necessary.

When they reached the counter, they both chose hot chocolate; she asked for hers to be topped with a homemade marshmallow.

The cashier took their order and directed them to one of the few tables in the café while they waited for their drinks to be made.

Joy sank onto the stool across from him as gracefully as a butterfly. Shrugging out of her jacket, she rearranged her sweater that had fallen haphazardly low down one creamy shoulder.

As she dragged it up to cover her skin, he bit back an involuntary protest. He ached to trace the tantalizing curve, first with his fingertips, then his mouth, and learn if she tasted as sweet as he remembered.

Now the sweater dipped low in the front, revealing a delectable glimpse of her plump breasts.

Joy caught him staring. Giving him an annoyed look, she wrestled the fabric up higher to cover her chest.

Desperate to banish images of her from his mind, he moved his attention to the chocolatier whipping up their drinks.

An incoming customer hurried to the order counter, leaving the door to the café open, and cold air dragged its sharp claws along his back. Hayes attempted to shrug it off. Even then, he shivered.

Her fretful gaze swept over him. "Should we head back to the hotel? Maybe you should lie down."

"I'm not sick." When she jerked back at his sharp tone, he struggled to modulate it. "It's just… I don't like Edinburgh."

Her intelligent eyes focused on his. He'd told her he hated this city once—but had never shared the reason behind his feelings.

Now that he'd brought it up again, she apparently sought to delve into it. "What happened?"

Before he could answer, the barista called their names.

"I'll get it." Standing, he bound his coat closer around himself and snagged their drinks.

When he returned to their table, he slid her cup to her and hoped she'd forgotten her question.

She barely glanced at the hot chocolate. "Why don't you like Edinburgh?"

He took a swig of the bittersweet liquid. "I don't talk about it."

Instead of sampling her drink, she drew the large marshmallow out with her thumb and forefinger and popped the entire piece into her mouth. She savored it with a low murmur, and he congratulated himself for feigning impassivity when all he wanted to do was drag her to him and taste all that sugar on her tongue.

"You don't talk about anything." She took a sip of her hot chocolate. "I've never seen you so layered up, though. What gives?"

Finishing the rest of his drink, he set the empty paper cup down on the table. "I was young and foolish here once. Being back brings up those memories."

Curiosity simmered from her pores as she hugged her cocoa close and leaned across the table. "Young and foolish how?"

"That's something that will remain between me and Scotland."

She tilted her head. "Does it have anything to do with Liselle?"

Fuck. How did she know her name? He never brought up his past with Liselle to anyone.

Clenching his fingers around his paper cup, he crumpled it. "I don't discuss her."

Joy, not surprisingly, refused to let it go. "Were you two together when you… pretended to date me?"

She had to go there, didn't she? He *had* used her to keep his company away from Liselle, but he'd never overlapped the two.

He tossed the remnants of his cup from one hand to

the other, like a deformed stress ball. "She and I were long over by then."

"But you used me to screw her over."

"She screwed me. You were—"

"A fool who thought you actually liked me, when all you were doing was playing me to keep something away from your girlfriend?"

"*Ex*-girlfriend," he clarified, but the similarity of the two situations didn't escape him. Would she back out of their current deal if she knew the truth? That he'd once again roped her in to stop Liselle from taking what belonged to him.

Joy finished her hot chocolate. "Well, am I right? Is she the reason you seem so out of sorts here?"

"My issue with my ex is none of your concern." He stood, taking both of their cups and disposing of them in a nearby trash can. "Let's go before it rains again."

# Chapter 7

Joy didn't press him as they walked back to the Royal Mile. Hayes clearly had history with Edinburgh—history he refused to share.

Joy had never been able to find much about Hayes's relationship with Liselle online, except that they'd dated at least once before. After their last breakup, he sold their startup, Poinsettia, from under her. He'd used Joy to secure a meeting with the buyer.

Guess Hayes Icefall was an asshole to all women. At least she hadn't been the exception.

She'd liked him once—more than liked. During their brief period of dating, she'd started visualizing what their kids might look like.

But it had all been pretend.

Instead, he'd used her, left her, and never apologized. Until he knocked on her hotel door yesterday, she'd only thought of him in the bitter hours of the night before swiftly shoving him from her mind.

Despite her feelings—her *indifference*—toward him, she itched to know what happened here between him and his ex, and when.

Was Edinburgh—and whatever had occurred here with Liselle—the reason for the callous man he'd become? Or had he always been a jerk?

As they continued along the Royal Mile, the charged air around them warned of an imminent storm. If they got caught in the downpour, Hayes would cut her sightseeing short and drag her back to the hotel.

She turned to him. "Maybe it's a good time for a lunch break?"

"Read my mind."

Narrow alleyways branched out from the Royal Mile, leading down stone steps to various pubs and restaurants.

Hayes waved toward one of the alleys. "Come this way. We'll check out the Devil's Advocate. You wanted to taste some whiskey. No better place for it."

When he settled his hand low on her back, hot recognition poured through her. He shouldn't affect her this strongly through her sweater and down jacket.

Dizzy, in need of space free of Hayes, she knew she should shake him off. Instead, she ignored her sprinting pulse and let him guide her down the steep steps.

When they walked inside the Devil's Advocate, the thick stone walls and low lighting made it seem like they'd taken a step back in time. The pub took up two levels, with a well-stocked bar downstairs and tables for dining upstairs.

Everyone must have had the same idea about lunch and whiskey, because the place was packed, but the hostess slid an appreciative gaze over Hayes and took them to one of the only two empty tables upstairs, tucked against the exposed stone wall. Handing them their menus, she promised that a waiter would come take their orders before drifting away.

Hayes glanced at his phone. "The Blairs want to know how our day is going."

"Tell them you've been mildly entertaining."

The suggestion didn't appear to amuse him. After sending off a quick text, he set his phone aside.

How deep did his relationship with the Blairs go? Not that he'd ever tell her. She'd have to ask them… which she would do as soon as she arrived at the farm.

Hayes pulled his menu closer. "They introduced me to this place."

"Must be good then." Joy perused the whiskey selections. "Did you know that more Scotch whiskey is sold in a month in France than cognac is sold there in an entire year?"

He filled her glass from the bottle of water at their table. "Then get the flight. But also get a solid meal. I need you of mostly sound body and mind today. We leave for the farm early tomorrow morning."

Her eyes scanned over the food menu. "You're going to continue to lie to the Blairs?"

"It's for their own good." He set down the water bottle.

"What you're doing is for your selfish reasons. Don't make it more than it really is. Why would you even put them through this? Just get your honey elsewhere."

His gaze flicked away. "They make good honey."

This couldn't be about honey, could it? Evie had once shared that Hayes was particular about things he liked, items in which he found comfort. He hated change. A funny trait for someone who sold the many businesses he founded without a second thought. But to fabricate a marriage to preserve access to his honey supply seemed far-fetched.

The waiter came to grab their orders. They settled on two whiskey flights, a roasted root vegetable dish for her, and fish and chips for him.

When the waiter returned with their flights several minutes later, she eyed the heavy pours with alarm. "This might add up to a whole bottle."

He repositioned the glasses until they aligned to his approval. "You don't have to finish them all."

The flight had been arranged geographically, starting with the Lowlands, followed by Speyside, the Highlands, the Islands, and ending on Islay.

"Start with the Lowlands one," advised Hayes. "It's milder."

Closing her fingers over the glass, she took a sip. Smooth and light, it warmed her from throat to belly.

Watching Hayes take a swallow from his own glass warmed her all over. Did the man have to be so beautiful even *sampling alcohol*? Disgusted with herself, she blew out a sigh of relief when the food arrived and distracted her dirty mind.

Digging into her plate of roasted vegetables, topped with fresh greens and crumbly feta cheese, she chewed a crispy sweet potato. Her gaze slid back to Hayes.

He cut into his fish and chips, his hands sure and steady on the utensils.

*Just great. Now I'm salivating over his use of a fork and knife.*

Concentrating on her own food, she let the silence stretch. Hayes wouldn't cut in with chirpy conversation, and she didn't wish to play nice with him any longer.

True, it hadn't been awful to have him as a companion on her outing. Exploring Edinburgh by herself would have been lonely and depressing, and she'd have jumped at anyone who even remotely resembled Ryder.

But Hayes had taken advantage of her before, and

was doing so again. He'd roped her into lying to the Blairs. How could she ever look them in the eye?

The familiar anger returned. *Good. Hold on to it. Don't let his cheekbones distract you from his cold, selfish nature.* He was a user, a cheater, *and a liar*.

She sampled the next whiskey in the flight. But as the whiskeys progressed, they grew smokier and peatier—something she hadn't expected.

"Ugh." She set down the last one in the lineup after the tiniest sip. "Too flavorful."

His throaty chuckle left her more lightheaded than the whiskey. When he swapped out her smokiest samples for his lightest ones, she eyed the move with suspicion. "You don't have to do that."

He shrugged. "I like the smokier ones better."

The dim lighting had turned his face sharp and angular, making him look dangerous and oh, so attractive. The thought made her set down her whiskey. *Okay, that's enough alcohol.*

Easing back in her chair, she focused on the low buzz of conversation around them—until a peal of cloying laughter cut through the chatter in the pub, the sound bouncing off the walls.

Across the table from her, Hayes froze. As slow as molasses, he angled his head toward the sound.

Recognition flashed across his face. Joy twisted to look at the newcomer too.

Definitely American, draped in faux fur over expensive athleisure, with an LV bag strung over her shoulder. Her chestnut hair, blown out in perfect spirals, cascaded to her snatched waist.

The woman turned from her built, tanned, younger companion and met Hayes's eyes. Hers filled with satisfaction, and she crossed to their table. "The Blairs told us we could find you here. We were in the shops nearby."

Hayes didn't speak. Just stared at the refined beauty next to them without expression.

If Joy had styled her own hair like that today, it'd have lasted all of five minutes in this rainy weather, yet the stranger's loose spirals were glossy and frizz-free. *How does she manage it?*

The woman turned to Joy and extended a manicured hand, the red nails long and dagger-sharp. "I'm Liselle, and this is my husband, Gene Garnier."

# Chapter 8

*This was Liselle?*

The ex? The one Hayes had used her to screw over? And Gene… as in…

*She married the Blairs' nephew?*

No wonder Hayes had lied to them.

Realization washed over her with the startling clarity of a cold ocean wave.

Hayes had manipulated her again. Not to buy the farm, but *to screw his ex yet again*. Clearly, he wasn't over her yet.

Joy realized she was staring when Liselle raised an arched brow. Not willing to be rude, she shook Liselle's hand—then Gene's. Gene fit his wife well, with his blindingly white teeth and Italian Riviera tan.

"I'm Joy," she said with a sidelong glance at Hayes, who had yet to so much as twitch.

Liselle looked at him too. "The Blairs mentioned you're interested in their bee farm. What a small world. Gene and I are making an offer, too."

Gene smiled brightly. "I used to stay at their farm every summer growing up. It means the world to me."

Hayes sat immobile, as though a venomous snake was slithering up his leg. He avoided eye contact with the beautiful Liselle, and he'd turned even whiter.

Liselle waited. When the silence stretched, she looked at Joy, expecting a response. Unsure of how to proceed, Joy reached for her whiskey and took a burning sip.

"A quiet bunch," said Gene jovially next to his wife. "Come on, Lissy. Our table is ready, and I'm starving."

Liselle's gaze ran over Hayes once more, and then she followed her husband to their table across the small space.

"Should we leave?" asked Joy.

Hayes reached for his own whiskey, and downed the glass in one swallow. "That was Liselle."

"So she said."

When Joy swiveled her whole body to look at Liselle again, he cursed. "Well, don't look, for God's sake."

Too late.

She and Liselle had made unmistakable eye contact.

Flipping back to Hayes, Joy stabbed an accusatory finger at him through the air. "You're using me because of her again."

He didn't deny it.

All the people breathing around them made the air too heavy. She needed space, but she refused to run. "I can't believe this."

"She means nothing to me."

Lies. More lies. He'd used her to get back at Liselle before, and was doing so again.

"Of course she does. Enough for you to lie to the Blairs to fuck her over."

"That's not true. I won't let her ruin the legacy that the Blairs built from the ground up." Shoving away from the table, he stood without further explanation and disappeared down the stairs.

Joy glanced behind her. Liselle and Gene chattered with the waitress, ordering who knew what off the menu. She took another sip of whiskey, ate some more food, waited. Hayes didn't return.

Maybe he did them both a favor and finally left her alone.

Unlikely.

Should she go look for him?

Before she could make her decision one way or another, Liselle's faux fur-clad figure moved past her and disappeared down the stairs.

She better not be going to search for Hayes.

Joy swiveled her head to check whether Gene was still around, and their eyes met across the crowded room. He flashed her a warmhearted smile and raised his glass in a semblance of a toast.

Unsure of what to make of him, she offered a corresponding smile that didn't quite reach her eyes and turned back to her half-eaten meal. Taking a healthy gulp of water, she studied the wall next to her.

When neither Hayes nor Liselle returned, Joy batted away her growing annoyance. She didn't care about either one of them. They could be screwing each other's brains out in the bathroom, and it would make no difference to her. It's not like she held any claim on Hayes.

But sitting up here, alone, waiting for him as though she had nothing better to do, wasn't her idea of a good time. Leaving her jacket on her chair so that the waiter didn't think they dined and dashed, she grabbed her purse and took the steps to the ground level.

The hostess glanced at her when she reached her at the maître d' stand. "Everything all right?"

Joy scanned the crowd in the packed downstairs bar, but didn't find Liselle or Hayes. "Where's the bathroom?"

The hostess pointed to a narrow corridor behind her. "Loo's through there."

Following the indicated path, she stopped when Hayes's familiar voice reached her through the closed door of the men's room.

"I have nothing to say to you," he gritted out.

Like a pervert, she stopped to listen.

Liselle's words seeped through the door like pancake syrup. "You'll have more to say to me soon. I know you expect to get that farm. Because you think you're so much smarter than everyone around you. But you're not. You're still as odd and awkward as I remember. And that farm is mine. The Blairs love me, and I'll make sure they love me even more this weekend."

His tone dripped with exhaustion. "Go away, Liselle."

Liselle harrumphed. "Why don't you do what you do best? Disappear."

Guess she wasn't the only woman he'd abandoned.

"You're the one who left me, Liselle."

"Fucking hated you."

"It's not what you said when you fucked me."

The door swinging open caught Joy unaware, and she faced a furious Hayes. He stormed past her, shoving his way through the crowds and out of the Devil's Advocate.

Liselle's hand touched her shoulder. The unwelcome contact made her recoil. "If I can give you a piece of advice, it's to stay far away from him. He only cares about himself. Always has, always will. I'd divorce him now, if I were you. He proposed to me, too, you know. I turned him down."

*Hayes proposed? Reclusive Hayes Icefall had wanted to spend his life with someone?* That was most definitely not on her bingo card.

"You're married to a liar," Liselle continued. "He only married you to spite me."

Well, that was offensive. "My relationship with Hayes has nothing to do with you."

Liselle smiled. "Doesn't it? I think it has everything to do with me."

The flash of Liselle's white teeth set Joy on edge. She didn't trust the woman. She didn't trust Hayes either. He'd played her before. Was doing so again. The common denominator? Liselle. And Joy, once again, was collateral damage.

She found him pacing in the gray cold just outside the bar.

"Deal is off," she said.

Hands in coat pockets, shoulders up to his ears, he faced her. "Excuse me?"

"This is about revenge. Or some warped foreplay between you and your ex."

His eyes flicked toward the Devil's Advocate. "What did she say to you?"

"Nothing of importance, but it's clear that this is some weird fetish between you two."

"There's nothing between us."

"One of you wants the other one back—and I can't tell which one. Leave me out of your sex games."

Turning on her booted heel, she turned for the pub— and her down-filled jacket—but his words stopped her.

"I'll cancel the Delices' funds."

The chill in the air nipped at her skin. The cropped sweater did little to protect against it. Crossing her arms and curling inward for warmth, she considered the stone-still figure across from her. "You would leave a family with a sick child destitute? That's how cold and callous you are?"

His stance widened. "I won't let Liselle have my farm."

"It's a pride thing then? She turned you down and you're bitter?"

"She's lying to the Blairs. She married their nephew to take the farm from me."

"And you're not? You told them you and I are married. You know what?" she said, tired of arguing, tired of the cold. "You two deserve each other."

With that, she strode back toward the pub.

He didn't let her get far, catching her elbow and halting her progress before she could take two steps. "You and I had a deal."

Wrestling her elbow out of his grip, she crossed her arms and glared. "That was before I knew you wanted to cheat the farm away from your ex-girlfriend."

His nostrils flared. "She and I were done a long time ago."

She didn't believe that for a minute. "First, you pretended to date me to get in front of Dr. Hutch and grapple Poinsettia away from Liselle. And now you're pretending to be married to me to take the farm from her."

His eyes turned the same frigid gray as the sky above them. "I won't let Liselle destroy the Blairs' legacy."

"You're destroying it."

"Never," he ground out.

Could she believe him? "Please, don't hurt the Blairs. They seem really nice."

His face softened. "They're the best people I know."

She wasn't sure whether his response mollified or terrified her. "I don't trust you, Hayes."

"Never asked you to trust me. Only asked you for six days of your time. You'd back away from your word?"

Bringing her palms to her temples, she massaged the growing ache there. "You made me give it under false circumstances. Don't pin this on me, buddy."

He paced away from her before stalking back, eyes flashing. "You come with me and play nice, or I'll make sure everyone in the SoCal hospital system hears that you were involved in your boyfriend's drug theft."

*What the hell?* "That's a lie! I didn't know about it."

"Doesn't matter what you knew. By the time I'm done, you'll be kicked out of your residency and no hospital will ever hire you. You won't be able to pay Evie back—or help her by babysitting. Actually, I'll expand beyond SoCal. How would it feel to move in, jobless, with Evie? Or your parents?"

The words struck her like a physical blow. "What is wrong with you? Is the human chip missing in your brain?"

"Six days, Joy. The why of it doesn't matter."

Her hatred of him blazed through her, warming her more thoroughly than the thickest coat ever could.

Squeezing her eyes shut against the challenge in his, she cursed. "I hate you. How you're related to Jackson, I'll never know. Fine, I can suffer for six days. But don't talk to me or be near me more than necessary. I'm going to hate every minute of it."

His cruel lips spread in a mockery of a smile. "Don't be so hasty. You may come to enjoy it."

# Chapter 9

He was an asshole.

A creep.

How dare he threaten her job to get her to bend to his will?

If he thought she'd take his threat lying down, he was in for a doozy of a surprise.

She may have fallen for his words—and his cheek-bones—before, but now she knew his true character.

He'd pinned her between two impossible choices: let herself be exploited again, or sacrifice everything she'd worked for and hurt the Delices in the process.

She'd go to that farm, pretend to be his wife, but she'd make sure Highlander Honey never belonged to Hayes.

That plan would begin tomorrow. Today, she'd retaliate in a more subtle way. She'd prolong their sightseeing expedition—let him suffer as a dawdling tourist in the raging downpour.

Nature refused to cooperate. The rain never arrived.

She dragged him from gift shop to gift shop anyways, buying Iona marble trinkets for her sister and mom, plaid scarves for her dad and Jackson—anything to protract their day outdoors.

Next on the list? A circuit through Holyroodhouse Palace. She set off toward the landmark, leaving him no choice but to follow.

"Really? You're not done yet?" he grumbled when she stopped at the main entrance.

Plastering on her brightest smile, she stalked to the ticket desk. "Not even close."

Hayes hovered near her during the audio tour through the palace, but she knew it had been as fascinating to him as a stroll through Costco. Served him right.

The sun had set by the time they surrendered their guides and exited the palace gates. "Enough playing tourist," Hayes muttered. "It's dark. It's cold. I'm hungry."

The sun did set early in Edinburgh in November, Joy realized. And truth be told, she was cold and hungry, too. Not that she'd let Hayes off the hook this easily.

Snapping her shoulder blades together, she ignored her grumbling stomach. "I'm going to enjoy my day in Edinburgh. You are the one who insisted on joining me."

"Day's over. I've been more than accommodating."

"*Accommodating?* You've been hovering in silence next to me since the pub. It's like touring the city with a grumpy ghost."

"If you wanted entertainment, you should have called the local stand-up. I don't have time to play tour guide. I kept my end of the bargain—day's done. It's time for dinner."

Her mouth dropped open to deliver a scathing reply… but the words never came.

Damn it. He'd never admit it, but he was in evident pain. She'd been too lost in her hatred of him to notice the gray cast to his face. When he hobbled two steps away, his gait was painfully lopsided.

She might detest him, but the doctor in her couldn't stand causing him physical discomfort on purpose.

Maybe she'd tired him out enough for today. "All right. Let's go back."

Relief flashed across his pallid face.

He hadn't been injured three years ago. What had happened to him since then?

They were a block away from the hotel when the clouds finally ruptured.

Hayes muttered a curse as the first fat droplets fell, snapping open his umbrella over her and stepping close. The familiar juniper and cedar notes of his aftershave surrounded her, shooting her right back to three years ago, when they had tumbled into her apartment, giddy on champagne and each other. He had pulled her into his body, told her how beautiful she was, how much he wanted her.

Just before she dropped to her knees…

And he walked away.

She had been so stupid then.

At least she was smarter now—and Hayes was a mistake she never intended to repeat.

*I'd rather get soaked in this torrent than be stuck under the umbrella with him.*

Before she could escape into the rain, the wind had another idea. A sudden gust pushed her square into Hayes's rock-solid chest.

In an effort to steady her, he curled his free arm around her waist, drawing her closer against him.

*Great. Just great. Time to step away.*

And she would have, right away. Just held her breath and done it. But another wind gust—this one even stronger—followed the first.

The hotel umbrella didn't stand a chance. Its canvas flipped inside out, leaving them fully exposed to the deluge.

The sudden drenching dissipated the tension between them more effectively than a cold shower.

*Guess nature decided to step in before things got too… serious.*

Blinking against the rain, she chanced a glance at his face. His very set, very annoyed face. Rivulets spilled from his soaked hair down his carved cheekbones.

He looked so waterlogged, she couldn't contain her amusement. "You carried around that umbrella all day and we got soaked *ten steps* from our hotel."

His eyes, already stormy with irritation, narrowed. Taking her hand, he pulled her toward the George. "Get inside. You want pneumonia?"

"Relax, Grandpa. You can't catch pneumonia from a little rain."

The doorman held open the door, allowing their soggy selves to slip through.

"Soaking out there," he offered as greeting.

With a silent glare, Hayes handed him the broken umbrella, never releasing her hand.

Leaving a dripping trail in their wake, they started through the lobby, but didn't make it far.

The concierge waved wildly at them from behind his desk, cutting off their escape. "Miss Campbell? A friend of yours left you a note."

The cold weather outside didn't compare to the ice that settled in her joints. If a friend wanted to reach her, they'd text. They wouldn't leave a note in a hotel in the middle of Edinburgh.

Hayes must have come to the same conclusion. Before she could ask for the note, he stepped between her and the desk and extended his hand. "I'll take it."

The concierge hesitated. The letter was, after all, addressed to her.

"It's okay," she told the staffer. Only then did he surrender the envelope and step away.

Hayes tore open the flap and withdrew a postcard.

When he flipped it over, the icy cold spread through the rest of her body. She knew that handwriting too well.

*I just want to talk. Unblock me. You owe me.*

Head spinning, she scanned the lobby, looking for her ex-boyfriend among the hotel guests, but encountered unfamiliar faces. Some guests waited at the check-in desk; others hovered near the entrance to the bar or gathered on the couches while they waited for the downpour to pass. Ryder Lewis wasn't among them, but he could be anywhere in the hotel.

*How did he find me in Edinburgh?*

Hayes locating her was bad enough, but *Ryder*? She waited for the paralyzing dread she'd first felt in San Diego and then again in London, but this time only anger prevailed. "That asshole."

Hayes slammed down the note. "Ryder."

Reflexively, her hand flew to her neck, the memory of being choked still fresh and painful.

The movement didn't escape Hayes. His face hardened.

She kept her voice low so Hayes couldn't hear it shake. "It's his handwriting. Do you think he's still here?"

Hayes waved the concierge back over to them. "Did the guy who dropped this off leave?"

"Almost straightaway. Said he had another appointment." The concierge glanced between the two of them. "Is everything all right?"

Hayes slipped him a business card and some cash. "If he returns, give me a call."

After the concierge assured Hayes that he would do so immediately, Joy tried to snag the postcard from Hayes, but he folded it and tucked it into his coat pocket.

"Bet leaving this place sounds like a good idea now," he muttered.

*Yes, yes, it was.* But she wasn't about to admit that to him.

"He has to snap out of it soon." She wasn't sure whether she was trying to convince him or herself.

With a final scan of the lobby, she strode to the elevator, struggling to feign indifference.

Their hotel room was stifling by the time they returned. Hayes must have left the heater on.

Overwhelmed by the arid air, she shed her wet jacket and hung it on one of the wall hooks to dry, but Hayes kept his coat on.

What was with him? No sane human being could possibly be comfortable in this dry sauna. Any minute now, steam was going to rise from her rain-soaked hair.

He hovered by the door, not releasing the handle. "Lock up behind me. I'll be back."

She understood his intent, and she didn't like it. "Don't tell me you're going to chase Ryder around Edinburgh."

The arrogant look he gave her grated. "I don't chase. I'll find him."

Balancing against the wall, she unzipped one boot and took it off. "Just leave it."

"And let him continue to terrorize you?" he asked, the door handle still in his death grip.

She pulled off the remaining boot. "There's nothing you can do. Soon, he'll realize I had nothing to do with him being fired."

"You didn't suspect he was an addict when you dated him."

A statement, not a question. The accuracy of it peeved her. "Is there anything you don't know?"

He thrust his hands in his coat pockets and glowered. "You tell me."

Always like a dog with a bone. "No, I didn't know he was an addict. I just thought he had a lot of… energy. He was charming and fun, and great. When he was fired, it's like a switch went off in him."

Her voice broke on the last word. Angry at herself for allowing the fissure of emotion, she sealed her lips and cleared her throat. She could freak out and panic on her own time. Definitely not in front of Hayes.

First of all, she didn't trust him not to use her vulnerability against her. And second, the man sucked with any emotional displays.

He proved her point when he walked past her.

Annoyed, she followed his movement. Striding to the table, he turned on the teakettle.

Wasn't the room stifling enough? He needed boiling water too?

Selecting a tea bag from the box, he tossed it in her cup.

*Is he… making me tea?* Unsure whether she was imagining it, she watched him rearrange the white cup on the table. It looked miniature next to his hands.

Those hands had once explored her body, sweeping from hip to breast with scorching possessiveness, tangling in her hair as he kissed her. She shook off the memory.

He remained silent while the kettle simmered and the rain drummed against the windows.

When the water boiled, he filled her cup and extended it to her. "Here."

Wrapping her fingers around the porcelain, she let the steam curl around her. "Don't go looking for him. He's not worth it."

He released an exasperated sigh. "He hurt you. He scared you. He killed your pets."

The reminder stung. She'd loved her goldfish. Feeling the familiar burn behind her eyes, she took a sip of the tea, as if it could wash away her grief.

When he tried to move past her, she blocked him. "He's not in his right mind. It's a waste of energy."

Hayes seemed poised to argue when lightning split the sky, illuminating the room in a flash of white. Almost immediately, thunder followed, the wind shaking the windows next to them.

He regarded the storm outside, as if deliberating whether or not to brave it. Finally, on a huff of frustration, he shrugged out of his wet coat and draped it over the chair, and she knew she'd won.

"Fine. I won't seek him out tonight. But eventually I will. I won't let him terrorize you."

"He just needs space," she said, keeping her voice deliberately gentle. The last thing she wanted was to witness Hayes and Ryder pummeling each other.

"Space, he'll get. We leave for the Highlands bright and early tomorrow."

She'd never admit it—not even under torture—but escaping somewhere remote for a few days was starting to sound like a good idea.

Now that he'd removed his coat, his black cashmere sweater hugging his broad shoulders made her long to trace the contours of muscle beneath the expensive fabric.

Setting the cup down, she sought safer ground. "I'm going to get out of these wet clothes and take a long shower. You want to go first?"

His darkened gaze stole the breath from her throat.

"I'll change in here," he replied, his voice a low rumble that seemed to vibrate through the charged air between them.

Retreating to the bathroom, she shed her clothes and stepped into the shower.

Did she linger under the rain showerhead to avoid him in the other room? Maybe. But a girl had to do what she could to protect herself.

When the cascade of hot water overheated her, she shut it off and stepped out of the glass cabin.

Just then, a murmur of voices reached her—Hayes's velvet baritone and another she didn't recognize.

She shrugged into a hotel robe. Who had he invited to their room?

Refusing to go investigate in nothing but a robe, she remained in the small space, brushing her teeth and applying her lotions, waiting for the stranger to leave.

Only when footsteps moved past the bathroom and the mysterious visitor left with a brisk goodbye, she slid open the bathroom door and stepped into the room.

Hayes must have cranked up the heat even more while she was in the shower. The feverish air grasped at her, made her want to shed the robe to survive the unbearable temperature.

And yet he'd kept his cashmere sweater on. His back was to her as he set something on the table between the teakettle and his tablet.

"Who was here just now?" she asked, approaching him.

Turning, he gave her a thorough once-over, his eyes lingering in places that made her throb with recognition. Between his smoldering gaze and the relentless heater, the air grew thick and heavy, and she struggled to breathe.

As if just now remembering her question, he pointed to the two small velvet cases on the table next to him. "Come look."

Curious, she did, approaching the blue velvet as carefully as one would a ticking bomb.

Although they looked like ring cases, with Hayes one could never know.

"What are those?"

He backed up all the way to the window and leaned against the sill. "Open them."

Narrowing her eyes at him, she snapped open the first case to uncover a gold ring, with thistles and Celtic knots flowing in a simple, unfussy vine. Her heart tripped as she pulled it from its velvet nest.

She knew it was all just pretend, but the distinctive Scottish symbols, weaved together in such a minimalistic design, captivated her.

Replacing it, she opened the second box. Another ring, also gold, this one a thin, simple band surrounding a round diamond.

"I know a local jeweler," Hayes explained from his perch at the window. He watched her with supposed indifference, but something she couldn't name smoldered just beneath the blue of his eyes. "He dropped off the rings for us."

She traced the intricate pattern with the pad of her finger, feeling every ridge and valley of the thistles and Celtic knots. "They're beautiful."

"They'll do." He pushed off his spot to cross to her and study the rings over her shoulder.

Not finding a third box, she turned to him. "And where's yours?"

He extended his left hand to show her that he'd already put it on. The gold gleamed against his tanned skin.

"We return them on Wednesday?"

He flexed his hand, as though the band irritated him. "And not a moment too soon."

Joy's fingers hovered over her rings, overwhelmed by the temptation to slip them on. But Hayes watched her too keenly. She wouldn't allow him to mock her misplaced eagerness.

Instead, she left the rings where they were and busied herself with the kettle—another cup of tea wouldn't hurt.

"You don't want to see if they fit?" he asked.

She kept her expression blank and her shoulder shrug—hopefully—casual.

"Guess it's not a bad idea to check the fit." Grasping for a tone of indifference, she withdrew the patterned band.

As she slid it on her fourth finger, it fit seamlessly. She stacked the diamond engagement ring over it. That one fit her perfectly too. How did he know her size?

*God, they are beautiful. Why did he have to choose such pretty baubles?*

"Why do the rings go on the fourth finger anyway?" she asked Hayes to distract herself. No way would she let him see her *admiring* them. "Why not the thumb? Or the middle finger? It'd be a fun way to flash it around."

Taking her hand in his large one, he smoothed the pad of his thumb over the rings. She fought to steady her breathing even as her heart pounded.

"Ancient Egyptians believed that there was a vein right here"—he touched the tip of her fourth finger before stroking along the sensitive underside—"called the vena amoris. A vein of love that connects straight to your heart."

She waited for him to step back, but he lingered, weaving dizzying little spirals across her skin. Who knew that such an innocent touch could be so arousing?

*What a silly thought*, she wanted to tell him. *All veins lead to the heart.*

But the words wouldn't come.

The whimsical story had riveted her even though she knew better. It was just a stupid myth—one he probably invented. She should get it together, pull her hand away from his, and stop staring at him like she'd been spellbound.

Yet she remained frozen, caught between the rational voice in her head and the warmth spreading through her veins from where he continued to trace patterns across her skin.

Clearing her throat, she withdrew her hand. "You just made that up."

He arched one eyebrow. "I don't make things up."

"I'm going to Google it."

"Are you always so suspicious of people?" he asked with a trace of amusement.

"Yes. I've learned my lesson." Refusing to look at his face, she concentrated on pulling the rings off her finger and returning them to their cases. "Did you know my ring size or is this a lucky guess?"

"Jeweler's guess." Tugging off his own ring, he set it next to the two boxes. "The Delices have their funds. We have our rings. We're set."

She lifted her chin so he knew she meant business. "Six days, and then you never, ever come near me again."

# Chapter 10

The next morning, after she slapped on four layers of foundation to cover the bruising on her throat, they powered through breakfast and checked out.

A McLaren waited for them at the hotel entrance.

Bundled in a fuzzy white sweater against the morning chill, Joy eyed the ride. "Really?"

Her make-believe husband shrugged at her unamused tone, coming around to the passenger side to hold open her door. "It's a rental."

"You and Jackson and your cars," she grumbled, but climbed inside the sports vehicle.

After Hayes dealt with their luggage, he slid into the driver's seat, started the engine, and pulled away from the curb.

He navigated the traffic like a Scot, weaving in and out of lanes and traversing construction blocks. It hadn't yet rained that morning, but the overcast skies above them warned of an impending thunderstorm.

The heat in the car stayed on full blast. It seemed like the very air in Edinburgh made him cold for reasons he'd never reveal, so she left the heater on, despite the sweat beading in the small of her back.

They looped around Edinburgh more times than she cared to count. Was he lost? Not that she'd point it out to him—he'd simply grumble that he didn't get lost. But the city, with its stone homes and narrow streets, flying past her window for the third time, said otherwise. The road widened as they finally exited town in the direction of the Highlands.

Hayes drove in silence, tension adding a sharpness to his movements.

Not used to mute car rides, Joy wished she could play some music or point out some of the sites they drove past, but he wouldn't appreciate the chatter. Besides, they weren't friends.

Twisting away from him, she studied the passing scenery.

It was he who spoke.

"I wound around Edinburgh a few times. If Ryder followed you, he got lost back in the city."

She whipped her head toward him. It hadn't even occurred to her that he was evasive driving on purpose. "I thought you were lost."

He slanted her an arrogant glance. "I don't get lost."

Biting down on the amusement his response drew from her, she looked behind them. "You think he was really following us?"

"He knew your hotel."

She sighed. "I don't understand his hyperfocus on me. It really wasn't me who got him fired. I didn't even know he did drugs."

"He lost his job and then he lost you."

"Murdering my goldfish and chasing me to the UK is not a way to get me back."

"Try telling him that."

If she hadn't been staring at his profile, she'd have missed the upturn at the corners of his mouth. She angled her head. "Did you just make a joke?"

"I don't know what you're talking about," he said, his expression impassive again.

Once they merged onto M90 and drove for several miles, Hayes seemed to relax. First, his fingers unclenched from the wheel, then he sat back against the seat and shook out his neck. Now loose-limbed, he reached for the blasting heater and turned down the hot, dry stream.

Interesting. It had been Edinburgh that had caused his chill, but why? What had happened to him there for him to react that way?

Hayes broke the silence in the car. "Did you ever visit Glencoe with your parents as a kid?"

She thought back. "I don't think so. Where is that?"

"I'll take you later, if we have time. A seventeenth-century massacre took place there. Government troops turned on their hosts—the MacDonald clan. Killed some forty people. Others fled, but died of exposure. I go visit when I can."

"That's really dark, Hayes."

"It's a good reminder for me—can't trust most people."

She remembered too well what happened the last time she trusted *him*. "No, one can't."

An hour ticked by in silence. How did he not find such muteness uncomfortable?

She ached to start up a conversation, but she reined herself in. Better to stay quiet and map out her plan of attack—identify the most honorable prospective buyers and ensure the Blairs selected them over Hayes.

As they drove farther, the scenery grew more striking. Every shade of fall weaved together across the flatlands, the colors intensified by the low-hanging clouds. She'd loved the moors when she'd seen them as a kid, and their sweeping beauty mesmerized her still.

The man next to her had yet to speak.

*Why is he always so silent?*

After another twenty minutes, she lost the fight with herself. "We never visited Glencoe." Turning to him, she resumed their conversation from earlier. "Or Loch Ness, though I've always wanted to see it. We first stayed in Edinburgh, and then made our way across the country. Saw a bunch of castles, most of which I don't remember, but I do recall Doune Castle—Evie and I *loved* playing there."

He didn't bother to look at her, but he did ask a question. "Was the castle your favorite part?"

Happy memories flooded her as she recalled all the places they had visited. "No, my favorite was a small village called Culross. To us as kids, it felt like we'd been transported back in time. Evie and I pretended to be princesses running around the cobblestone streets. To me, at that age, it was better than Disneyland. I doubt the ice cream shop is still there, but it was the best ice cream I've ever had. It's the one place I *have* to visit before I return to California—I'll go after our time on the farm is done."

*Six days of lying from now*, thought Joy with a pang of guilt.

Hayes didn't respond. She waited for a whole minute before she refocused on the scenery around them, and let the awkward silence resume.

***

Hayes couldn't pay attention to the fallscape that seemed to have gripped Joy. The sweeps of the russet red reminded him too much of spilled blood, and the sprawling clouds threatened rain. A thunderstorm would only delay them.

He glanced at Joy, who rested her head against her seat as she watched the moors fly by. Her scent—that distinctive warm beach fragrance—curled around him. It clung to her skin, even in the frigid Scottish air.

She'd been a surfer when they met. Did she still surf? He'd spent three years deliberately avoiding her, and now all his suppressed curiosity rushed back.

He had to get this week over with and get some much-needed distance between them.

Because he knew himself.

He fell hard. He couldn't fall for her.

# Chapter 11

The hills, beautiful in their starkness, whizzed by until Hayes turned onto a narrow vein of an unpaved road she would have hardly noticed.

Passing a bubbling brook hidden by dry vegetation somewhere to their left, they reached freshly painted white gates that had been left wide open in welcome. Above them, a simple metal sign said *Welcome to Highlander Honey Farm.*

She had assumed the farm would be a gigantic production, with rolling fields as far as the eye could see. After all, Hayes liked nice, lavish things. Yet the bee farm was not at all what she'd expected.

They navigated along the gravel path, past dormant garden beds and a slumbering orchard. Joy couldn't begin to guess at the fruit they grew here—the only way she'd know an apple tree was if it lobbed a Granny Smith at her.

An array of trees had been planted around the property, and their leaves, from blazing red to burnt orange and yellow, contrasted markedly with the dark-green evergreens that bordered a portion of the land. The quaint farm charmed her.

They passed a large barn that looked brand-new, its white paint and sharp red roof immaculate.

Hayes must have noticed her staring at its bright-red

doors. "That's where they extract, filter, and bottle the honey."

Cruising around the barn, they drove farther inward until they stopped at the main house. It looked lovely, but not massive by any stretch of the imagination. Made of brown stone, it stood at two stories. Its purple door and lilac shutters gave it a whimsical quality. Smoke drifted from the chimneys in tantalizing white swirls.

The front door swung open, and Maisie and Cal Blair stepped onto their stoop, welcoming them with cheerful waves.

Guilt made her nauseated. They were actually *happy* to see them. Meanwhile, she and Hayes were lying to them.

She slanted a peek at her faux husband. Did his conscience eat at him too? After all, they were his friends, not hers. But the man didn't seem guilt-ridden. Apparently, when the asshole had his eye on the prize, he didn't care who he hurt.

She'd been trapped in his games before. How did she end up here again?

Hayes drove behind the house and parked his car next to two others.

Had the other prospective buyers arrived, or were these the Blairs' vehicles?

As she reached for the door, his fingers clasped her wrist. Surprised, she looked at him. "What?"

He leaned across the console, and lowered his voice. "I held up my end of the bargain with the Delices. You better bring it as my wife."

"Don't worry." She pulled free of his hold. "I'll be the best fake wife there ever was. Because it'll get you out of my life forever."

Before he could respond, Cal and Maisie hurried up to them, waiting a few feet away.

When she and Hayes exited the vehicle, Maisie instantly went in for hugs. Her floral perfume enveloped Joy. "You're here! We're so happy to see you. How was the drive? Nice car, Hayes. Looks like one of those Hot Wheels toys, just life-sized. Oh, my goodness, I didn't notice the ring earlier!" Maisie reached for Joy's hand. "It's gorgeous. And what a nod to Scotland."

The diamond engagement ring and gold wedding band sparkled in the diffused sunlight. She shifted her hand back and forth so the stacked rings caught more light. Gorgeous, yes, but they were a symbol of their lies, not of love. The reminder hit with a pang of conscience, and she returned her hand to her side.

As Cal grabbed Joy's suitcase and led the way to the house, the guilt that swept over her thickened. The Blairs were so kind, and genuine, and welcoming. She shouldn't be lying to them.

Maisie directed them through the front door and small mudroom. On the way upstairs, Cal pointed out parts of the house they could see: the living room to their left, the family room to their right. The staircase branched into two halfway to the top: one fork led to a closed door straight ahead and the other fork swooped to the right and ended in a hallway.

"This here is our bedroom." Maisie pointed to the shut door ahead of them. "But we'll go up this way to yours."

She led them up the remaining stairs until they stood in a rectangular hallway no more than thirteen feet long.

Maisie opened the door to their immediate left. "This is your bedroom. We always think of it as Hayes's room. It's the biggest of our guestrooms and has its own bathroom." Before letting them in, she pointed to the door next to theirs. "That room is empty, Joy, but not big. Hayes can use it for work calls so he's not disturbing you." She nodded across the hall. "I've put Gene and Liselle in that room over there, and Kenna and her laddie in the one next to it. That door next to Kenna's room is the bathroom. They'll have to share it, but they can use the one downstairs if they need to."

Joy had expected the farmhouse to be large, with wings and extensions that would give everyone some privacy. Hayes had told her that the farmhouse had five bedrooms, after all. She hadn't expected that four of those bedrooms would be clustered in one compact rectangle of a hallway. Thankfully, she and Hayes were at one end of that hallway and the other two couples at the other, but barely four yards separated the two ends.

Hayes's house in Nevada was a mansion chiseled into a desert mountain. How would he adjust to a farm that couldn't be more than 2,500 square feet?

At least they had their own bathroom for the week— and an empty room *right next door*. She would have to figure out how to shove Hayes into it when the others weren't looking.

If she could avoid sharing a room with him, she might even enjoy the enchanting farm and the Blairs' delightful company.

The bedroom had been painted a cheerful yellow and decorated with watercolor paintings of flowers in full bloom. Floral curtains framed the large windows, which provided unencumbered views of the fallscape outside.

Thunderclouds zoomed across the sweep of hills toward the house.

*Hayes is going to be cold again.* Not her problem, because he'd be in the other room. She chanced a glance at the bed.

Big enough for two people only if they were side sleepers and didn't mind spooning, the charming spindle bed was covered in a yellow bedspread and piled with fluffy, white pillows. She couldn't wait to climb under the covers later that evening. The drive had taken over two hours, and though the scenery had distracted her from the trip, Hayes's presence had kept her tense and agitated. Stretching out here while he slept in the other room was just what the doctor ordered.

Cal set Joy's suitcase in the corner; Hayes dropped his right next to it. That was fine. As soon as the Blairs went back downstairs, she'd insist that Hayes figure out a way to move into the small room next to theirs. Maybe he could say she snored, and he needed some shut-eye. She didn't care. As long as he stayed far away from her every night for the rest of their stay here.

"We'll leave you to settle in." Maisie stepped into the hallway.

"Kenna and Benjamin are on their way, but Gene and Liselle are running late." Cal followed his wife into the hall but hovered at the threshold. "We'll see you in the kitchen when you're ready. After lunch, I'll give you, Joy, the farm tour. Unless, Hayes, you'd like to? You know this place as well as I do."

How was Hayes as acquainted with this farm as the beekeeper living here? Not that the secretive grouch would tell her. Maybe the Blairs would, though. She'd have to get them alone and ask.

"You lead the tour, Cal," said Hayes. "I imagine Joy would appreciate an insider perspective."

Cal beamed and closed the door behind him and Maisie. Joy heard them chatting happily to each other all the way down the stairs.

"You're sleeping in the empty room next door," she told her unwanted fake husband.

"Fuck no. That's an office. There's only a puny couch and an old desk in there. And how do you expect me to sneak in and out between the two rooms with the others across the hall?"

"I'm sure if you put your mind to it, you can figure it out."

He kneeled next to his suitcase. Unzipping it, he pulled out his neatly folded clothing items and began to hang them up in the armoire.

"You sure you want to continue this farce?" She sat on the edge of the bed.

Not bothering to look at her, he grunted. "We have a deal."

"Is there nothing you'll stop at to get your way?"

He didn't respond.

Crossing her arms, she watched him work. "There's still something between you and Liselle."

*Why did I have to bring her up? Now he's going to think I'm jealous.*

This time, he glowered. "There's nothing between us."

She didn't buy it. "Yet you spent a fortune on the Delices to get me to lie for you."

"This farm means something to me. I won't let her have it."

Joy doubted anything was sacred to Hayes.

The muscles under his sweater shifted as he rearranged the hangers to be just so, and closed the armoire doors. Forcing herself to look away, she walked over to her own luggage and began to pull out her clothes.

He extended his hand. "I'll hang them up for you."

She eyed the open palm with suspicion. "I can do it."

"You'll mess up my system."

Not caring enough to argue, she surrendered her clothes to him and watched as he hung up her things next to his.

***

When he finished rearranging her items, he stepped back to make sure the hangers looked right.

"You're not sleeping here," she said, as though it were a given.

She assumed wrong, but he wasn't about to start an argument now. He adjusted a stray hanger. "We'll discuss that later."

It's not like he itched to share the room with her either. Joy was too distracting, and he refused to get sidetracked.

Being back felt good, though. He'd last been on the farm for Christmas—both to see the Blairs and to avoid Joy at the family gatherings. The familiar smell of this house— the trace of ash from the fireplaces, the sweet notes of honey and vanilla that seemed to linger in the air, the tang of wet pine—set him at immediate peace. It was home.

He often escaped here when work got tiresome and he needed a break. He never thought he'd be bringing Joy here, or lying to Cal and Maisie. But it was for their own good.

"Do the Blairs know about your history with Liselle?" Joy asked in a low register, as though she was afraid sound carried in the house.

He brought his attention back to her. "No."

"Why not?"

"What would I tell them?"

"Oh, I don't know." She flung her arms out wide. "How about Liselle is my ex. Don't sell her the farm?"

If only it were that easy. He'd never once told them her name. Not while holed up in this very room over a decade ago, healing broken bones and battling depression. Not after he and Liselle reconnected years later. As far as the Blairs knew, he'd lost touch with the woman he had once thought he loved. How could he tell them the truth now?

"She's their new niece—she married their nephew. They don't need to know our history."

"You deny it, but you want her back."

How many times did he have to have this argument? "I want her out of my life. I'll do so without embroiling the Blairs in our past."

Her nose scrunched. "I don't believe you."

Stepping around her, he went to unpack the rest of his suitcase. "You don't have to believe me."

"If I find out that this is foreplay for you two, I will make you pay. Hard."

The very word shot a jolt of need through him. He could show her exactly how hard she made him. The hours in the car with her had been torture—her scent, her soft sounds of appreciation of the vistas around them, her sheer *presence* in the passenger seat made concentrating on the road almost impossible.

More than once, he'd been tempted to pull over onto some isolated side road and take her there, while the wind battered their car.

The chatter of voices just outside their door cut through his lascivious thoughts.

# Chapter 12

The other prospective buyers had arrived.

It was easy to tell—their unfamiliar voices carried through the small upstairs space.

*Here we go. This farm would go to the most deserving ones if it killed her.*

A few minutes later, the strangers' excited prattle grew louder as they passed their door on their way down-stairs.

"I guess we should go downstairs too," said Joy when the chitchat faded, though dread weighed her down.

She hated lying—pretending to be married to the man she despised was going to take a lot of acting chops. Meanwhile, she only had six days to find the most authentic buyers. What if she chose wrong and the farm went to monsters? It's not like she had a great track record with picking the right people—first, she thought herself in love with Hayes, then she fell for an addict who killed her pets.

Hayes looked as excited by the prospect of meeting the newcomers as she did, but he threw open the door and motioned for her to precede him.

They followed the prattle through a bright, ginormous kitchen—by far, Joy was certain, the largest room in the house. The L-shaped counter wrapped the length of two walls. A rectangular table anchored the space, with ten slat-back chairs arranged around it. Against the left wall, a plush, butter-yellow couch nestled between two windows, flanked by matching armchairs on either side. A flame point Siamese snoozed in one of the armchairs.

"That's Malik. He runs this place. He'll come say hello later." Hayes indicated the cat.

Because Hayes never paused, she couldn't pet the feline or study the family photos that lined the wall above the sofa. Instead, she followed him into the glassed-in sunroom.

The sleepy farm stretched beyond the glass walls, storm clouds rolling across the horizon. Against the gray backdrop, the cozy space reminded her of an oasis. Plants of every variety lined its perimeter like a miniature jungle. In the middle, two well-worn love seats and a couple of deep armchairs framed a coffee table arranged with miniature potted plants. A floor-to-ceiling bookshelf brimmed with books in the corner. As soon as she could sneak away later, she'd return here, pick a novel, and curl up in one of the armchairs.

A couple sat on one of the love seats—a cute redhead with a button nose smattered with freckles, and her gangly, dark-haired man. They looked up at her and Hayes with unmistakable curiosity and rose to their feet.

Maisie, in an armchair next to the couple, jumped up too and the wattage of her smile tripled. "Hayes, Joy, this is Kenna Ross and her fiancé, Benjamin Buchanan. Kenna, Benjamin, meet Hayes and Joy Icefall."

Joy had to remind herself that for the next six days, that was her name. She'd accepted Hayes's deal and there was no backing out now.

After they shook hands, Maisie directed them to sit across from Kenna and Benjamin, all the while giving a quick background of how she and Cal knew the young couple. "Kenna grew up on the sheep farm next door.

She's a good friend of our son's. We've known her pretty much her entire life."

"When I heard that Cal and Maisie were selling," said Kenna, "I convinced Benjamin that we have to put in a bid. A developer keeps phoning my parents. He's offering a ridiculous amount for their sheep farm to build a fancy tourism development there instead. No way am I letting that happen to Highlander Honey Farm either."

"We'd never sell to a developer," said Maisie.

"I know that," Kenna assured her with a warm smile. "But what if the next owner would?"

Was that why Hayes and Liselle swarmed this place? Did they see the farm as an investment opportunity? Joy had no idea how much the developer was offering, but she'd bet good money it was more than the Blairs' asking price.

Kenna's fiancé jutted out his pointy chin and wrapped a bony arm around Kenna. "We want our kids to grow up here, to grow old here, not to see this place torn apart and turned into a playground for the rich."

Tucked against her fiancé's shoulder, Kenna glowed. "I've got so many ideas for the farm, like selling jam along with the honey. And beauty products too, made with farm honey and beeswax."

Hayes, next to Joy, groaned.

"We'd move to the farm, of course," said Benjamin. "It's not too far from where we live now, so it wouldn't be much bother."

Joy knew that Hayes would not make the same commitment.

Maisie backed out of the sunroom. "I'll be right back. Lunch is nearly ready."

"Can we give you a hand?" asked Kenna.

"No, no, you sit and get to know each other."

"What do you guys do?" Joy asked after Maisie disappeared into the kitchen. So far, she liked Kenna and Benjamin, but she needed more intel.

When Kenna looked at her fiancé, her face softened with pride. "Benjamin owns several coffee shops."

"And Kenna's a speech therapist." Benjamin nuzzled the crown of Kenna's head before redirecting his attention back to Joy. "Maisie was just telling us how you're a doctor down in San Diego. We've always wanted to visit. How long have you lived there?"

Finally, someone to have a conversation with. While Hayes sat silently beside her and studied Kenna and Benjamin with conspicuous suspicion, she told them more about her residency program and asked them questions about Kenna's job and Benjamin's cafés.

Too soon, Maisie interrupted. "Is everyone hungry? Lunch is ready."

With that, she shuffled everyone to the set kitchen table.

Hayes claimed the chair next to Joy.

Couldn't he give her some space? His familiar scent made her want to straddle his lap and take a deep whiff of his neck like a horny vampire; she resisted the urge like the big girl she was.

In need of a distraction, she turned to their host. "Maisie, please let us help."

Maisie waved off her offer, ladling out lentil soup into everyone's bowls. After setting a tray of ham and cheese sandwiches on thick-sliced bread in the middle of the table, she took her own seat.

"Where's Cal?" asked Hayes, clearly oblivious to Joy's charged thoughts.

Maisie smiled. "He went out back for his mead."

"What piqued your interest in the farm?" Kenna's aqua eyes moved from Hayes to Joy.

Hayes's lips flattened. "I like the honey."

"Oh, he does love our honey." Maisie laughed. "But Hayes has come out to visit at least once a year for over a decade now. When our barn went up in flames some years ago, he had it completely rebuilt, and made it state of the art."

*How did he meet the Blairs in the first place?*

Hayes shifted in his seat, and the top of his nose bridge turned red.

"You're embarrassing the lad, Maisie," chided Cal as he appeared in the doorway. Waving a dark glass bottle in the air, he grinned. "Who wants to try my new mead flavor? I made it with our heather honey."

After Maisie helped get everyone glasses, he poured the bubbling gold liquid while chattering about his mead-making process before taking a chair next to Kenna.

Joy brought her glass closer and took a ginger sip. The effervescent liquid tasted like how she imagined a heather meadow to smell—floral and warm. The bright sweetness played across her tongue.

"Oh wow." She savored another swallow. "Cal, this is incredible."

"Isn't it?" Her host grinned. "Mead from the best heather honey around." His gaze flicked to the farm beyond the glass windows and the corners of his mouth tipped down. "We are proud our lad made a life for himself in New York, and we look forward to being closer to our grandkids, but we'll miss this place."

Joy's heart twisted at Cal's forlorn sigh.

"I'm sure whoever buys it would want you to visit," she offered softly. In fact, she'd try her hardest to ensure it.

Kenna laid her hand across Cal's. "And to stay as long as you like."

"This will always be your home," Hayes added.

Maisie blinked furiously. "It's a good thing to move closer to our grandbabies, but this place has been a part of us for so long. Cal grew up here. We raised Alexander here. It'll be a change for us all."

Joy took another draught of the mead, guilt at lying to the Blairs skyrocketing.

Hayes must have felt her dilemma, because he laid his hand on her knee.

In comfort or warning? She couldn't tell, and she fought the urge to shake it off. He was the one who had made a liar out of her.

"How did you two meet?" Kenna turned her pixie face to Joy.

Hayes's grip on her knee tightened. "We met through our siblings."

"Oh, how romantic!" Kenna exclaimed. "Are they pals?"

"His half-brother, Jackson, married my sister, Evie."

Benjamin scooted his chair closer to his fiancée. "And how long have you two been hitched?"

Joy cleared her throat. "Feels like barely a day."

Kenna's eyes widened with delight. "Newlyweds! How nice!"

Joy tried to move the subject to anyone but her and Hayes. "How about you two?"

Pulling over her mead, Kenna took a long drag. "Oh, we're only just engaged."

"Love at first sight with these two," supplied Maisie. "They met at Benjamin's coffee shop. Kenna stopped on her way to her parents' farm—and the rest is history. Have you two set a date yet for the big day?"

Kenna faltered. "Erm, not yet."

Benjamin looked like he wanted the ground to swallow him whole. "Not yet," he echoed and reached for his mead too.

A doorbell chimed before Joy could ask a follow-up.

Maisie rose to her feet. "That must be our nephew and his bride. Remind me how you two know each other again, Hayes?"

His shoulders drew together. A muscle twitched beneath the clean-shaven skin of his cheek. "We met a long time ago."

He didn't add anything more, but Joy doubted the Blairs noticed, as they both dashed off to let in the last of the prospective buyers.

She and Hayes stayed in the kitchen with Kenna and Benjamin and dug into the laid-out lunch while the Blairs settled the Garniers upstairs.

All too soon, Liselle and Gene's voices—hers cloying, his cheery—grew louder. Hayes jerked at Liselle's saccharine laugh.

Dread twisted Joy's organs. She did not like Liselle, but Vacation Barbie and her young husband appeared in the kitchen all too soon, the Blairs just behind them.

Maisie insisted that everyone finish lunch before the farm tour, seating her nephew and Liselle at the other end of the table.

As usual, Liselle looked flawless, with not a curl out of place. Her ridiculously dewy skin made it seem as though she'd just woken from a twenty-four-hour nap that involved IV hydration. No wonder Hayes was still obsessed with her. In comparison, Joy must have resembled a gremlin after the car ride.

Twisting toward her with a bright—Joy would have bet

anything—*fake* smile, Liselle took a delicate sip of the mead Cal had poured her. "Maisie tells me you're newlyweds."

Ugh. *Here we go.*

Her whole body burned as though she'd fallen into a pile of poison oak. Fighting the itch searing her skin, she plastered on a smile as bright as Liselle's. "We are."

"Gene and I just moved to Aberdeen." Liselle twirled a glossy lock of hair around her manicured finger. "You're a new doctor. Won't it be hard to find a job in Scotland as a medical professional without much work experience? Or are you two planning on living in the States?"

One thing was certain. Joy would *never* let Liselle have this farm. Joy didn't even know her, but boy, did she dislike her. Maybe it was her overpowering perfume, or that overly exaggerated laugh, or the way she spoke down to her. Either way, if a developer came calling with an offer, Liselle would be the first one to line up. The Blairs' place deserved better than that.

"We'll split our time." She gave Hayes what she hoped would pass for a lovey-dovey look. "Highlander Honey means a lot to my husband."

Hayes covered her hand on the table with his, raising it to his lips. His eyes never left hers as he brushed an unexpected kiss to her knuckles.

The PDA was calculated; she wasn't an idiot. Just an act for their audience. Yet heat sparked where his mouth had touched.

Uh-oh. She'd waded too far. She tried to reclaim her hand with a subtle tug, but his fingers tightened around hers, zinging misplaced need to all her sensitive areas.

Frustrated by her own reaction to something as simple as a *peck to her hand*, she resorted to yanking it away under the guise of requiring both to eat her lunch.

The acts of affection, the glances, the caresses were all a blatant lie.

*Remember that, Joy. Don't fall for it again.*

And yet as Hayes topped off her mead, she couldn't help but notice the thick length of his fingers and remember how they had felt against her bare skin.

Across from her and Hayes, Kenna and Benjamin looked head over heels in love. They sat with their hands interlaced, and he'd lean to brush a brief kiss across her shoulder, her cheek whenever he thought others weren't looking.

Out of all the vultures circling the farm, they seemed the most genuine. She still had six days to learn more about them, but so far, she had a good idea whose team she was on.

# Chapter 13

After lunch, Cal and Maisie invited the newcomers—namely, Joy and Liselle—on a tour of the farm. To Joy's immense relief, the others tagged along too. A tour with just her and her fake husband's ex-girlfriend would have been plain awkward otherwise.

Cal and Maisie led the way, with Hayes, Joy, Kenna, and Benjamin at their heels. Liselle and Gene brought up the rear.

Kenna pointed to a row of Scotch pines that bordered the farm on one side. "My folks' property is just across the trees. The developer's been calling and texting them nonstop. I'm surprised you haven't been hounded?"

"Not yet…" Maisie responded. "They can probably guess what our answer will be."

The fence line began where the pine trees ended; Cal pointed out the raspberry and bilberry bushes that grew wildly along it.

As they walked past the orchard, Cal spoke of the apple, pear, and plum trees with obvious pride. They passed a chicken coop, a greenhouse, and a pumpkin patch scattered with bright-orange pumpkins, and rows of beehives.

"The bees are low maintenance when it's this Baltic out," said Cal, stopping next to the apiaries, "so we check up on them about once a month or so, but we don't like to bother them otherwise."

"We use Smith hives," Maisie added, looking between Joy and Liselle. "They're smaller than the ones you see in America. The bees do all the cooling and heating of the hives themselves, and the smaller hives make it easier for them to keep their home toasty in the winter months."

"Scottish beekeepers prefer them for another reason too," said Cal. "Beekeepers from the Lowlands drive up their bees to the Highlands for heather blooming season, and the smaller boxes make it easier for them."

When they stopped in front of the new barn, Maisie threaded her arm through Hayes's. "Here's the new barn that Hayes had rebuilt. It's got an extraction room and bottling equipment now. We're so grateful to you for this, Hayes."

Hayes cleared his throat. "It was the least I could do."

What inspired him to rebuild their barn?

How did a reclusive American entrepreneur come to know a pair of Scottish honey farmers?

Questions bubbled, and she burned to ask them, but wouldn't that be something Hayes's wife would know? Asking Cal or Maisie about their connection to Hayes might make them suspicious. And as much as she detested lying, she and Hayes had a deal.

Throwing open the barn doors, Cal led them into the large space. Though the stainless-steel machines had been cleaned and stored away for the winter, scents of wildflower pollen, earthy beeswax, and sweet honey lingered in the cool air.

The Blairs walked them through their small operation—the serrated knives they preferred to heated ones to uncap the ready honeycombs, the uncapping machine in the corner that Hayes had purchased for them but they had yet to use, and the swing cage basket extractor that spun to sling honey from its combs into a vat.

"This is our old-fashioned honey filtering system," Maisie said with a note of pride, stopping by a collection of metal sieves—the coarse ones for the first filtration, and the fine ones to strain out the smaller particles. "We don't heat honey in any way."

As everyone studied the sieves, Hayes used the opportunity to slide his hand along her arm and clasp hers, threading their fingers together.

She knew what he was doing: playing the role of doting husband to impress the Blairs. It was a ruse. Completely fake. And yet the simple act ignited a wildfire beneath her skin.

*This has got to stop.*

*I don't like Hayes. I don't trust him.*

Her body didn't seem to care.

Apparently, Joy wasn't the only one who found Hayes appealing. Liselle kept sneaking charged glances his way too. Quite inappropriate for someone whose husband hovered on her other side.

The bite of possessiveness surprised her.

*Great. There I go, falling for the ruse again.*

Hayes wasn't her territory to defend; he was a con artist duping a good family and he'd made her his unwilling—though very active—accomplice.

Guilt swamped her, and she tugged her hand out of Hayes's, pretending to fix her braid.

As Cal walked them around the extractor, Gene and Liselle jostled too close. Before Liselle's sharp elbow could connect with her rib cage, Hayes tucked Joy securely against his side, settling his hand on her hip like it belonged there.

He smelled like the wintry air outside and his expensive aftershave. Covertly, she glanced up at him— at the strong sweep of his jaw, the easy way his lips curved as Cal elaborated on the equipment. When she finally wrenched her gaze away and tried to focus on Cal's words, they hovered just out of reach.

Hayes's hand released her hip to splay across her lower back as they proceeded to the next piece of equipment, this one used for heather blossom honey.

"This is called a loosener," said Cal. "Heather honey is much thicker and more gelatinous than wildflower honey and much harder to extract. This beauty right here helps us out loads. It gets the honey out but keeps the combs intact."

He described the process of the machine using pins to prick through the honey caps, but Joy—distracted by Hayes at her side—couldn't pay attention. Forcing herself to move as far away from him as possible, she surveyed the barn.

Beekeeper suits hung neatly by the barn doors. Helmets, gloves, and accessories she couldn't identify lined the shelves built into the opposite wall.

When she asked the Blairs to explain the trappings, Cal happily obliged. "Those on the top shelf are smokers. They calm our babies before we open their hives. And those are bee brushes. We use them to nudge the bees away when we need to get at the honey frames."

"Do you give them sugar for winter?" Joy asked, curious.

"We leave them with honey and make sure they

have plenty of it," Maisie replied, "because honey has the nutrients and vitamins our bees need. We do provide fondant to supplement when winter's particularly cold."

"As they say, bees don't freeze, they starve," added Cal.

After the barn, the Blairs walked them to the shed where they stored jarred honey, along with portioned honeycombs, bee pollen, and blocks of beeswax, ready for sale.

Together with a dedicated team, the Blairs sold their honey at local markets and shops, through several distributors, and online. How Hayes was going to manage all that from the States, Joy had no idea.

They took a closer look at the coop next, where a dozen chickens grazed in their paddock.

As they continued the farm tour, Joy grabbed Hayes's wrist, maneuvering him to the back of the group.

"I can't believe you made me do this," she said after the others walked far enough ahead. "They are so kind, and you're taking advantage."

"I'm protecting them."

She didn't believe that for a second. He had always only prioritized himself.

Hayes held to her side throughout the rest of the tour, the very image of a doting husband. He'd lay his hand on the small of her back to guide her in a certain direction, or lean close to murmur a droll comment.

*Don't fall for it. You know it's an act.*

Her body reacted, regardless.

When Cal and Maisie stopped at the far edge of the farm to discuss an upcoming fence replacement project, the wind picked up, sending a shiver to skip across her skin.

Hayes, somehow perceptive to her discomfort, stepped behind her, wrapped the edges of his coat around her, and pulled her shivering frame into his warmth.

Saturated by the very essence of him, she stiffened—torn between her desire to lean into him and her need to escape.

When he angled his head and placed a kiss along her cheek, she not only let him—she settled her hands over his on her waist and melted against him.

*Just putting on a show. Acting as any newlyweds would.*

She was *not* enjoying this—she *had* to play along to lull him into a false sense of safety before she determined the farm's rightful owners and ensured Highlander Honey went to them.

*It's all a game to him anyway,* she reminded herself, even as her hands on his tightened.

# Chapter 14

The rain started just as they finished the walk-through of the fence line. Because no one had thought to bring umbrellas, they dashed into the house a soggy mess and hurried to their respective rooms to change.

Hayes waved her ahead of him into the bedroom, stripping before he even shut the door.

Joy tried really, really hard not to stare. Truly she did. But it was as though her eyes had grown a mind of their own.

He shed his damp coat first. The sweater and the white undershirt beneath came off at the same time.

She'd seen plenty of shirtless men before—she was a doctor, after all. Even men as built as him. And yet the shock of seeing Hayes—who tended to layer up around Scotland—made her gawk.

*He has a tattoo.*

A poinsettia, etched in black ink over his heart.

Before she could look away—because, honestly, she meant to—he reached for the button of his jeans, worked down the zipper, and then—*bam!*—shoved them down his muscular thighs.

His boxers were black silk. Of course. Leave it to Hayes to even surround his junk in luxurious comfort.

Breath bated, she wished he'd drop the silk boxers

next. But he kept them on. Only after he strutted to the bathroom to grab a towel did she finally stop gawking.

He brought a towel out for her too, extending it to her before drying his soaked hair.

When had he gotten the tattoo? Was it a nod to the company he sold, or was Hayes a secret Christmas fan?

Realizing she was staring again, she wrung out her braid into the waffle weave cotton. Still, she couldn't let it go. "Your tattoo is new."

His gaze shuttered. "Got it a couple years back."

Curiosity pierced her. *Why would stick-up-the-ass Hayes get a tattoo?*

Attempting to appear disinterested, she shrugged out of her down jacket and wiggled out of her sweater. "Any meaning behind it?"

He stalked to the table. "A reminder that people can't be trusted."

Guess that was his life motto. Whittling any more out of him would be futile.

Her jeans had gotten soaked too; she peeled them down her legs until she wore nothing but a cream-colored tank top and underwear. Trying to act nonchalant, she peeked at Hayes through her lashes, wondering whether he was as interested in her stripping as she had been in him.

Her pride took a beating because he wasn't. He concentrated on his iPad instead.

*Humbling.*

Trying not to feel insulted—and failing—she shook out her jeans and went to the armoire to grab a hanger so they could dry.

Suddenly, he was next to her—all hard muscle and bronzed skin.

Feeling very naked, even in her tank, she backed up. And bumped into the edge of the bed hard enough to yelp. Had it always been there?

Without sparing her so much as a blink, he reached for a change of clothes in the armoire.

She pinned her gaze to his face and kept it there. Straying any lower would lead to disaster. And some very bad choices.

"What?" he asked, and she realized she'd been caught staring.

*Crap.* She struggled for something to say. "Nothing. Just… I don't like this."

Not bothering to look at her, he pulled on a slate cable-knit from a hanger. "The farm?"

She lowered her voice because the walls were thin. "Pretending."

Not an ounce of sympathy softened his features. "You're going to have to get used to it."

For a businessman like Hayes, lying was par for the course. Not for her. Especially now, when she'd gotten to know the Blairs better.

He'd never understand.

Careful to avoid getting too close to him, she hugged her own change of clothes to her chest and retreated to the other end of the room to dress.

***

A clothed Joy Campbell was beautiful, but an almost naked Joy Campbell? Hayes forgot his own name.

He should have stayed far away. Instead, he moved before he caught himself—and then he was next to her.

Her tank was an obstacle his hands twitched to tear

111

out of the way. How easy it would be to tug down the fabric and learn if her nipples tasted as sweet as he imagined. Three years ago, he'd kissed every inch of skin her silk dress had left exposed, but he'd stopped himself from stripping her bare.

"Why are you looking at me like that?" she asked.

He lifted his gaze away from the rapid rise and fall of her breasts. "I'd think it's obvious."

"Well, stop it, will you? I don't want to be ogled."

"Really? Because earlier you were upset I hadn't… ogled you enough once before."

Her gold-flecked eyes narrowed. "That's not why I was upset. Besides, my days of wishing to be… ogled by you are long over."

"Is that a fact?" he murmured, and stepped closer. "One day, you'll beg me to take your pretty nipples in my mouth."

"Your mouth is never coming anywhere near my nipples."

"You say it as though you haven't spent the entire day thinking about it."

"I haven't." The tinge of pink in her cheeks belied the statement.

At least her blush made her easier for him to read.

"Must have been just me then."

He shouldn't have touched her. When it came to Joy, a single touch had never been enough. He did it anyway, cupping her face with a gentleness that surprised him.

The pulse at her throat thundered—not from fear. No, she wasn't afraid of him. Despite their time apart, the pull between them hadn't lessened. He wasn't misreading it. For once, he was certain.

He had no business wanting her. She was all beauty

and effervescent energy, and strictly off-limits, but when she looked at him like that, he was powerless to resist.

Her cheek, gilded a rosy pink by her earlier fib, felt cool beneath his palm. He traced his thumb across the chilled velvet.

"What exactly were you thinking about?" she asked in an unsteady voice.

"Stripping you… I'd make you stand naked in front of me, lift your breasts and beg me to taste them."

Her eyes darkened at his admission.

"I'd never beg you," she shot back on a ragged breath, but she didn't shake off his hold.

"You would," he murmured, leaning in close enough to brush her cheek with his lips. "I'd do so eventually, take them in my mouth and nibble and lick until you're dripping for me… but not right away. First, I'd kiss down your belly, taste that sexy little ring, spread you—"

Flattening her hands on his chest, she gave him a not-so-gentle push, giving him no recourse but to let go.

"What a wild imagination." She tucked a wet lock of hair behind her ear. "But that's not happening. Not now, not ever. Now, can you stop toying with me so I can change?"

"Change quickly. I'm sure Cal and Maisie have the rest of the afternoon mapped out."

He wasn't wrong.

By the time they joined the others in the family room, Cal had dragged down a large whiteboard and set out a collection of colorful markers.

Kenna grinned at them. "Just in time for Pictionary."

He'd have expected Joy to jump on board, but her "Great!" sounded lukewarm at best. Maybe she'd been as affected by their earlier interaction as he was. Or was he projecting?

Benjamin gave Hayes a pained look and held up a bottle of beer in silent commiseration.

"I've got a headache coming on." Liselle rose from the couch. "I'll sit this one out."

Gene wrapped his arm around her shoulders. "Come on, darling, I'll head up with you. Want something for your head?"

Hayes pitied the poor bastard. When Liselle cut him loose, he wouldn't know what hit him.

"We should play men against women," Kenna offered. "Loser gets to… perform a dramatic reading of their last few text exchanges over dinner."

Next to him, Joy snickered. "Oh. We are going to *win*, ladies."

Hayes loathed group activities on principle, but Joy's competitive spirit apparently matched his own.

She was up first.

"Make it good," he taunted.

Her pretty eyes flashed, and she lifted her chin. Challenge accepted.

The breakneck battle thundered on as the storm raged outside. They called it only when the sun set, with Joy's team winning by one point.

Tossing her head back, Joy did a little dance around the coffee table before stabbing her finger through the air at him. "Get your text messages ready, fellas!"

He'd expected to be bothered by the defeat. Instead, her delight shot unsettling possessiveness through his veins.

Realizing that, as her husband, he could touch her, he crossed the short distance until he was next to her. Her breath caught when he lifted her in the air, spinning her around before planting a kiss to her surprise-rounded lips.

The chatter around them died away as he looked into her shining face. Unable to resist, he took her mouth again. This time, she met him halfway—pulling him closer as she kissed him back.

Someone whistled. Fucking Benjamin.

As if remembering where they were—and what they were to each other—Joy shoved away from him. He let her go immediately—but caught her as she stumbled.

"Better be prepared for your dramatic reading, Icefall," she muttered, before sinking into the far corner of the couch and reaching for her tea.

# Chapter 15

Liselle and Gene joined the group a few minutes later. The energy shifted, like mud thickening water.

At first, Joy thought she'd imagined it, but Kenna and Benjamin had gone more reserved, and Hayes had shut down completely.

In an attempt to return the energy to prior levels, Cal and Maisie amped up their ribald humor, and Joy accepted this new normal with the Garniers in the mix.

"Fancy a movie before dinner?" Cal suggested, already moving to the big screen. "We've turned this room into a cinema of sorts with our new telly."

Liselle and Gene claimed the couch. Kenna and Benjamin nestled together in one of two oversized armchairs; the Blairs took the other.

Refusing to sit next to Liselle, Joy slid to the floor, leaving Hayes to stand awkwardly in the middle of the room before he settled next to her.

*Was there no escaping him?* Grasping at excuses to get him to move away, she leaned close. "You sure you shouldn't sit on the couch? Floor can't be good for your… injury."

"I'm not injured," he muttered.

What was with the strange limp then?

"Don't you two look cozy," said Maisie.

Hayes offered their host a smile, wrapping his arm around Joy's shoulders and pulling her against him.

She knew the gesture was intended for those around them, but it made her ache in places that should know better. Telling herself that she was just playing along, she settled more comfortably against him, and savored the soft brush of his lips against her hair—another one of his make-believe moves.

As the movie played on and Tom Cruise jumped off a cliff on a motorcycle, she snuggled closer into Hayes. The house was adequately heated, and a fire danced in the nearby fireplace, but a draft across the floor prickled at her.

If she felt cold, she knew Hayes's teeth would soon be chattering.

With a fluid motion, Hayes reached behind himself with his free hand, snagging a throw from the sofa arm without disturbing her position against him. He draped it over them both.

Just as she melted against him, he readjusted his hold to weave lazy patterns across her shoulder. Cars chased each other on-screen, but Joy couldn't focus, her attention absorbed by each idle stroke.

*He's doing this on purpose for the audience. Don't read into it.*

But the movie in front of her blurred as his clever fingers sent her pulse points throbbing.

This wouldn't do at all.

Yet plastered against his side as she was, moving away would draw attention. She could make up an excuse—she had to use the bathroom, or fill a glass up with water. A breather to get her raging hormones under control because, with Hayes, one had to always lead with one's brain.

He was too wily, too clever—he'd take advantage of any perceived weakness. The hospital gala fiasco three years ago was Exhibit A and here, pretending to be married, was Exhibit B. How many more exhibits did she need?

And yet he smelled so good, and was so warm and solid. All she wanted to do was nestle closer. Foolishly, she did just that.

*But it's okay*, she told herself; *you still don't like him. He's just a heat source.*

After the movie ended, Cal stood to start dinner. "Joy, we're having pan-seared steak, but I'm making you fish. That sound good to you?"

Separating herself from Hayes, Joy rose. "You don't have to cook separately for me. I'll be fine with the soup from lunch, or some toast."

"Nonsense. Steak and potatoes for us, fish and potatoes for you."

"Need help?" Hayes asked Cal, setting the blanket aside and standing too.

"I got it. You all relax before dinner. I need a half hour—tops."

"And I'll need three hours to clean up after you. Come on, I'll help clean as you cook," said Maisie, crossing to Cal.

***

After dinner, everyone retired to their rooms.

Hayes retreated to their bedroom to work, but Joy stayed downstairs, undoubtedly waiting for everyone to sleep so she could kick him out into the small office.

The tiny space—with its half-sized couch—wasn't

ideal, but he'd take it. The alternative was walking around with a permanent erection in the room he shared with Joy.

When the other couples finally settled, he set aside his tablet and went to get his wife.

He found her reading on one of the love seats in the sunroom, lit by the pale glow from the table lamp next to her. Malik, ever the smart one, had found his way to her lap.

Closing her book, she looked up, as if expecting him.

"Everyone settled?" She scratched between Malik's ears. The cat closed his eyes and purred in resounding bliss.

*Great, now I'm jealous of a cat.*

Her sweater rode low off one shoulder, exposing the deep cut of her tank and a mouthwatering glimpse of full breasts.

He jerked his chin in a semblance of a nod. It was the most he could do with the blood rushing from his brain.

Irritated with himself, he proffered his hand. "Time for bed."

But she didn't take the assist. Moving the cat gently from her lap, she rose on her own and kept a few feet of space between them.

Resigned, he waved her ahead of him.

Once inside their room, she marched to the bed, undoing the neatly tucked corners. "Take the duvet with you. And there's more blankets at the bottom of the armoire."

No way in hell was he taking the thickest blanket from her. The weather outside dipped into bumfuck freezing at night. "You'll be cold. Keep the duvet."

"I'll be fine."

"How do you propose I sneak in and out with all the blankets?" he asked, pacing to the armoire.

Her full lips thinned. "You claim to be smart. Figure it out."

He wanted to bite that sharp tongue of hers.

Ignoring the urge, he hunted out the extra quilts at the bottom of the wardrobe and tossed them on the bed. "Gonna shower first."

Her eyes slitted with annoyance. "*Now?* You couldn't have done it while I was downstairs?"

"No. Had work to do."

"And you couldn't have gotten me after?" she asked in a pitch high enough to send dogs running.

Interesting. Maybe she wasn't as immune to him as she claimed.

He let his smile spread. "Think you can't resist joining me if you're a couple of feet away?"

Crossing her arms, she raised that dimpled chin of hers. "I can resist joining you."

His gaze slid over her breasts—thrust higher by her interlaced arms. "You'd look so fucking hot in nothing but soap bubbles."

"I do look hot in nothing but soap bubbles," she returned with a smile. "But you don't get to experience that. Ever."

He appreciated a challenge.

What would it take to feel her lips close over him again, to pump into her mouth, claim her throat?

The creak of a nearby door and voices in the hallway cut him off mid-thought. "You hear that?"

Tilting her head, she listened. "Probably one of the other couples using the bathroom."

Kenna's frustrated hiss reached him.

"Shush," Benjamin interrupted.

Guess it wasn't all premarital bliss for them after all.

He'd suspected that something was off with those two from the moment he met them. They were too lovey-dovey, too… smiley. Like they were playing at house.

He stalked to the door.

"What are you doing?" whispered Joy. "Are you eavesdropping?"

Kenna and Benjamin's footsteps got closer as they moved past their door on their way to the stairs.

Where the fuck were they going? Wouldn't returning to their room to argue make more sense?

Their tread faded as they reached the bottom of the steps.

A few seconds later, the front door slammed shut, jarring the floor beneath his and Joy's feet.

"Who goes out in a cold, wet night? It's unnatural. Something is off with those two." He reached for the doorknob, pinning Joy with a warning glare. "Stay here."

She gave him a dubious look. "You're not serious. They're having a fight and need privacy."

In a rainstorm? "I'll be right back."

"I'm going with you."

Arguing with her would only waste time. "Fine. Hurry up."

She prowled behind him down the stairs. "I'm only coming to watch you make a fool of yourself."

"You gonna apologize when I'm right?" he asked over his shoulder.

In the mudroom, he pulled her jacket off the coatrack and held it out for her. She slid her arms through the sleeves and zipped the puffer to her throat. "This is insane. We're being stalkers right now."

Shrugging into his own coat, he opened the front door. "Stay close to me."

"You're trying to find something incriminating on them to leverage it to get the farm," she said as she walked past him.

He followed her into the frigid evening. "I don't trust them."

"You don't trust anyone. Kenna seems nice—so does her fiancé."

"Everyone seems nice at the beginning."

Although the rain had stopped, layers of clouds obscured whatever moonlight would have otherwise reached them. The porch sconce provided the only source of light. Once they left its coverage area, inky darkness submerged them.

When Joy slowed, Hayes turned to her. "Don't dawdle."

"I can't see."

When he took her hand, it felt oddly right. Logic screamed to let go; he threaded their fingers together anyway. "Come on."

"How do you even know where they went?" she asked. "Wait… I hear them."

He heard them too. Keeping her hand securely in his, he sped up his stride.

"What are you trying to do?" Joy whispered, walking faster to keep up with him.

"What do you mean? We're moving closer."

Through the darkness, she gave him that dubious look again. "How are you going to explain us wandering around in the bitter cold?"

Squeezing her hand, he brought it to his mouth and laid a kiss across the delicate skin. "A romantic stroll through the woods."

Her eye roll spoke volumes.

Kenna and Benjamin had gone as far as the barn.

What the hell were they doing out here? The air bit at each exposed inch of his skin. Why would they risk frostbite for privacy?

The scrape of a match against the striker cut through the silence. A pinpoint fire sparked in the darkness. It arced through the air, lighting a cigarette.

"Are they smo—" Joy began.

He squeezed her hand in a reminder that sound carried.

"I can't keep doing this," said Kenna, her voice crystal-clear in the quiet evening.

"It was your fucking idea," Benjamin growled. "Now here we are."

"I know that. Here, give me that."

The cigarette migrated from his hand to hers.

"Since when do you smoke?" Benjamin asked.

"Since tonight." She released a long breath. "I hate this."

"Me too."

"Did you hear that?" Kenna's question reached them along with the acrid cigarette smoke.

Joy gripped his hand—hard.

There was no fucking way Kenna could have heard them. They hadn't even moved. Did the woman have the hearing of a bat?

If they backtracked now, the soggy crunch of leaves and grass beneath their feet would give them away. Their only recourse was to stand still.

"No. What?" said Benjamin.

Kenna handed the cigarette back to her fiancé. "I think there's someone behind the barn."

*Behind the barn?* Hayes had pretty good hearing himself. Concentrating, he strained to detect what Kenna had heard.

Benjamin took a drag of the cigarette. "No one is here, Kenna."

That's when Hayes heard it too. Retreating foot-steps.

*What the fuck?* Dropping Joy's hand, he sprang in the direction of the intruder.

Kenna and Benjamin yelped as he ran past them.

Benjamin found his voice first. "Hayes?"

Hayes didn't stop to chat. He ran at an all-out sprint, but by the time he reached the other side of the barn, it was too late. Mud sprayed and tires squealed as a motorcycle peeled out. The driver kept the taillights off, and Hayes could only guess at the make and model. Fuck.

Joy, Kenna, and Benjamin caught up to him as the bike disappeared through the open farm gates.

"Who was that?" asked Benjamin, wheezing next to him.

Hayes threw him a glance. "Buddy, if you're this out of breath after *that* distance, it's time to quit smoking."

Joy laid her palm on his forearm. "Did you see who it was?"

"No." Instinctively, he covered her cold hand with his. If it was her ex, he'd make sure it was the last time he dared set foot on his farm.

"Creepy," Kenna murmured.

Drawing Joy closer, he scrutinized Kenna and Benjamin. "Were you two meeting someone out here?"

Were they here under false pretenses, taking advantage of the Blairs?

The irony didn't escape him. But his situation was different. He couldn't let Highlander Honey go to Liselle.

Benjamin put out his cigarette underfoot. "No way, man."

"You think… it was a stranger?" Joy asked. The slight shake to her vocal cords said enough—she, too, suspected Ryder Lewis.

Kenna threaded her arm through her fiancé's. "Are the Blairs expecting another buyer?"

A reasonable question or playing dumb? Hayes would find out. "Why were you out here in the middle of the night?"

The couple exchanged a glance.

Joy tugged on his sleeve. "Maybe it's none of our business."

"We were just having a smoke," confessed Benjamin. "The Blairs don't know I smoke, and Kenna reckoned they'd frown on it. I came to the barn to sneak a cig."

"And I wanted one too," added Kenna.

Hayes saw through their bullshit. They both looked disproportionately guilty, but he knew better than to interrogate them now. Let them think they'd fooled him. He'd learn their secrets soon enough.

He jerked his chin toward the house. "Go inside. I'll lock the gate."

As they moved past him, he claimed Joy's icy hand.

The elevated rush of her breath triggered a fresh bout of anger. Someone had dared frighten what was his—for the next five days—to protect.

Her head swiveled as she searched the surrounding shadows, and he could practically hear her thoughts: *How had Ryder found her in the Highlands?*

Let the bastard return—he'd show him exactly what happened to men who came after what belonged to him.

By the time they returned to the house, Kenna and Benjamin had retreated to their room. After leaving her coat in the mudroom, Joy did the same. But Hayes stopped by Cal and Maisie's bedroom on his way upstairs.

Maisie opened the door as soon as he knocked. "Is everything all right?"

"Someone was loitering behind the barn just now," said Hayes. "He rode off before I could catch him."

Cal joined his wife at the threshold. "Did you clock what he looked like?"

"No. But I locked the gates. Keep them closed, will you?"

# Chapter 16

*Ugh, finally morning.*

Lifting her head from the crumpled pillow, Joy reached for her cell phone on the nightstand and checked the time. Not even close to seven, and she'd been awake for hours. Thinking. Worrying.

How had Ryder found her here? Now that he knew her location, what would he do? How could she have been so blind as to not see this side of him? There must have been signs… how did she miss them?

On a dejected sigh, she fell cheek-first back into her pillow.

The debacle with Hayes three years ago had left her insecure, vulnerable, and Ryder had swooped in at the right time. Somehow, she'd missed his crazy. Just like she'd overlooked Hayes's selfish, lying nature too.

*Maybe I need therapy.*

Flipping to her back, she stared at the ceiling above her as nausea chomped at her stomach. An entire day of dishonesty loomed ahead of her.

Yesterday was bad enough, and it had only been a half day. She'd have to pretend the entire day today. It was too much.

She actually liked almost everyone here—with the exception of Hayes and Liselle, of course.

Those two deserved each other. They should get back together and leave the rest of the world alone.

Maybe she could pretend to be sick? No one would want to hang out with her if she was hacking up a lung. She could throw a couple of wet snorts into the mix for good measure. Then they'd leave her alone and she'd stay up here and pretend to be Hayes's wife from afar.

Anything to be away from Hayes.

Despite knowing better, she still felt that foolish drum of excitement under her skin whenever he was near her. How dumb was that? After everything that had happened, her body still wanted him. Like some sort of perverse joke.

Just as she flipped to her side and told herself not to think about him, the door opened and Hayes crept inside. She hadn't even heard his footsteps.

He clearly hadn't expected her to be awake. When he realized that she was—the man apparently had some great night vision—he shut the door and said, "Good morning," in that devastatingly sexy voice.

She shoved any thoughts of him being sexy from her mind.

He had coerced her to be here, after all. No part of him should be attractive to any part of her.

Grumbling a response, she threw back the covers, climbed out of bed, and turned on the light.

He'd changed out of his pajamas and into casualwear. On him, the thin, gray cashmere sweater and jeans somehow looked formal. Must be his rigid posture—hard not to have a ramrod-straight back when you had a stick shoved up your ass.

Setting his pile of blankets at the foot of her bed, he continued to the bathroom and shut the door.

Grateful for a few more minutes of respite, she padded to the wardrobe and pulled out her own outfit for the day. After tugging on the merino wool tights Evie had gifted her years ago and a burgundy knit dress, she secured her hair into a ponytail and waited for Hayes to emerge so she could brush her teeth.

When he came out a few minutes later, with his face freshly shaved, smelling of toothpaste and his signature shaving lotion, she took a heedful step back.

*Remember, no part of him is attractive to any part of you.*

Even then, she took a surreptitious whiff of him as she glided past him to the bathroom.

Face washed and teeth brushed, she joined him in the bedroom. The sun had yet to show any sign of rising.

Hayes sat on her bed and tapped away at his tablet. He looked up when she entered, and his gaze swept her from head to toe.

Irritated at herself for enjoying his blatant perusal, she crossed her arms and scowled.

Before she could tell him to stop staring, he set aside his iPad and closed the distance between them. Anger stormed his face as he surveyed her neck. "Does it hurt?"

She'd forgotten about the bruising there. Arrested by the emotion in his expression, she had to clear her throat before she could answer. "No. They're almost all healed by now."

Just as she was about to step back, he trailed a devastatingly gentle finger along each mark.

Although she knew she should move away, his careful touch held her welded to the floor.

He lifted his hand.

*Okay, good. Moment over.*

She spoke too soon. Before she could retreat and go about the rest of her day, he leaned down and put his lips where his fingers had been.

*Whoa.* The surprise at the dry press of his mouth to her skin didn't outweigh the shock of her reaction to it. Her skin tingled, her breasts swelled, the intimate area between her legs throbbed. She doubted she'd be able to step away if her life depended on it.

He made sure to kiss each mark. "He will never get this close to you again."

"I kneed him pretty hard," she reminded him. "His voice went up a few octaves."

His lashes lowered as his thumb skimmed across her jaw. Lulled by the raspy caress, she covered his hand with hers, unsure of what she'd intended to do. When he tipped up her chin, she let him. When he lowered his head, she almost canted into his kiss. The man could always make her crave him.

*Except he is nothing but a user—using me, using the Blairs, and probably using the farm to boot.*

The reminder worked.

Curving her fingers over his hand, she drew it away from her face.

"Let's save the PDA for an audience," she told him, surprised that her voice didn't falter.

"Didn't know you had an exhibitionist streak in you."

She shot him a look. "I don't. But our deal doesn't include… whatever this is."

"Maybe we can renegotiate. See if we can make our little arrangement a little more"—he dropped his gaze to her mouth—"fulfilling."

***

What would she do if he kissed her again? Their brief exchange yesterday had only made him want more. More of kissing her, more of touching her, more of… her.

He'd long ago learned to go after what he wanted. She might hate him for what he'd done to her three years back—might despise him even more now. But he'd bet the entirety of his investment portfolio that she wanted him too. That was enough of a beachhead.

Her dimpled chin lifted. "Thanks, but no thanks. I'll find my *fulfillment* elsewhere."

That didn't sit well with him. She wore his ring on her finger—whether she liked it or not, until Wednesday, she was his.

"And where do you plan on looking?" he asked in a deceptively mild tone.

"That is none of your business, Icefall." She turned away from him as though she deemed the conversation over, busying herself with making her bed.

What would she do if he tumbled her into it and messed up her hospital corners?

"For the next five days, you're my wife."

"*Fake* wife," she reminded him.

"Fake wife or not, I won't have you doing…" *Who the fuck would she run into on a remote farm?* "The local milkman."

Amusement flickered in her expression. "Are those even still around?"

"You want to get off while in Scotland," he leaned close enough to smell that beach and sun scent of hers, "you come to me."

She smiled sweetly at him. "As memory serves, that wasn't very fulfilling the last time."

He hated being predictable, but her taunt worked. He

had her flat on her back before she could so much as squeak, pinning her into the just-made bed.

Her chest rose and fell against his in rapid surges. Outrage or desire? Loosening his hold, he gave her the option to shake him off and stand, but she stayed where she was.

He brushed a stray lock of hair from her forehead. "You're so beautiful."

"Are you role-playing the milkman?" Her lips twitched.

"Just demonstrating what you're missing, sweetheart," he murmured against her ear, and slid his hand to her bountiful breast.

Her breath caught as he cupped her, but she didn't push him away.

"I've had fantasies about this." He slid his thumb over her nipple until it tightened, distinct even through the layers of fabric. "You, on your back, under me."

She arched into his palm, shifting her legs wider apart to cradle his throbbing hardness.

"Have you ever wondered what it would be like to be naked under my mouth?" he continued, stroking across her taut peak.

Waiting for her response, he lifted his gaze to hers—the wariness in her face froze him. Even to him, it was clear as day.

Releasing his hold, he rolled away from her. "Fuck. Sorry. I took it too far."

She sat up, fighting to steady her fragmented breathing. "This is why we should stick to our initial deal."

She was right.

Because once again, he'd misread the situation.

# Chapter 17

The silence ticked like a bomb.

Guess he was done talking. What did she expect? Him to take it a level further and strip for her?

Shooing him off the bed, she straightened the duvet and strove for a tone of normalcy. "How'd you sleep?"

"Couch in there is about half of me, but it was better than the floor."

A tendril of guilt urged her to offer him the bed for tonight, but she crushed it. He was the reason they were here—he could suffer on the couch.

"Is it too early to sneak some breakfast?" she asked, grasping for a reason to leave the small room.

He extended his hand. "Let's go see what we can dig up."

Avoiding the offered palm, she skirted around him. "Give me a minute to slap some makeup on my neck."

When she was done layering foundation, she led the way into the hallway. The other doors remained closed. Not wishing to wake their neighbors—since lying would then have to begin before breakfast—she crept downstairs without flipping on the lights.

Hayes seemed to have the night vision of an owl, and he followed her down the stairs without tripping once.

When they hit the bottom step, the light in the kitchen drew them like moths.

Maisie, already awake, fussed at the stove while Malik sat at her feet.

She turned as they walked in and greeted them with that sunny Maisie smile. "Good morning, you two. I knew Hayes rises early. Did it rub off on you as well, Joy?"

*Hayes* just rubbed up on her upstairs, but she kept that thought to herself.

"Come and sit," Maisie continued. "Joy, would you like tea or coffee?"

"No need to trouble yourself," she assured the woman. "I can make my tea."

Maisie walked over to the teapot she'd already managed to brew and withdrew a cup from the cupboard above her. "Nonsense. It's no trouble. You're my guests." Pouring the dark liquid, she slid it across the table to her. "Sit, sit. Enjoy."

Hayes, ever the dutiful husband, pulled out her chair. With the chair waiting and the tea steaming and ready, Joy found no other option but to sit.

"Hayes, I've got your coffee here," Maisie continued, lifting a jar of the instant kind. "Do you want it black as usual?"

"Thanks, Maisie." He walked over to the counter to take the coffee from her. "I'll make it."

"The water in the kettle just boiled."

Hayes stirred the freeze-dried grounds into his cup and drowned them in steaming water. When Malik wove figure-eights around his ankles, he kneeled to pet him. "You got your breakfast, buddy?"

"He's had two breakfasts." Maisie laughed.

With one final scratch for the cat, Hayes returned to

the table. When he took a seat next to Joy, he moved his chair ridiculously close, and his calf brushed hers.

Pretending to reach for the sugar bowl in the middle of the table, she scooted out of his way.

What just happened upstairs could never repeat—she had already locked it away with all the other memories of him. Why did he think she'd welcome his touch here, in the kitchen, with Maisie?

Ah, of course… Maisie expected to sell the farm to a happily married couple. Hayes had slipped into the act well enough.

The Blairs deserved better than to pass on their treasured farm to her scheming faux husband.

Maisie returned to the stove. "I've got some bacon and sausage for the meat eaters. Joy, do you eat eggs? I've about finished scrambling them. Beans and tomatoes and mushrooms are ready."

"What can we do to help?" Hayes asked.

"Get your plates, eat. The others won't be up for ages, and I've been meaning to spend some time with you two."

At her bidding, they took their plates from the stack she'd set out on the counter, loaded them with food, and brought them back to the table.

With her own plate full, Maisie joined them. Hayes poured Maisie a cup of tea.

"Thank you, Hayes. It's good to have you back." Her gaze encompassed Joy. "Were your parents upset about the elopement?"

Er… elopement… that's right… another one of Hayes's lies.

"Not at all," Hayes offered smoothly.

She guessed that *was* the truth—they weren't upset

because there was no elopement. Her parents and his knew nothing about this strange charade.

"Her sister and Jackson had a recent-enough wedding for our parents to have all the wedding excitement they could possibly want," he added. "And Nate got married not that long ago, too. My parents are weddinged out."

As Maisie, clearly delighted, asked questions about his two brothers' weddings, Joy's gaze drew to the rings on her left finger. They looked so authentic. To Maisie, she and Hayes were a real couple, having breakfast in the brightly lit kitchen, prattling away about their siblings' nuptials. Maisie looked so darned happy to see them together.

An itchy burn spread from her chest to her throat. *Not again.*

She scratched at it.

Replacing her hand on the table, she noticed that her foundation had come off and gathered under her finger-nails. Damn. Did any of the bruises look obvious now?

Would it be suspicious if she excused herself to check in a bathroom mirror?

Hayes continued speaking, weaving some tale she couldn't follow. "Wedding… Joy walking toward me… knocked the wind straight out of me… threw herself into my arms like we've known each other forever…"

"Aww," breathed Maisie.

Wait… what had Hayes just said?

The burning itch spread everywhere—now the tops of her breasts burned under her dress.

Trying not to focus on her stinging skin, she strained to pay attention to Hayes's story—now he was in the middle of a particularly funny recount of Jackson (re)marrying her sister.

Joy remembered that wedding too well.

Seeing Jackson's brother that day—with his ramrod-straight posture and standoffish scowl—had made her want to shake the rigidity out of him. Instead, she hugged him. Hayes had clearly not expected that. He froze against her, and they stood that way—him like a statue—as seconds ticked by. Just when it started to get uber awkward and she attempted to move away, his arms wrapped around her and he hugged her back. At the contact, prickling awareness surged through her. Separating herself, she took several steps away, her heart pounding. Lusting after one's brother-in-law's brother was never a good idea. If only she'd heeded that thought.

At the kitchen table, Hayes turned to her, and her heart tripped at his easy smile. What had he been saying?

She could get lost in him if she wasn't careful. He'd made her forget herself before—when he'd pretended to date her. One would think she'd have learned her lesson by now.

He was at ease here, on this farm, with Maisie. She hadn't seen him be this relaxed… well, ever. Clearly, he valued Maisie.

And yet he was lying to her.

*They were both lying to her.*

The rash burned more.

He must have noticed the hives spreading across her skin, because the warmth in his eyes flipped to alarm.

Maisie spotted the rash too. "Joy? Are you all right?"

"Yes." Oof. That was much too squeaky. She cleared her throat. "Yes." Now, that was too *low*. She tried again. "Yes. Just fine. A little hot."

"Do you need a glass of water?" Maisie asked, rising to her feet.

"Don't trouble yourself—" Joy began, but their host was already moving toward the refrigerator.

Hayes's fingers hovered at her collarbone. He didn't make contact, but she felt him all the same.

He lowered his hand to her knee and squeezed. "You okay?"

She shook her head.

"You want to go upstairs?"

Maisie returned with a glass of water. "Here you are, my dear."

Joy reached for it with a—to her own surprise— steady hand and took a gulp. The cool liquid soothed her from the inside, and took her mind, temporarily, off her hives. Taking a deep breath, she exhaled slowly. "Thanks."

"Do you have a food allergy?" Maisie asked, eyeing the hives that had yet to ebb.

"No, no allergies." Joy smiled, and prayed the smile reached her eyes. It wouldn't do to make Maisie suspicious. She took another sip of water. "Just… tired."

Maisie's eyes probed hers. "I see."

Did she see? Did she see that she and Hayes were lying to her?

Her cheeks now flamed too.

Hayes squeezed her thigh. "Want to go lie down?"

She shook her head, even though she wanted to escape the room, the farm… at this point, freaking Scotland.

After a beat, Hayes lifted his hand, but his eyes remained dark with concern.

Setting down the glass, she twisted away from him and reached for her fork and tried to distract herself by eating.

The conversation around her resumed, with Hayes and Maisie idly chatting away.

"Joy's never been to Loch Ness."

Hayes's statement yanked her out of her thoughts, and she realized she hadn't been paying attention.

"You've never been to Loch Ness?" Maisie exclaimed. "Oh, we must remedy that! Hayes will take you today."

The last thing Joy wanted was to spend a day alone with Hayes. Sure, being away from all these lies might be good for her skin, but a deal was a deal. He'd covered the Delices' bills, and she would stick around… she just had to find some antihistamines first.

Plastering on a bright smile, she shook her head. "Oh, no, we couldn't. Hayes wants to spend more time with you here, and I've had a great time on the farm. I'll see Loch Ness another time."

"Nonsense! You're already near enough to it. Might as well go," Maisie insisted.

When Hayes settled his hand on top of hers, Joy startled at the contact. Why did he keep touching her? Turning, she met his gaze.

"We'll go see Loch Ness," he said.

Not wishing to argue in front of Maisie, and to an extent desperate to spend as little time lying as possible, Joy offered him a bright smile she hoped looked genuine to their hostess. "All right. We'll go today."

Maybe she could get Hayes to drop her off and return for her in a few hours. Or, even better, maybe he could give her the car and she'd drive herself—though, no, driving on the wrong side was intimidating enough, much less driving his very expensive sports car.

He released her hand as the silence stretched. Lifting her cup of tea, she took a generous sip.

"And take her to Fort Augustus," said Maisie, and launched into the history behind it.

The impending outing settled Joy's nerves. She practically felt the hives recede.

Too soon, Kenna and Benjamin, Liselle and Gene, and—fresh from a morning run—Cal joined them in the kitchen.

The crowd exclaimed their appreciation for Maisie and the hearty breakfast. Maisie waved off the thanks and ordered the newcomers to fill their plates.

As they settled around the table, Hayes scooted closer to her until nothing separated their two chairs. The large table allowed everyone their own chunk of personal space, and yet he pressed close enough to be on her lap. Under the guise of sipping her tea, Joy looked past his shoulder to see who was on his other side.

Ah.

Liselle.

So that's what he was doing. Using her to make his ex-girlfriend jealous.

If Liselle hated Hayes enough to buy the farm he wanted, why would she sit next to him out of all the other places at the table? Even with the four couples all seated, there were two extra chairs. She could have picked any one of them. And yet she chose to sidle up to Hayes.

Gene sat next to his wife on her other side, chomping on a piece of bacon.

Hayes's hand covered hers on the table.

She might as well have expected that.

Show off his new wife to the ex he still wanted.

As Maisie updated everyone on Hayes and Joy's impromptu upcoming day trip, Joy tried to extricate her hand from his, but the subtle tugging didn't work. He held fast.

"We should go." Hayes turned to her. "Get an early start."

Rising, he pulled her up with him.

Everyone murmured their goodbyes as they dropped their plates off at the sink and left the group to finish their breakfast.

Did he not mind leaving the Blairs with the other two couples? Didn't he want to be here to make a good impression?

The trip to Loch Ness made no sense for someone needing the Blairs to like—and choose—him over the others.

When they entered their room and Hayes shut the door behind them, Joy finally wrenched her hand free of his grip. Yet the electricity his touch had sparked continued to buzz beneath her skin.

Irritated by the attraction she couldn't seem to shake, she lashed out. *"Stop touching me.* I agreed to lie for you—I don't want to be fondled too."

She expected Hayes to bite back with something callous or conceited, but he frowned instead. His hand at his side flexed. "It won't happen again."

"Good. We'll just be one of those couples who doesn't do PDA."

He didn't acknowledge her statement with any sort of reaction. "Your hives go away?"

She touched her neck. "Yes."

"Figured a few hours away from this place might help. You turned so red, I couldn't tell your skin and your dress apart."

Whose fault was that? "I hate that you're making me lie to them."

Clearly unconcerned, he sifted through the hangers in the closet, extracting her thickest sweater. "The end justifies the means."

She disagreed, but before she could voice a counterargument, he handed the sweater to her. "Layer up. It'll be cold."

Curling her fingers into the wool, she sank to the edge of the bed. "We're not really going to Loch Ness, are we?"

"You've never seen it. I'll take you."

Asking him to drop her off would sound petty. Instead, she opted for a question. "You've been before?"

"The Blairs took me." He extricated his own pullover, slipping it over his lighter layer.

*The man looks good in everything.* She twisted her face away. "You are very close with them. I hadn't realized."

"They saved my life."

The low-worded statement was the most intimate admission Hayes had ever divulged.

She swallowed, waiting for him to expand further. When he stalked to the dresser and selected a scarf, she couldn't hold back any longer. "What happened?"

Instead of answering, he dug out another scarf—this time, her checkered emerald one. He tossed it to her. "Get dressed. I want to beat the rain."

Guess she'd never pry anything out of him that he didn't wish to share. She changed out of her dress into jeans and the indigo sweater. Wrapping the scarf around her bruised neck, she grabbed her purse.

Now that she'd committed to going to see the infamous Loch Ness, a frisson of excitement fizzed through her.

An escape from lying—even for a bit—would be worth the silent car ride with Hayes.

# Chapter 18

As Hayes navigated away from the farm along the windswept planes of the Highlands, he slanted a glance at Joy. She'd twisted her body to look out her window, leaning so close to the glass that another quarter inch would fuse her to it.

An escape to Loch Ness wasn't just for her benefit. He needed a few hours without making small talk with Benjamin or being blinded every time the sun glanced off Gene's teeth.

Five more days until the farm belonged to him—and Liselle returned to whatever roach nest she'd scurried from.

He missed his home in Nevada. It was quiet, and solitary, and peaceful. No one ever bothered him near his mountain. He wanted to be there now. Away from the Blairs' guests. Just him and Joy.

Hayes almost slammed on the brakes. Where had that thought come from? They weren't really together— why would she be at his Nevada residence?

Yesterday, he'd gotten used to touching her whenever he wanted, and reaching for her hand at the table that morning had been unconscious. He liked the feel of her soft skin against his, the way her breath always caught at first and then she'd nestle closer. The accusation that he'd been fondling her when she didn't want to be touched struck at the core of him. He'd never forced himself on a woman. He'd misread her signals. Again.

Somehow, since they arrived on the farm, he'd convinced himself that she liked when he touched her. Meanwhile, she'd only been fulfilling her end of the bargain he'd coerced her into.

Angry with himself for forgetting—even momentarily—that she wasn't his wife, he brought his attention to the road.

Once the farm was his, he'd go to Nevada alone, and Joy would return to California.

Better that way, anyway. When you let people in, they eventually betrayed you.

"The landscape here is so striking." She broke the silence. "It's nothing like I've seen anywhere else."

If Scotland hadn't been tinged with the pain of fractured bones and a broken heart, he would feel the same. For him, the only spot of warmth and beauty here was the farm, made so by the Blairs.

They drove in silence as they navigated toward Loch Ness—just how he liked it.

Dark clouds encroached from the horizon, casting gray shadows over the moors. He waited for Joy to say something—the woman loved to chatter—but she stayed mute.

He drove for another ten minutes… let it stretch to eleven. Still, she said nothing. Had she caught a cold?

For a man who considered silence the best gift, the quiet car rubbed him the wrong way.

On minute twelve, he gave up. "Cal brought me to Loch Ness years ago—it's the only part of Scotland, besides the farm, that doesn't make me physically ill."

Pushing back from the window, she swiveled her entire body to face him. He wasn't positive, but he was pretty certain she stopped breathing.

Unsure of why he'd even mentioned it when he'd never intended to speak to her of the Blairs, he attempted to focus on the road, but her silent curiosity drew out his next few sentences.

"They came into my life when I needed them. I owe them everything."

The unexpected brush of her hand along his shoulder felt like a coup. "How'd you meet them?"

Guess there was no backing out now. "By chance. I proposed to Liselle when I was twenty-four years old. Young and so stupid. I thought I loved her. Back when I was an idiot. I know better now. Love's nothing but hormones and psychosis."

She gaped at him. "You proposed to her in *Scotland*?"

"Yep. At the Dome."

Her hand on his shoulder curled into him, and she leaned closer. "The restaurant across from my Edinburgh hotel?"

"I thought it would be romantic to do it under all the holiday décor. She thought it was tacky. Turned me down."

"You dodged a bullet."

"I know that now. Back then, I was devastated. She'd been shocked. It was as if everything between us had solely been in my head."

He could still see the disbelief and dread in Liselle's wide eyes when he'd presented her with the ring that had taken him weeks to pick out.

*What the hell are you talking about?* she had said. *I don't know how to respond.*

Tightening his hand on the wheel, he continued. "She said she didn't see a future with me, and walked out. I remember feeling lost, the world crumbling around my ears. I had nowhere to go—it's not like I could go back to our hotel room because she was there. I wanted to escape. So, I started walking. I don't even know for how long. I just kept going. It began to rain. Then hail. I kept going. I didn't realize I was on the side of some isolated road until a car pulled up beside me. A group of guys got out—big, brawny. Drunk. I was a puny kid then—scrawnier than Benjamin."

She whistled. "That's saying something."

"They demanded my wallet. I refused. They took it as a challenge. Beat me up bad. Broke two ribs, dislocated my hip. Gave me a nasty concussion, knocked out two teeth. I recall being cold. Colder than I've ever felt before, and then I wasn't cold anymore. That's when Cal found me. Hypothermic, confused."

The physical recovery was rough. The emotional one? More so.

Her hand drifted along his arm. "Hayes…"

He glanced at her. Uncomfortable with the pity clear on her face, he twisted back to the road and finished his story. "My bones hurt here. My hip's healed fully, but soon as I landed, I felt it again as bad as the day it was dislocated."

"I didn't know," she murmured.

"No one knows. Except the Blairs. That night, I lost my wallet, the passport I stupidly had with me, everything. They left me for dead on the side of that road. Cal was driving to the farm—I still don't know how he saw me. I had no money on me, no identification. He took me to the hospital, stayed with me. He was there the following morning, when I woke up."

Hayes hadn't planned to tell her the most shameful part of all, but at this point there was no turning back. "I called Liselle from the hospital, told her what happened. She refused to come see me. Said we were over and she owed me nothing. My first ever real girlfriend, and she didn't care if I lived or died."

Joy tended to prattle. The current silence was telling—he'd shocked her.

He didn't know why he even gave her the background. Maybe, deep down, he didn't want her to look at him and see a monster.

"Thank you for trusting me." She settled both her hands on his arm.

It would be so easy to release the wheel, to take her hand in his, but it would show weakness. His history with Liselle was nothing to him anymore. He was sharing only to explain how much the Blairs meant to him.

"Once I was released," he continued, "Cal took me to the farm, as though I wasn't a stranger. I was depressed. Too ashamed to tell my brothers what happened. Or my parents—optics is everything to them, you know that. I'd always been their golden child. Cal and Maisie insisted I stay with them. And I did. For months, until I recovered. They didn't know me, but they took care of me as though I were their own kid. I owe them my life."

Joy's brows drew together in accusation. "But… you got back together with Liselle."

He'd been an idiot the second time around.

"I didn't learn from my first mistake." Not wishing to dwell on his ex, he finished his story. "I ended up staying in the UK to do my PT here. I worked on launching my company from the very bedroom you're currently occupying. When I sold it years later, I made bank. I offered half of what I made to the Blairs. They refused—refused fifty million dollars. They said they didn't want money from me. Even my parents—who you know are more than well off—asked me for a ski chalet."

"I've only known Cal and Maisie for a few days, but I believe it. People mean more to them than things. But Hayes, we are lying to them."

"The farm is everything to me. It brought me out of a dark place. But the Blairs mean more. I'm doing this for their own good. Cal and Maisie are too kindhearted. I have to protect them from themselves. If Liselle buys their farm, she will destroy it for no other reason than to spite me. She holds a grudge and doesn't care who she hurts."

"Why didn't you tell the Blairs that Liselle is your ex-girlfriend?"

Emotion tightened his throat. "At first, I didn't know how to say it without sounding bitter. And my history with Liselle shouldn't influence their decision."

"I don't think they'd sell the farm to someone you hate."

"She isn't the one who mugged me."

Fog rolled in, making it difficult to see the road ahead. Focusing on getting Joy to Loch Ness safely, he said nothing else as they drove into the mist.

***

The fog that curled around them made it impossible to see.

Although Hayes seemed at ease navigating the sports car, his eyes stayed sharp on the road.

After he'd lied to her three years ago, she'd always thought of him as a jackass. The story he'd shared about him and the Blairs had shaken that opinion. Then again, maybe the story was yet another lie—a way to win her over. With Hayes, one could never know.

Attempting not to look obvious, she glanced at him.

He wasn't cold-hearted enough to lie about his affection for the Blairs… was he?

No, his love for them was indisputable. The story he'd shared explained it.

Darn it. Now she felt *sympathy* for him. Unacceptable. She couldn't allow any feelings for him because he was deceitful, and selfish, and he used people.

*He used* me. *I have got to remember that.*

Did the fog get thicker? She could no longer make out a thing in front of them. How was Hayes driving in this? Shifting in her seat, she narrowed her eyes through the windshield, as though that would help them navigate better.

"We're almost out of it, I think," Hayes said, undoubtedly picking up on the tension that gripped her.

"I can't see anything."

To her relief, he was correct. They drove out of the fog into a clear part of the Highlands. Among the dry grasses to her right, a group of large, auburn, long-haired animals contently munched away.

"Are those some sort of bison?" she asked.

He threw a quick glance at the livestock. "Highland cattle."

They drove past the animals and continued toward the swelling storm clouds.

Just over two hours after they left Highlander Honey Farm, they reached Fort Augustus, a quaint village on the southern tip of Loch Ness.

As Hayes pulled into a compact parking spot,

several locals turned to look at the car, which seemed ostentatious next to the other vehicles on the street. Hayes didn't seem to notice as he walked around to her side.

Grabbing her purse, she exited the vehicle onto the wet pavement.

Hayes settled his hand on her back—then dropped it. He must have recalled their earlier conversation about groping her.

She'd been upset with herself for her reaction to him, not at him, but it wasn't as if she could backtrack at this point. Pretending not to notice, she smiled. "Where to?"

With a comically dramatic flourish, he motioned just ahead. "Nessie awaits."

Wind battered at them as they made their way to Loch Ness. Crisp moisture and the scent of thick vegetation filled the air around them. In this weather, the loch and the sky were the same blurred shade of gray, but Joy didn't care. It could start raining frogs right now, and she'd still insist on exploring. The chill nipping at her cheeks and nose only added to the excitement of Loch Ness in the fall.

"Want a photo to send to your family, since you never made it out here as a kid?"

Touched that he had remembered, she extended her cell to him.

He snapped some pictures before handing the phone back. "Let's take a stroll around."

As they made their way along the loch, he launched into a colorful tale about the legend of Nessie.

She'd have never guessed that grumpy, surly Hayes could be such an enchanting storyteller. Although she knew that he recalled facts easily, she'd never heard him weave them together in such an intriguing way. In his line of work, he had to be great with words, but she'd rarely managed to squeeze more than a dry sentence or two out of him.

Lost in the anecdote, she made a foolish mistake. She peeped at his face while he was at a particularly humorous part. The glimmering, tropical hue of his eyes contrasted with the gray dreariness around them, and the sparkle sucked her in.

Even worse, she let her attention drift to his mouth—to his animated lips that turned up at the corners as he spoke. How could a man be this beautiful?

His usual aloofness had vanished, making him seem warm and disarmingly charming. She wanted to taste this Hayes she didn't know existed.

She hadn't realized she'd been staring at his mouth until his lips ceased moving—and she had no idea what he'd just said.

Her eyes flew to his. Silent now, he watched her with a quizzical expression. Did he ask her a question? Would it sound off if she requested him to repeat it?

The wind picked up around them. Before she could suggest they find a warm café, he brushed his fingers along her cheek. The simple touch thawed her chilled skin, and she slanted into his caress.

Either he stepped closer or she did—she didn't know, couldn't tell. Before she could process his sudden proximity, he caught her face between his large hands.

*Whoa. How did we get here?*

He stroked across her skin, as if savoring the texture under his fingertips.

The sensible part of her screamed to pull away, but, lost to the energy beating between them, she stayed.

His eyes darkened to the same slate gray as the loch next to them, and he claimed her mouth with his.

# Chapter 19

Kissing him was like kissing a firestorm. No gentle brush of lips or teasing strokes of tongue here. He took her mouth with an intensity that swayed her into him, and then he hauled her closer still. The kiss licked fire across her skin, melting her from the core.

Need battered her as fiercely as the gale-force winds around them. When the thick beat of his heart reached her through the layers of clothes, she wondered whether he could feel the corresponding pounding of hers.

As though the heavens themselves wished to end their hasty make-out session, the skies above them split open and rain unfurled like heavy fabric. The sheets of ice water smacked them.

Hayes gripped her hand as the two made a mad dash through the torrential downpour back to the village.

The ridiculousness of the situation—kissing her archenemy and then being punished by the Scottish gods for it—didn't escape her, and laughter fizzed. She didn't bother to contain it, and was fighting tears by the time they reached the nearest building and pressed themselves against its walls.

Hayes seemed to find the whole thing just as funny, because his rich laugh wove around her, even as the rain tried to claw them out from the overhang where they sheltered.

"I'm never destined to be warm." He shook off the water from his short hair.

She glanced at the stone wall against which they were currently plastered. An inn and restaurant… with a very inviting, shiny door. "Let's go in here. Might as well get an early lunch while we wait for it to taper off."

The dark-paneled inn was packed with people escaping the same storm, but Hayes and she snagged the last available table for two in the corner by the crackling fireplace.

When Hayes, standing at the table, burrowed deeper into his wet outer layers, Joy reached for his lapels. "Take your coat off—it's soaked. You'll be warmer without it."

Dubious of why she was fussing over him and refusing to dwell on it, she liberated him from the wet wool and tossed it over the back of the chair closest to the fire to dry.

"Come sit here." She motioned to said chair.

He didn't sit. With a bit too much familiarity, Hayes unzipped her jacket and helped her out of it.

Because of the overfull neighboring tables, it was impossible to maneuver the other chair closer to the flames.

Laying her puffer over the back of the chair closest to him, he motioned to the chair next to the fireplace. "You sit there. You're not used to this climate."

"You're not used to this climate either—you live in the desert," she pointed out, but because she knew he wouldn't budge on this, sank into the chair he'd indicated.

Sitting, he grinned at her from across the small table. "The good news is this is Scotland, and whiskey cures everything."

Before she could dispute his statement, he weaved

his way around the clustered tables crammed with guests and pushed his way to the bar.

Joy tore her gaze from the wide expanse of his back in the cable-knit sweater and pulled out her phone.

Her sister and parents had sent several texts to check in, and she used the lull to respond—and to send the photo of herself in front of Loch Ness.

The snapping fire warmed her back as she typed away. By the time she sent the last of the texts, Hayes returned with two steaming mugs.

She recognized the drinks instantly. "You got hot toddies? It's like you read my mind."

He slid her cup to her and took his seat.

Leaning closer, she inhaled scents of honey, lemon, cinnamon, and whiskey. The hot mug warmed her hands as she took a generous sip and let the liquid defrost her.

Hayes watched her over the rim of his cup as he drank. "Got food coming too."

The waitress arrived a quarter hour later with a tray piled with steaming dishes: fish and chips, haddock chowder, leek and potato soup, and stovies with oatcakes. The enormous plates barely fit on their tiny table.

He rearranged them just so. "Figured we'd share."

Another unexpected turn to the day. Joy didn't like him enough to share a meal with him, much less split four plates of food, and yet she found herself salivating over the dishes.

"I got the vegetarian version of the stovies," he said as her fork hovered over the stewed potato dish.

The *for you* part remained unspoken, but the tweak to the order didn't escape her. She knew Hayes loved his meat.

The conversation and laughter around them mixed with the crackle of the fire and the steady fall of rain outside. His wedding ring glowed against his tanned skin as he reached for the hot toddy.

"Why don't you just explain to the Blairs why they shouldn't give Liselle the farm, even if she is married to their nephew?"

"The farm means a lot to them, and they will sell it to the buyer they deem worthy."

Suddenly, she understood. "You want them to choose you of their own free will. To make the win over Liselle sweeter."

"It's not about Liselle."

"If it's not about her…" The picture cleared. "It's about *you*. You want the Blairs to find you more worthy than they find her of their own accord. That's why you won't go out and just *tell* them what she did to you."

A subtle tic of a muscle in his jaw belied his calm exterior. He took another sip of the toddy before he spoke. "She'll destroy the farm if she takes it from the Blairs. I want them to feel good about who they're selling it to—and yes, you're right, I need to be the one they choose to trust with their legacy. And not by default, because I ran crying to them about my past with Liselle."

Just as she was about to prod at the fact that he was lying to them, he continued. "I hadn't expected her to marry Gene. It threw me for a loop, and yes, I panicked and lied that you and I were married."

"You never panic."

"I did when it came to this."

"Will you eventually tell them we're not married?" She popped a bite of potato into her mouth. "Or will I have to go visit them with you for the holidays and bring along fake children?"

He ate a fry. "We'll cross that bridge later."

Oh boy.

Joy took another nip of her drink. "I can't believe *Liselle* was your first ever girlfriend. Have you seen you? I'd have imagined girls fell at your feet in high school."

Hayes's lips curved. "They did not. I was awkward in high school. Shy. Quiet. My brothers were my closest friends. Still are. I didn't go out much. School was my comfort zone—I took all AP classes and enrolled in a few courses at the local community college to supplement. When I actually got to college, I took on three majors. Didn't leave me much room for a social life."

"*Three?*"

He sliced into the flakey, battered haddock. "Computer science, business, and art history."

Joy forked a piece of the fish he'd just cut into and slid the steaming morsel into her mouth. "Why those three?"

"Computer science was a passion of mine, so that was a no-brainer. My dad wanted me to follow in his footsteps and insisted I major in business. That was my least favorite major."

"How come?" she asked, curious.

"Hated my classmates. They talked a lot but said nothing."

Joy replaced her fork with her spoon and sampled the chowder. "Ooh, all of these dishes are so good. And art history?"

"Since childhood, Oliver had been into ancient Greek sculptures. I took the classes so we had something to talk about."

Oliver—Hayes's youngest brother—was now an art history professor at UCLA. Unlike Hayes, he was chatty and jovial.

"I like that you're close with your brothers."

Hayes ate a bite of the stovies. "Me too. We're different, but we get each other."

"I see what you mean, though. All that schoolwork didn't leave you much room to date."

"Dating never came easy to me. Still doesn't. I misread social cues. I hate small talk. It got me into a few uncomfortable situations in high school and college."

The flush of red across his cheekbones said enough. Reluctant to prod at a sensitive subject, Joy tried a taste of the leek and potato soup, ready to change topics to spare him embarrassment.

When Hayes continued unprompted, she froze in surprise.

"I remember liking this one girl in high school and thinking she liked me. Turned out, she was merely being nice to me and had a boyfriend. Others know the difference between flirting and being friendly, but nonverbal communication isn't intuitive for me. When her boyfriend found out, he told everyone in school. It wasn't pleasant."

Her heart broke for little teenage Hayes. "I'm so sorry, Hayes."

"In college, I thought my TA liked me. Turned out, she was just trying to get hired at my dad's private equity firm." He took a swig of his toddy. "When Liselle asked me out, I thought I'd misheard her. But no. She flat out wanted to go on a date with me. Unlike all my prior dates, which were awkward or boring or both, our first date had been spectacular. I told Liselle I loved her that same night."

Joy plunked her utensil on the table. "*What?*"

Hayes gave an indifferent shrug. "I was head over heels. I mistook lust for love then. I know better now. But back then, I thought myself in love—and assumed she felt the same. Learned the hard way that I was wrong. My brothers tried to warn me. I didn't listen."

"Sometimes love can blind us."

He gave her an arch look. "Hormones and neurochemicals blind us."

There's the pragmatist she knew.

"Did your parents like her?"

"Yes. They enjoyed showing her off to their friends, and she fit well into their country club world. On the rare occasions my parents talked me into attending any of their fancy events, I would leave early or say something that someone would find rude. Liselle was a good counterbalance. She loved attending galas and dinners with them."

"At least your brothers saw right through her."

Hayes's gaze softened. The affection for his siblings was clear. "Yep. Almost instantly."

Her phone lit up with a low battery warning.

Joy groaned. "Ugh. I hate this phone. I just charged it before we left the farm. I sent a handful of texts—and the battery is drained. It's not even that old."

A stillness came over Hayes. He extended his hand. "Give me your phone."

Confused, she did, placing it into his open palm. His expression went from still to thunderous.

She leaned across the table. "You're freaking me out. What is it?"

Hayes cursed. "That's how Ryder knew where you were in London and Edinburgh. He's tracking your phone."

"What? That's impossible."

Flipping the phone so that the screen faced her, he showed her the app she didn't even know she had.

"You have a thousand apps on this thing," he grumbled. "That's how you didn't notice this one. He's tracking you."

Nausea clamped her stomach. "Turn it off."

Diving into her phone with the concentration of an eagle, Hayes dug around for several minutes before he raised his head. "No other malware. Bet Ryder heard about this app in a forum or something, but it's easy to remove."

She tucked her shaking hands under her butt on the chair. "He's been tracking my location this whole time? Did he have access to anything else? Like my camera?"

"No. All that app does is share your location with him. But he knows you were at Highlander Farm, and he knows you're in Loch Ness now."

"He must have installed it when we were still together." Disturbed, violated, she searched the bar, feeling as though a thousand roaches marched up her spine. She shivered in disgust. "Think he's here now?"

Hayes shook his head. "I haven't noticed. But I don't like that he knows you're at the Blairs'."

Realization made it hard to breathe. "Then that really was him last night by the barn. Do you think he could hurt Cal and Maisie?"

"Right now, he seems focused on you, but I don't want to take any chances. I'll warn Cal. He refuses to let me set up cameras or a security system, but I'll remind him again to keep the gates locked and to be vigilant." After he sent the text message to the Blairs, he glanced through the window with clear regret. The rain still pelted away.

"We can't drive in this weather," she said, understanding his thoughts.

"No, we can't. Maybe it'll slow down soon."

# Chapter 20

By the time they finished eating, the rain turned to snow. Big clumps of it dropped from the sky and rapidly coated the ground.

Hayes groaned; the horde around them, having noticed the same, groaned too.

But Joy laughed in undiluted enchantment, her eyes wide as she watched the snowfall through the window. "It's snowing! I haven't seen snow in *so long*."

The white obscured the ground at warp speed, effectively trapping them inside the inn.

He studied the piling layers of snow. "The roads will be a mess."

Joy didn't appear to share his concern. "Maybe it'll stop soon."

"Not by the looks of it."

Rising, he strolled through the adjoining lobby to the front desk and got in line. More people wishing to stay at the inn joined behind him, and by the time he reached the front desk, the line stretched around the small lobby.

His original plan was to reserve two rooms, but as he saw the number of individuals in need of a hotel for the night, he booked just one. He and Joy didn't need the extra room, and someone else might.

When he returned, the plates had been cleared away and Joy sat by the fire, watching the snowfall.

"Snagged us a room." He tossed two sets of toiletries he'd gotten from the front desk on the table between them.

"Good thinking. There's going to be a lot of people in need of a hotel tonight."

"Want to head up, or have another drink?"

Standing, she reached for their coats. "Let's go up."

The room was small but clean and the bed was big enough—just barely—for two. They could do a lot worse, he decided. Then remembered that she was going to make him sleep on the floor again. And this floor was unforgiving hardwood.

"Sharing a hotel room is becoming a tradition," she murmured, exploring the compact space.

Although his hip had healed years ago, the cold, wet weather made it throb. A subconscious, more than a physical, reminder of what had once occurred, and yet sleeping with it crammed against the hardwood floor would kill him.

Joy blasted the heater before turning to him. "Is this warm enough?"

"It's fine," he bit out in a cooler tone than he intended.

The realization that she'd made the room warmer for him caused all sorts of funny feelings to swell through him. Ones he refused to dwell on. He'd fallen head over heels for a woman once, and it had backfired spectacularly. Fortunately, he'd finally learned from his mistakes. He wouldn't let Joy fussing over him get into his head. She was just being nice.

She spread out her jacket across the back of one chair, then did the same with his coat and the other chair.

"Don't know about you, but I'm getting out of my wet jeans," she told him, reaching for the top button.

"They didn't really dry in the pub downstairs, but the fire made the soggy fabric nice and toasty."

In one quick move, she had the jeans off and her long, toned legs fully bare. The sweater covered just enough of her to make him salivate. Fighting the urge to tug up the fabric and explore, he turned to the window, willing his erection to subside.

"Aren't you going to take off your pants?" she asked behind him.

"In a minute." The thick sludge of his voice gave enough away.

As he battled with his body, she walked over to the narrow credenza holding the teakettle and took it to the bathroom to fill it with water. Returning, she set it to boil and hopped on the bed.

"I understand why you got one room," she said. "There were a lot of people in need of shelter tonight. But why the one bed?"

It hadn't occurred to him to ask for a double. "I'll sleep on the floor."

"No, don't do that."

The refusal surprised him. He twisted his head to look at her.

"You favor one hip when it's cold or wet out. I know why now. You can't sleep on the floor." She paused, before adding with a playful crinkle of her pert nose, "And I don't want to."

"My hip's healed. The pain, it comes stronger when it's cold, yes, but it's mostly in my head."

She patted the spot next to her. "We'll share the bed tonight like the fake-married couple we are."

Charmed by her sudden impishness, he took a step toward her. "Think you can keep your hands to yourself?"

Her eyes sparkled as she chewed her lip in mock concern. "I don't know. You may have to tie them."

Painfully hard, he fisted his hands at his sides. At least he managed not to pounce on her.

Her eyes rounded as she realized she'd taken it too far. "Sorry. You're fun to flirt with because you're so serious all the time. Makes me want to say things to get a reaction, but I still don't like you."

He wasn't sure whether she was reassuring him or herself.

She patted the bed again. This time, he took her up on the invitation and sank to the thin mattress next to her.

"Can I ask one question that's been bothering me?" she asked him, her eyes serious. "Why did you date her a second time?"

Of course she wouldn't have let that part go.

How to explain something he himself didn't understand? "After I sold my company, Liselle reached out. I thought she missed me, that she wanted me for me. Like an idiot, I overlooked our past. When she asked if she could help with my new company, I gave her a small role. It's not often easy for me to read between the lines, but eventually I saw that she never wanted me—just the lifestyle I could provide. I broke it off. She went ballistic. Tried to sell Poinsettia from under me."

"How could she do that?"

"She started dating the CEO of the company that was about to acquire Poinsettia. Made him think I abused her. His security wouldn't let me within yards of her—or him. When I heard he was the keynote speaker at your hospital gala, the easiest way to get to him was through you. I lucked out because he was smart. Saw the truth— way faster than I would ever have. He dumped her, and we finalized the acquisition. Liselle's been on a rampage ever since. I don't know how she found out about the Blairs selling Highlander Honey, but she did."

"So… you aren't pining away for her?"

The idea was so ridiculous, he threw back his head and roared. "No. The very thought of her reminds me of having my hip popped back in."

"Why do you think she's this obsessed?"

"Because someone she once rejected—someone she'd called awkward and weird—dumped her."

"You're not awkward or weird."

He gave her a look.

"You're not," she repeated. "She's the weird one."

"It's not the first time I've been called that." He leaned back on his arms, at ease in this space. At ease with *her*. "I know I can be antisocial and particular. Women barely glanced my way until my bank account got all those extra zeroes. Now they tolerate me for the Michelin-starred meals."

Her lips ticked up. "Maybe they're using you for your body."

He answered her teasing smile with one of his own. "Good. Then I won't cancel the gym membership."

# Chapter 21

Although Joy was prickly around him when awake, in deep sleep she was a cuddler. Hayes didn't snuggle, but when she all but crawled on top of him in her sleep and her arms fastened around him like rubber ties, he wasn't as annoyed as he'd expected to be.

Her hair smelled of sun and surf and tumbled around him like mulberry silk. Only a short, cotton shirt and a skimpy pair of underwear covered her, and her warmth seeped into him, chasing away the chill that being back in Scotland, in the vicinity of Liselle again, had brought.

With a content little sigh, she climbed higher up his chest, and snuggled in under his chin. As he wrapped his arms around her, he felt steady for the first time since he'd arrived in Scotland. With her around him like his very own weighted blanket, he succumbed to sleep.

Hayes sprang awake as he always did—all at once. He never slept this late, and the light seeping through the thin curtains disoriented him. As did the woman in his arms.

At some point in the night, Joy had shifted away from him, and he'd apparently followed, now curled around her, his dick aching to be inside her.

He should ease back, give her space. Instead, his arm tightened, and he scooted closer. Just two more breaths wrapped around her, and then he'd loosen his hold, lift his arm, and roll away.

Hayes knew the moment Joy came awake. The ease fled her muscles, and her breath caught. He could almost see her brain processing the situation—his erection straining against the crack of her ass.

Neither one had expected to wake up spooning. He wondered whether she was coming to enjoy this momentary respite as much as he did.

Her breathing settled—becoming slow and steady as she adjusted to his proximity and relaxed against him. He could have sworn she shifted closer. They stayed that way, pretending to be asleep, unwilling to shatter the moment.

Her hair tickled the tip of his nose, and he let that summer scent of her fill his lungs. His hand splayed across her stomach, the pearl navel ring pressing against his palm.

He'd had a few one-night stands the last three years, but he couldn't remember the last time he'd woken up with someone in his arms. If it had been anyone but Joy, he'd have left the room by now in search of solitude. But here, caught in each other's warmth in the quiet room, he couldn't imagine being anywhere else.

*He wanted this forever.* The split-second thought froze him as effectively as an ice storm. He didn't do forever.

Better to let the moment pass, and get their day started. Time to return to the farm, anyway.

Just as he was about to pull away, her hand covered his where it splayed over her stomach. He held his breath, waiting for what she'd do next.

Her belly rose and fell under his palm as she deliberated. He knew the moment she made her decision.

Curling her fingers over his, she guided him upward to her breast.

He molded his hand around the generous mound, treasuring this unexpected offering. When he squeezed, she responded with a quiet gasp. Through the thin cotton of the shirt she'd worn to bed, her hard little nipple pushed against his palm. As she arched into his touch, pressing herself more firmly against him, a triumph surged through him. *Mine*.

He circled the straining nipple through the fabric, basked in her murmur of approval.

"More," she hummed.

Yes, he needed more too.

Slipping beneath the cotton, he cupped warm, responsive flesh. "I've thought about this a thousand times, remembering how you felt, wondering what you taste like."

Her hips nudged back into his erection at his quiet confession.

"My biggest regret is never seeing you naked," he continued, capturing the sensitive bud between his fingers. "I still picture you in that silk dress—all that bare, tanned back. I wanted to tear that dress to shreds."

Her sharp intake of breath encouraged him. "I bought that dress for you."

"And when you sank to your knees in front of me—"

It was the wrong thing to say. Joy sprang away from him like she'd been scalded.

Landing on the ground with a hard thud, she gave him a look of pure loathing. "You just had to remind me, didn't you? Asshole."

Her ashen face undid him.

He scrambled off the bed after her, but she already reached the bathroom.

"Joy—wait."

The door slammed shut. *Fuck.*

Breaking it down was out of the question.

Cursing, he tracked to the window and threw open the curtains. A layer of snow covered the rooftops and shaded patches of ground, but last night's clouds had dispersed, and the startling blue sky taunted him.

The sooner they returned to the farm, the better. The Blairs were making their decision soon, and lollygagging here would give Liselle an edge he couldn't allow.

It was time he looked into Kenna Ross and Benjamin Buchanan too. He'd been too distracted by Joy to do it sooner, but if the Blairs were to pick them over him, he'd do his due diligence and ensure they were entrusting their farm into good hands.

Not having a change of clothes, he threw on last night's layers—which were still ridiculously damp—just as Joy emerged from the bathroom.

The white shirt she'd slept in barely covered her tummy. What would she do if he stepped into her and cupped her through her lace underwear? Claw his eyes out, that's what.

She looked at him with the seriousness of a soldier primed for battle. "That was a mistake."

Her voice still held that morning throaty quality, and it sent his blood draining from his brain. "Didn't feel like a mistake to me."

Stalking to the wardrobe, she snapped her clothes off the hangers. "We should head back."

He remained rooted where he stood. "Unless you'd like to crawl back in bed and… snooze longer?"

The look she gave him would have withered a lesser man. "No more snoozing. And definitely not with you."

Her skin glowed in the faint morning light. Slipping her jeans over her perfect ass, she zipped them over her glinting navel ring. He couldn't recall ever wanting someone with such intensity.

Her gaze flicked to the window—a clear attempt to change the subject. "It stopped snowing. Think the roads are clear?"

Yep. And they'd have to get back on the road. The moment was most definitely over.

He cleared his throat. "By the time we eat? Should be."

The mention of food had its intended effect. Joy's eyes lit up. "I'm starving."

Despite knowing she hadn't intended the phrase to sound sexual, his mind took him there and wouldn't let go. Visions of taking Joy across the bed in this small hotel room played across his brain.

She watched him with guarded eyes. "Why are you staring?"

"I want to fuck you."

Releasing a humorless laugh, she wiggled into her sweater. "It's good to want things."

"You want it too."

Didn't she?

"I wanted it at one point in the past, yes," she allowed, raking her fingers through her hair in an effort to work out the tangles. "But we both remember how that went."

He recalled the feel of her hot, willing mouth around his cock. If his conscience hadn't gotten the better of him that night, he'd know what it would feel like to bury himself in her pussy.

Refusing to dwell on what could have been, he stalked to the bathroom to brush his teeth.

When he emerged, she stood by the window, her hair falling in a thick braid down her back.

He reached her in three brisk strides.

With a terse, frustrated exhale, she turned to face him. "Should we talk about what—"

He silenced her mid-sentence, gripping the nape of her neck as he crushed his mouth to hers.

There was no hesitation in her response—almost as if she'd anticipated his move. Wrapping herself around him, she kissed him back, mewled when he slid his lips along her jawline to her collarbone.

God, they were meant for each other.

The intensity of the thought scared him. He pulled away so abruptly she stumbled.

His hand shot out to steady her, but she shook him off. "Stop. We can't do this. We should go."

# Chapter 22

The drive back was painfully quiet.

Joy hated silence, but Hayes seemed to be in a mood. One minute, he was kissing her; the next, he was withdrawing so quickly, she almost tumbled head-first into his chest.

*Why had she allowed the kiss?*

Hayes had fooled her into thinking he liked her before—how many more times would she fall for his games before she learned her lesson?

They returned to the farm, walking into a house that smelled of just-baked pastries, melted butter, and caramelized sugar. What goodies was Maisie whipping up?

Maisie popped out from the kitchen, meeting them by the door as she wiped her hands on an embroidered kitchen towel. "You're back! I'm glad you waited out the snow. Roads were hellish last night. Joy, grab some tea and pastries and get yourself changed. I'm taking us lassies into town. Hayes, you boys will have to fend for yourselves for a few hours."

Relieved, Joy perked up. A break from Hayes was an unexpected boon. "I just have to take a super-fast shower, and I'll meet you downstairs."

She couldn't escape Hayes fast enough, but she knew he watched her all the way up the stairs.

When she emerged from the shower, Hayes waited for her in their room, sitting at the table, the iPad in front of him.

Not expecting to find him there, she tightened the towel more securely around her breasts. "You hiding up here?"

His darkened gaze swept her from head to toe. "Had work to do."

"Stop leering. It's not going to happen."

"Give me a minute to convince you otherwise."

His husky words wrapped around her. It would be so easy to drop the towel, lower to his lap—

"A century won't be enough. Now, can you go so I can change? Maisie is waiting."

Hayes didn't budge, but the suggestive gleam left his features. Just like that, he was all business. "While you're out and about today, ask Kenna some questions. Make sure she is who she claims to be."

Hurrying to the wardrobe, Joy pulled out a turtleneck and a wool skirt. "Stop trying to find fault with everyone here."

"They're too into each other. You don't find that suspicious?"

"No. I think it's sweet."

Hayes's glare told her he was calling bullshit.

Instead of retreating to the bathroom to change or asking him to leave the room again, she stayed exactly where she was. Hayes had toyed with her before. He deserved a little payback.

Presenting him with her back, she dropped the towel.

Hayes groaned. "Fuck. No fair, woman."

She schooled her features before pivoting to face

him, deliberately giving him an unobstructed full-frontal view.

His hungry gaze roamed over her naked form as she closed the distance between them.

Leaning close, she brushed her lips across his. "After Wednesday, we're through."

She moved away as he reached for her, and his hands grasped empty air. Retreating to the dresser, she selected a hot-pink bra and matching underwear. Flashing him had been thrilling, but she was grateful for the layer of coverage the lingerie now provided.

"Share your location with me on your phone."

The brusque tone grated.

"Why?" It was bad enough Ryder had tracked her. Now Hayes intended to do the same?

He kept his gaze locked on her face. "Ryder can't trace you now, but on the off chance that something happens, I need to know where you are. You can end the location sharing when I'm with you. When I'm not, it stays on."

"That's ridiculous. I don't need you to watch me twenty-four-seven."

"Share the location, or you're not going."

*The arrogance.* "You can't tell me what to do."

"Watch me."

She stepped into her skirt. "Fine. Then I'll skip the outing."

"Great," he countered. "We can stay in our room and pick up where we left off earlier this morning."

Pulling on her turtleneck, she freed her hair from the high collar. "There's nothing to pick up."

His tone softened. "Look. Ryder is still somewhere out there. What'll it hurt if I keep an eye on your location for a few hours?"

When he sounded reasonable, it made it harder to argue.

Walking to the nightstand where she'd left her phone to charge, she unplugged it and tossed it to him. "Here. Share my damned location with yourself. But I'm turning it off as soon as we're back."

The rest of the day passed in what Joy could only describe as a forced way to get to know each other.

Because Maisie already knew Kenna, she focused most of her attention on Liselle and Joy, but Kenna didn't escape the interrogation either. The farm purchase might very well come down to which of the three answered Maisie's outlined questions best.

The drive to town, the casual stroll down the shop-lined main street, the grocery run, and their snack and food breaks felt like one extended interview.

"How many children do you want?" Maisie asked them during a stop at Benjamin and Kenna's coffee shop.

"Will you raise them here?" she queried during lunch at a local pub.

"Do you think your kids will enjoy growing up on a farm?" she pressed after dessert arrived.

Their son had refused to pursue the family business, and Maisie intended to select someone who, in turn, would pass the farm on to the next generation.

The farm was clearly dear to her. If she were Maisie, she'd choose someone who ticked off all her boxes too.

The questions didn't bother Joy. What bothered her was the lying. Because she and Hayes weren't married, they'd never have children together, and they certainly wouldn't raise those kids on the farm.

Hayes might go on to settle down someday—if he found a woman crazy enough to take him on. And sure, maybe they'd raise their family at Highlander Honey—but that wasn't Joy's journey. She'd be in San Diego, focusing on her career and helping her sister.

Hayes could do whatever he wanted.

And yet the image of him surrounded by another woman's children brought a bitter taste to her tongue.

What especially annoyed Joy was Liselle. The woman seemed to have prepared for the questions as though she had found a cheat sheet. She answered every inquiry in that annoyingly pleasant voice and batted her lashes and spoke with such awe about the children she'd raise there that Joy had to unclench her jaw before she ground her teeth to the bone. No way would Liselle stay married to Gene long enough to bear his offspring.

Joy couldn't bring herself to answer in the same bogus way. It was bad enough to lie about being married, but to fool Maisie into believing she'd settle down in Scotland? That crossed a line.

Instead of making up pipe-dream scenarios, she told Maisie the truth: she worked hard for her career and, sure, she wanted kids eventually, but she had a life in Southern California and she couldn't move to Scotland.

"Oh. I see," said Maisie, alarm blotching her fair skin.

"I can't promise you that we'll raise our children on the farm. I'm sorry."

"What about you, Kenna?" Maisie took a small bite of dessert.

Joy didn't hear what the woman said because Liselle's triumphant smirk flipped her stomach.

# Chapter 23

Hayes checked his watch for the millionth time. The platinum hand ticked away against the ice-blue dial.

Cal, Gene, and Benjamin focused on the game across the big screen in the family room. Hayes hadn't registered a single play.

Why the hell was Maisie keeping them out this long? A girls' trip shouldn't take more than a couple of hours.

Grabbing his phone, he checked it again. No text messages. No calls.

Like a lunatic, he pulled up Joy's location. Throughout the day, he'd watched her move from a café—where they spent more time than buying a coffee required—to a pub—sure, it had been lunchtime, but how slowly did they eat?—to a grocer's. How long could grocery shopping take?

Why did he ever allow her to leave when she had an ex stalking her? Maisie and Kenna would be of little help if Ryder found her during their outing, and Liselle would push Joy into his waiting arms.

He checked his watch again. This was the longest they'd been apart since Wednesday, and he didn't like it. The farm—his haven—seemed bleak and lonely without her.

Cal, on the opposite side of the couch, didn't look away from the screen. "They'll be back soon enough. Drink your beer and stop scowling."

Realization struck him harder than a Glasgow kiss. He was pining after his wife—*fake* wife.

Reaching for his bottle of brew with an unsteady hand, he took a swig.

Gene and Benjamin gave him a sympathetic look from their armchairs before returning their attention to the TV. He usually preferred his laptop for company, but socializing wasn't bad when no one attempted to talk to him.

How long did Maisie intend to keep Joy away from him—er, from the *farm*? Would they stay out for dinner too?

The wind rattled the windows behind him. Great, just what the day needed. What if it rained? Or, worse, snowed? It wouldn't be safe for them to drive in those conditions. Their car could skid off the road or someone could T-bone them at an intersection. Joy's fragile bones wouldn't survive that.

They better be on their way home.

Once again, he peeked at her location. And, once again, it hadn't moved any closer.

Should he call her and demand she come right home? He knew exactly how that directive would go. She'd tell him to shove it and stay out longer on purpose.

Was he… missing her? Impossible. Sure, he liked spending time with her. She had a natural tendency to put people at ease. She put *him* at ease. Not a lot of people managed that—few were even allowed to try.

Maybe he'd go work upstairs—take his mind off Joy for a while. He had back-to-back work calls scheduled with New York anyway. Despite his current focus on Highlander Honey, the Auclair-Icefall Hospitality Group did not run itself. The second of their nightclubs had opened in New York City—and they were expanding to Chicago. His brother pulled his own weight and was as hands-on as Hayes, but with a toddler and an infant at home, Jackson's hands were full.

Hayes would handle the calls without him, and follow up on the background check he'd requested on the other prospective buyers. He should have had it in his inbox by now, and didn't appreciate the delay.

Rising, he backtracked out of the family room and went upstairs. An hour and a half later, he finished his last call, pored over the background checks, and still Joy wasn't back.

Needing something—anything—else to do, he grabbed his coat and scarf from the mudroom and slinked outside. If the women weren't home in the next hour, he'd drive out and drag them back himself.

Checking on the fence line and surveying what improvements the farm might need would pass the time until then.

A half hour later, just as he cleared the barn, his eyes settled on Maisie's car, parked in its usual spot.

*Joy is back.*

He sprang toward the house—then stopped. What the hell was he doing?

There was nothing to get worked up over. Joy wasn't his real wife, and he wasn't about to chase someone who wanted nothing to do with him. He'd learned his lesson from Liselle, and he'd learned it for life.

*Slow the fuck down.*

He may have modulated his pace, but he failed to calm his soaring heart.

Skin prickling with anticipation, he eased open the

front door. The mix of excited voices reached him from the kitchen. He bet Joy would be there too, probably helping herself to tea.

Hayes suspected the purpose of the trip was for Maisie to get to know the women, and finding out what they talked about should be his top priority. Instead, he wanted to hear about Joy's day.

What the hell was wrong with him?

Joy was an indulgence he couldn't afford.

Avoiding the kitchen—avoiding Joy until he could get a handle on his reaction to her—he set a direct path to the bedroom upstairs.

When Hayes walked into their room, he expected to find it empty. Instead, the woman he'd come up to avoid lay on the bed. *Guess she skipped out on the kitchen social.*

At first, he thought she was asleep. Lightening his footsteps, he edged closer.

She'd kept her skirt and top on from earlier, but had taken off the tights. The wind whipped at the windows, and although the room was adequately heated, she could get cold while sleeping on top of the covers. But when he reached for the throw at the foot of the bed, ready to cover her in its soft layer, her lashes fluttered open and she regarded him with clear, wide-awake eyes.

He released his hold on the throw. "Thought you were asleep."

She closed her eyes again, seeming to sink deeper into the bed. "I'm awake. I'm just so *exhausted*. My boots got soaked through as soon as we got out of the car. And all that lying… My feet are killing me, but not nearly as much as my conscience. I needed a break."

The heavy fall of her lashes across her pale cheeks confirmed how tired she was. Reaching for the blanket again, he drew it over her. Her eyes flew open, and she started to protest, but clamped her lips together and let him cover her with the throw.

Knowing he should leave her to nap, he took a resolved step away from her. Yet, that was as far as he got. He hadn't seen her all day, and for some inexplicable reason, he missed her… wanted to spend some time in her presence. She was about to sleep, which he should let her do, but still he lingered.

Before he could talk himself out of it, he sank to the edge of the bed. "What about a foot rub?"

One eye slitted open. Suspicion gleamed. "What's the catch?"

"No catch. You spent the entire day with Maisie, Kenna, *and Liselle*, and we both know you did it because I got you into this situation. The least I can offer is a massage."

She considered his response, then exhaled. "I like Maisie and Kenna. Maisie's interrogation aside, we had a good time, even with you-know-who there. But I won't say no to a massage." She gifted him with a mischievous grin, and lifted her foot toward him. "Start with this one."

As he sank his thumbs into her sole, she released a throaty moan. Jesus, this was a bad idea.

Drawing a steady breath, he focused on the task at hand and tried to ignore her sultry sounds of pleasure.

***

The cool room air contrasted with the velvet warmth of his hands as his thumbs explored her sole. She shouldn't have agreed to this, but she had, and it felt glorious. When he pressed into a particularly tight knot, she couldn't fight the gasp of relief.

180

Readjusting her foot more comfortably in his lap, he settled into the massage. He knew the places to knead to release the tension, and the places to notch it higher. With slow, sensual circles, he worked the tightness out of her stressed tissue. When he surged deep into her arch, she moaned, wanting his hands all over her, but he stayed focused on the tender curve.

Hayes worked her foot like the most elite of reflexologists, knowing the exact points that made her purr.

Squeezing her eyes shut, she refused to give him the satisfaction, and then he pressed deep on a particular pressure point and her inner walls fluttered.

What the—

Was that even possible?

Could he be doing that on purpose or was she simply in dire need of some human touch?

She shivered in anticipation as he lifted her other foot to his lap. His clever fingers soothed across the outer edge, stroked along the inside curve, sank deep into her sole, his movements equally relaxing and arousing.

His skillful hands continued to rock into her pressure points. She fisted the bedding under her, fighting the urge to pull him to her and feast on his mouth. He continued the slow torment until she was dizzy, and then he slid to her calf.

"Oh my God," she gasped. Realizing what she'd just done, she bit her tongue.

*Don't let him know the effect he has on you. This is Hayes. He will use it to his advantage.*

He worked the knotted muscle of her calf until the pressure released. Lost to the sensual glide of his fingers over her skin, she gave in and let his touch sweep over her.

When he stopped, she bit back a whine of protest. Guess the massage had come to its inevitable end. Soon, she'd have to move off the bed and pretend like her bones hadn't turned to mush.

Lifting her heavy lids, she met his watchful gaze, as if even a flicker of hesitation would signal him to stop. Whatever he saw etched in her features must have satisfied him, because the tension in his face eased.

Her breath caught as he traced a slow path from the curve of her knee to her sensitive inner thigh. She waited for him to go farther, all the way to where she wanted him, but he stopped and lifted his hands away.

*What... Wait...*

Lightheaded, she couldn't manage a word.

When she sat up, the room spun. Her breasts ached for his touch. She almost grasped his arm to haul him back. Thankfully, he left the bed before she embarrassed herself.

His breathing was as erratic as hers, and color rode high on his cheekbones.

The massage hadn't left him unaffected either.

Struggling to focus, to chase away the need that seemed to tether them together, she cleared her throat. "How are you so good at this?"

His voice was thick when he responded. "The first business I ever opened was a reflexology studio. Granted, it's easy to do when your father gives you the money for it. He was my first investor."

She hadn't expected that. "Reflexology studio? When was this?"

"I'd just gotten to college. Needed a way to make a living, and figured owning a foot massage parlor would be easy money. I had a couple of reflexologists working there, but took the classes myself so I knew what it entailed. Eventually, I scaled it into a wellness-chain. Sold it when I graduated."

"You've had a hand in just about every industry."

"A few," he allowed.

She crossed her legs to ease the tension that gathered there and studied him from her perch on the bed. "Do you like what you do with Jackson?"

"I like working with him. We share a similar work ethic. We've made Arlo Las Vegas one of the highest grossing nightclubs in the States—and Arlo New York isn't doing too shabby. The Chicago expansion has been tricky, so I'm far from bored."

"You think you can manage all that and the farm, or will you sell Highlander Honey?"

His resolute eyes held hers. "Never. You know what this place means to me."

He edged toward the door. The tension had grown too thick, and he plainly needed an out.

Yet she didn't want him to leave yet.

She'd missed him during her day away.

If he'd tagged along, he'd have quipped about the slow service at Benjamin's coffee shop or commented on the gaggle of tourists taking up most of the main street. His surly attitude used to annoy her, but today, she found herself missing it. What happened?

They were probably spending too much time together. It needed to stop.

His hand stilled on the brass doorknob, and he flipped back to face her. "Did you have fun today?"

Although the question hinted that he'd missed her as well, one never knew with Hayes. He was always playing three-dimensional chess.

She patted the spot next to her on the bed, though she knew she shouldn't. "Yes. Come sit, and I'll tell you."

What a fool.

When he moved toward her, her heart tripped, then raced. He sat next to her, his expression one of genuine interest.

Remembering the meal at the pub, she grinned. "Lying and walking in soggy shoes aside, it was *so* fun. The pub owner, who said he knows you—how does he know you? Then again, everyone seems to know you. Anyways, he brought over a raspberry dessert he called cranachan, and—what?"

He watched her mouth with eyes that had turned feral.

"Um, Hayes… what are—"

That was as far as she got before he dove across the small space between them and slanted his mouth over hers.

The shock of the kiss should have frozen her. Instead, it spurred her. Fisting her hands in his sweater, she dragged him closer and met his skilled tongue with hers.

He growled his approval, kissing her with a wildness that singed her skin.

Sliding her hands around the corded muscles of his neck, she pushed her heavy breasts against his rock-hard chest to ease the aching pressure.

Not lifting his lips from hers, he readjusted her legs until they settled around his hips, and her throbbing center pressed into his erection.

She should have hated this, should have hated him. Instead, effervescent joy spread from the pit of her stomach as he kissed her blind.

A small, increasingly insistent voice buzzed in her eardrum, urging her to pull away.

Eventually, she listened.

Curving her hands around his shoulders, she drew away from him. It took several seconds before she had enough air in her lungs to speak. "What is this, Hayes?"

Instead of responding, he scraped his teeth along her jaw, almost making her forget the question.

She leaned farther out of reach as she waited for him to answer.

When his turbulent eyes finally met hers, they had as many questions in them as hers did. He didn't know what this was either, she realized.

For some reason, that was enough for her right now. When he fake-dated her three years ago, he'd remained cool and unaffected. Now, the raw need and sheer confusion that radiated from him settled her misgivings. He wasn't kissing her to get her to do what he wanted. This pull between them had left him powerless too. Mollified, she returned her mouth to his.

He tasted of hops and mint, a heady combination she sought to explore. When his fingers curled around the edge of her turtleneck and he pulled back with a question in his eyes, she swept it over her head herself.

He didn't pause to admire her lingerie. Tugging the straps of her lace bra down, he pulled at the cloth until her breasts sprang free.

"I've missed these," he murmured, cupping her with a reverence that unraveled something deep within her. "I've missed you."

*Don't fall for it.*

*This is what he does.*

*He can't be trusted.*

"I've dreamed of this," he continued, mapping the sensitive undersides.

She swallowed. "Of tormenting me?"

"Of having you in my arms again."

Words. They were just words. Words didn't mean anything. And yet the deep timbre of his voice chipped away at the painful memories she'd layered around herself like armor. They'd been in a similar situation before—and not that long ago.

Before he walked away.

She attempted to hold on to the resentment she'd once felt for him, but all that surrounded her now was need. Where had the anger gone?

She'd end up repeating her mistake…

"Don't get used to it," she managed, but it came out all breathy and wrong.

Busy stippling soft kisses along her collarbone, he didn't seem to hear her anyway. The pad of his finger skimmed between the slope of her breast and the dusky pink areola.

"I love the contrast here," he crooned. "Velvet and silk." Leaning forward, he replaced his fingers with the raspy tip of his tongue. "You're so sweet. One taste is never enough."

Delicious tingles frothed across her skin, and she arched into his touch.

More. She needed more of him, all around her.

Instead of pulling the hard bud into his mouth, he teased along the delicate rim before shifting his attention to her other breast… avoiding the swollen flesh that demanded him most.

When he lifted his mouth away completely, she released a frustrated groan.

Heat licked along the axons in her body. Why was he stopping?

"What—"

His fingers dug into her hips. "Shh," he soothed. "We'll get there."

Returning to her breast, he flicked her nipple with his tongue before drawing it into his mouth.

"Yes. Finally," she managed.

He chuckled as his fingers closed over the other peak and tugged.

Fighting for air, for sanity, she scored his scalp, the back of his neck, any exposed area of skin as she tried to anchor herself amid the swell of sensation.

Did he know it was her he was kissing? With an insistent jerk, she brought his mouth back to hers to remind him.

As though he understood, he whispered her name against her lips. The rough murmur soothed her qualms, slipped past her defenses.

She opened to him, and he took, fusing their mouths together as his hands flowed along her spine, her hips, the backs of her thighs.

"I love the way you taste," he whispered against her lips. "The way you always smell like summer vacation." He homed in on the pulse at the base of her neck, pressed there before nibbling at the sensitive spot just below her ear. "The throaty way you gasp when I touch you."

His lilting revelations fractured the last of her control. Frantic to feel his mouth on her breasts again, she moved him there.

Hayes's appreciative groan spread through her like warm honey.

"I'm going to tear your panties away and put my mouth on you." He punctuated the statement with a bite where neck met shoulder.

Arching her neck, she encouraged him to feast. "Hurry, I need you."

He went feral, taking her mouth with his as he rocked her into his heavy erection, the cotton of his shirt deliciously rough against her sensitive nipples.

The drugging massage, the sweltering words, the velvety glide of his tongue against hers launched her over the peak without warning.

"*Hayes.*"

The word ripped out of her as pleasure exploded from deep in her belly.

Consciousness came to her in pieces: his firm shoulder under her cheek, the soft words he crooned in her ear, the tantalizing circles he soothed over her back, the harsh beating of his heart.

His hardness throbbed against her through the layers that separated them.

Lifting her head, she settled her hands along his neck, let the rapid beat of his pulse remind her that this craving between them was real, reciprocal, as overwhelming for him as it was for her.

What would happen when it overwhelmed them?

He'd run, and she'd be left to sift through the shattered pieces of her heart. The image was so clear that it immobilized her.

His lashes lifted and his passion-glazed eyes met hers. He must have noticed the change in her, because he hesitated, concern replacing hunger. "What's wrong?"

When she leaned away from him, he loosened his hold, though his arms remained around her for support. With a definitive shake of her head, she scrambled off his lap and, for good measure, off the bed.

Realizing that her bra was bunched around her waist, she maneuvered it back on before facing Hayes.

Just a few years ago, she thought herself in love with him. Now she knew better… and she still got all heart-eyed.

Hayes had *coerced her*, made her lie to the Blairs for him, and would never think about her once he got what he wanted.

She wasn't made of the same callous stuff as him. Even now, she knew she'd think about him after their stay here ended, and the ache would gnaw at her.

How could she have allowed herself to get this close to him? She was willing and ready to—

No, if she were to sleep with him, it would be on *her* terms—when she was certain that she could do so without engaging a single emotion. Not a one.

Lulled by his foot massage, softened because she'd missed him today like a clown, she had almost stripped him just now…

What if she developed feelings like last time? She couldn't handle him crushing her like that again. Three years ago, he'd walked away. He'd do so again now.

If anything were to happen between them, she had to be in the right mindset. And right now, her mind wasn't the one doing the thinking.

Finding her turtleneck, she pulled it back on before backtracking to the door. "I need some space."

Even as she twisted the handle, she lingered, waiting—stupidly hoping—he'd ask her to stay, but he kept silent.

The disappointment that rushed through her confirmed that she was making the right decision.

# Chapter 24

Dinner a few hours later was… awkward.

Joy sat next to Hayes at the large kitchen table while the other couples around them chomped and chatted, and yet the easy rapport between her and Hayes had disintegrated into terse looks and brittle silences.

The others could tell, she was sure. Maisie scrutinized them from across the table. She could almost read her thoughts: *What had happened between the return to the farm and dinner?*

Liselle lapped up the rift between them like a satisfied cat. Sidling closer to Gene, she'd dot a kiss across his cheek or lay her hand on his shoulder. The very epitome of a couple in love.

Cue the eye roll.

Kenna threw Liselle and Gene a dark look too, but when she redirected her attention to Joy, her smile brightened. "Joy, you never finished telling us what other places are on your list of things to see while you're in Scotland. Did you visit every location from your childhood that you wanted to, or is there anything left?"

"Almost all except for two. I still need to go to Doune Castle and Culross, but that's it."

"Hayes, will you take her?" asked Kenna. "If not, Benjamin and I'd be happy to tour Doune Castle with you, Joy. I haven't been in a while."

"I'll take her," he bit out, looking as enthusiastic about it as she felt.

"Want to keep her all to yourself, do you?" joked Cal from across the table, taking a sip of his mead.

When Hayes looked at her, a brooding emotion simmered just beneath the surface. Taking her hand in his cold one, he lifted it to his mouth. "You got me."

As Maisie launched into a story of when she and Cal first started dating, Hayes kept her hand in his, stroking his thumb across her skin as though he'd forgotten they weren't really together.

Cal tacked on a colorful detail to Maisie's tale, and the other couples hooted. Hayes chuckled too, his fingers playing with hers.

This didn't feel like pretending.

She couldn't fall for his ruse yet again.

After dinner, Hayes escaped upstairs. The others gathered in the family room for movie night, but she declined. It had been a long day. She wanted her bed, a book, and maybe a long scroll on social media.

Hayes would be in his small room by now, and she could finally have a break.

On her way upstairs, she ended location sharing to his phone. She already had one stalker; she didn't need two.

When she entered their room, she almost choked on her own saliva.

The man was shirtless again.

*Look away, Joy.*

Moving her attention to the window, she fought for a measure of control. "Er… um… warm tonight?"

He didn't seem to notice her sudden embarrassment. "Yep. The blankets I found are meant for a polar vortex."

"You should keep one when we leave this place."

"Yeah. Maybe I'll do that." Shrugging into his tee, he strode to the door. "Night."

When he left, Joy felt like punching a wall. Instead, she plopped on the bed and groaned into a pillow.

That's when she heard a voice.

Liselle's voice, to be exact. She'd recognize that fake purr anywhere.

Setting the pillow aside, she crept to the door and listened.

"You and the missus have a fight?" asked her fake husband's ex-girlfriend.

"What makes you say that?" Hayes evaded.

Joy could practically see the practiced lift of Liselle's tanned shoulder. "I'm not surprised. I can't see you two together. You always preferred your women…" Her voice lowered, and Joy failed to catch the last part. She pressed her ear tighter to the door to hear better.

A thud against the wall next to her jolted her. Had Hayes bumped into it?

"I left something in the other room—was going over to get it," he said.

"And Friday night?" queried Liselle. "I heard you sneaking off too."

"Had to work—Joy's a light sleeper."

Liselle snorted out a derisive sound. "Joy. What a silly little name. What are you doing with a doctor, Hayes? You weren't ever one to go for someone so stodgy and boring. You've become so settled. It's making me want to…" The words morphed into another low murmur.

Now she was insulting her profession? She wasn't stodgy or boring. Settled, sure. But it was good to be settled.

The rumble of Hayes's familiar laugh cut off the rest of Liselle's words. "One thing Joy isn't is stodgy or boring. Now, I'm going to get back to my wife."

It didn't sound like Liselle would back down that easily. "You and I had it good though, didn't we? Sometimes, I still think about that night at the Waldorf. Do you remember? You made me come so hard, the neighbors called security. They thought you were murdering me."

That was an image Joy neither wanted nor needed.

Hayes's tone chilled. "Go back to your room."

"Gene won't stop blabbing about your little side deal. I won't let it go through, you know."

*What side deal?*

"I'm done with you, Liselle."

The woman purred. Again. Ugh. The practiced hum grated.

"Liselle. So formal. That's not what you used to call me when…" Her voice turned low and sultry.

Joy couldn't catch the words, but she understood the gist. How dare she hit on her fake husband?

Outraged, she swung open the door. The sight dropped her jaw square to the floor—Liselle had pinned Hayes against the wall like an out-of-luck butterfly.

Joy raised a brow. "I suggest you take your hands off my husband."

Liselle gave her that annoying, self-satisfied smirk and stepped back. "We were just catching up."

The only reason Joy didn't punch Hayes was because he looked furious, a muscle in his jaw jerking as he extricated himself from his ex-girlfriend.

"Catch up with your own husband." Joy stepped back inside her room. Hayes followed. She didn't bother to see what Liselle would do as she shut the door.

He raised his hands, palms out. "That was not—"

She whirled on him. "Your ex hitting on you?"

"Liselle only wants things other people have."

Realizing that he was right, her stance softened. "She thinks I have you, so she wants you. She knows the Blairs love you, so she wants them to love her more."

"Yep."

"And she wants this farm because you want it."

He nodded.

"Well, she can't have it. Liselle is *not* this farm's next owner."

Then again, neither would Hayes be, if she could help it.

The realization dawning in his features made her uncomfortable. "You're jealous. Nothing happened. I wouldn't—"

"*I'm not jealous!*" Oof. That came out much too loud. She lowered her voice. "Why would I be jealous? You and I aren't really together, are we? You think I forgot that? I simply don't like her. She thinks we are married, and she hit on you. And she called me boring and stodgy. I'm not boring and stodgy. I'm insulted, if anything. Not jealous."

Maybe she *was* protesting too much…

His eyes creased at the corners. "I told her you're not stodgy or boring."

"I heard." She paced across the room, still not calmed. "And it's good to be settled."

He offered an easy shrug. "Agreed."

His concurrence didn't pacify her. "If she felt settled, she wouldn't be going around trying to sleep with other people's husbands."

*Fake* husbands, but still.

"I was trying to get to my room," he pointed out.

"And she was watching, biding her time. Tonight, you're sleeping here. Take the bed—I'll take the floor."

"She's back in her room by now. She won't emerge again tonight—you scared her." He stepped into her personal bubble. Before she could scamper back, he pressed a kiss to her cheek. "I like it when you get jealous."

"I'm not jealous," she repeated, scowling.

Chuckling, he headed for the door. Confirming no one lurked in the hall, he slipped out, his footsteps retreating as he strode to his small, assigned room.

"I'm not jealous," she repeated again—to remind herself—and went to brush her teeth.

By the time she emerged, Hayes was in her room again.

She crossed her arms over her pajama-clad chest. "Didn't you leave?"

"Heard Gene skulking around. Figured I'd work from here until everyone settles down."

She sighed. "Just sleep here. It's fine. I think we can both keep our hands to ourselves."

His gaze traveled up her body. "I better take the floor."

# Chapter 25

Hours later, long after everyone else had retired for the evening and the sounds of Cal's snoring resounded through the house, Joy watched Hayes doze on the floor beneath her bed, wrapped in a blanket like a jumbo burrito.

The man was attractive even in sleep, with his chiseled features and perfect lips. What was wrong with her that she could still want him after everything he'd done to her? Worse, it was nearly two a.m. and she couldn't sleep, too preoccupied with thoughts of him.

They had two full days left on the farm. On Wednesday, after Cal's birthday, she'd return to Edinburgh, find a different hotel, and enjoy Scotland for the rest of her vacation. By then, her part of their deal would have been met, and Hayes would have to leave her alone.

Now that Ryder no longer tracked her phone, it's not like he'd be able to find her.

If she could figure out a way to see both places in one day, she'd visit Doune Castle and Culross Village before her flight on Friday.

Returning home would have its own challenges— like taking out a restraining order on Ryder, and finding a new place to live. No way would she return to her old apartment—if he was still rampaging, she'd be a sitting duck.

Flipping to her back, she suppressed a frustrated grunt as the reality of what awaited her in San Diego intruded.

Maybe she could make the most of her time here. Take a little break from her problems, and just have some stupid, no-holds-barred fun.

A few days of hot, steamy sex to let this attraction between her and Hayes run its course so that she never thought about him again.

So long as they both knew it was nothing but sex until their stay with the Blairs was over, who could it hurt? Her, if she grew feelings for him. But that ship had sailed when he'd left her the last time. She was smarter now, wasn't she? Yes, and she knew exactly what she was getting herself into.

Climbing off the bed, she tiptoed to him on the floor. He was a light sleeper, she knew that, and he'd jolt awake as soon as she got near. She closed the distance anyway, sinking to her knees next to him.

He was alert and sitting up before she even hit the ground, his sleep-hooded eyes sharpening on her face. "Are you okay? What's wrong?"

Settling more comfortably on the hard floor, she folded her legs under her. "Let's have sex."

She'd always been direct, had never taken long to mull her decisions, but Hayes clearly did not know that.

He scrutinized her with mounting concern. "Are you sleepwalking?"

She leaned closer, brushing her lips along his jawline. "What's the harm? We part ways soon—"

He was on her before she could get another word

out, as though worried she might disappear. One second, she sat facing him; the next, she was on her back under him, and his tongue was sweeping past her lips to tangle with hers.

Grasping handfuls of her button-down pajama top, he ripped it in half with a quick flex of his biceps. She didn't even have time to yelp.

"I thought you'd never ask." He caught her swollen nipple with his fingers, twisting gently. "You going to take all of me tonight?"

"If you hurry." Framing his face between her hands, she redeployed his mouth back to hers, needing an anchor amid the churn of need his eager willingness unleashed.

Slipping her fingers between them, she grasped the top monogrammed button of his flannel pajamas. Haste made her clumsy, and she fumbled her first attempt. Brushing her hands aside, he shredded the fabric in one swoop. The buttons scattered, pinging across the floor.

Pulling back, she stared, absorbed by the sheer expanse of bronzed muscle so close to her. "You weren't this ripped three years ago."

He shrugged out of the remnants of his flannel. "Had to find a way to get you out of my head."

She froze under him. How many women had he screwed to get this shredded?

Amusement flickered in his eyes as he clarified. "At the gym."

Oh. That was acceptable then. "I thought—"

He reached for her bottoms. "I know what you thought."

Finally naked, she pushed him to his back, his heavy erection between them. Riveted by the perfect shape of him, she closed her fingers around him—

With one swift move, he had her on her back on his makeshift bed yet again. Kissing down her belly, he homed in on her piercing.

"This sexy little pearl suits you." He tongued the navel ring. "An unexpected surprise. Like you."

She sifted through his short hair. "I've wanted one since I was a teen. Finally got it for my birthday last year."

"I've always liked the rebellious streak in you."

Widening her legs to make room, she gave him a gentle push. "Show me how much."

Hayes released a purr of satisfaction, scooting lower and spreading her wider.

"You're perfect," he murmured, settled between her thighs.

*Hayes Icefall's face is between my legs.*

The surreal realization fled quickly, chased from her mind by his warm breath against the core of her.

"I've wanted to taste you since the day we met," he rumbled against her arousal. "Once won't be enough."

The man knew what he was doing. Joy bucked off the makeshift bed as he learned her with long, languorous strokes of his tongue. He crooned soft words against her skin, telling her how good she tasted, how long he'd dreamed of this, how much he wanted her.

Struggling to hear him through the rush of blood in her ears, she boosted her hips. "I'm so close…"

The smug smile he gave her was distinctly Hayes. And that was when the real show began.

He pushed her to the edge where gasps slurred to moans, to raw, primal sounds she barely recognized as her own. Lifting into him, she sought her own release, but Hayes refused to allow it. He encased her hips in a steel grip, overriding her movements.

Her desperate sobs seemed to fuel him further, and he closed his mouth over her swollen bundle of nerves and sucked, tearing a hoarse cry from deep within her as she splintered apart.

Several minutes ticked by before she could form a coherent thought. "Did I—? Was that sound—?"

Guess she still couldn't form a sentence.

He flashed a self-satisfied grin. "Did you scream? Was that sound you? Yes."

Great. She'd hoped the howl he'd torn from her had stayed in her head, not bounced off the walls of the small farmhouse.

"Everyone will know what we're doing in here now." But the languid afterglow made it hard to care.

He stroked along her ultra-sensitive inner thigh. "This is hardly a scandalous activity for a married couple."

Surrendering, she melted into the improvised bedding. "I don't think I can move."

He levered over her for a rough kiss that made her inner muscles clench. "Good thing I want you on your back."

Waking him up tonight was the best idea she'd ever had.

Hayes continued to kiss her as though he couldn't get enough, taking her mouth in a series of wet, biting kisses that made her writhe for him again. He nibbled along her lower lip, teased her cupid's bow, the corner of her mouth.

Gripping his shoulders, she kneaded the flexing tissue, slipped her palms up and down his rock-hard biceps, along the strong column of his neck, and into his closely shorn hair. The strands felt like cool silk under her finger pads.

When she scored his hot scalp with her nails, he

rumbled in pleasure, skating his lips along her jaw to nuzzle the sensitive hollow just below her ear.

His teeth closed around her straining neck tendon, making snowflakes of sensation dance across her skin.

Lifting into him, she rubbed her aching nipples along his chest. His large hand immediately cupped one heavy globe, his thumb teasing across the throbbing peak just before he closed his mouth over her and suckled.

She squeezed her eyes closed at the sharp pleasure.

Hayes continued to worship her breasts, alternating playful flicks of his tongue with long, drugging pulls that made her hips buck involuntarily, seeking him.

"I need you. Now, Hayes, *now*."

Joy felt him smile against her breast. "I forgot how impatient you are."

With one mischievous lick across her nipple, he pushed away and padded to the nightstand—his impressive erection bobbing.

*Don't stare, girl. Play it cool.*

Boy, was that hard to do.

He moved like a panther—all primal self-assurance and slick, flexing muscles. She ached to feel him fill her, to lose herself just for a little while.

"Bed or floor?" He stood over her. Lifting the condom packet to his mouth, he tore it with his teeth.

*Bed later.* "Here. Now."

"Are you going to scream for me again?"

Why was he toying with her? Now wasn't the time. She reached for him. "If you make it good."

His low chuckle felt like a caress. "I'll see what I can do."

Wrapping her fingers around his sheathed member, she scooted closer. "Less talk, Icefall."

He needed no more invitation than that. His dark, dilated gaze locked on hers as he filled her in one thick glide.

Lost to the feel of him, she let her heavy lids fall as she wrapped her legs around him, digging her nails into the flexed muscles of his back.

God, he was hot—inside and around her. For a man who tended to layer up like a hiker through the Arctic, when you stripped him of all those layers, his body radiated heat. Who needed one of those fancy bladeless Dysons when you had Hayes? There was no comparison. A giggle escaped her throat.

"What's so funny?" He brushed his lips across her forehead, coaxing her to open her eyes.

She gave in to her merriment, her muscles closing around him with each wave of laughter. "Just thinking that you can thaw me from the inside out better than any swanky heater."

She fixed a kiss to his lips and smiled, dropping her head back against the pillow. But he continued to watch her, his own expression careful.

What did he seek to find? What did her face reveal? She wished she could mask her emotions as easily as he could—but pretense had never been a skill she mastered.

Whatever he read in her expression snapped the silken ties of his usual control. He crushed his mouth to hers, his tongue staking claim as he retreated, only to push deeper.

"I've craved this," he murmured, withdrawing almost fully again before plunging home with a satisfied snarl. "I've craved you. Imagined what you'd feel like wrapped around me. Not even my wildest fantasy compares to the real thing. To you."

He stoked the liquid fire higher and higher, but refused to let her detonate. Easing back whenever she whimpered, so close to release, he kept her on a maddening precipice until she clawed at him, cursed him.

Only then did he give in to them both, his thick cock swelling inside her as the world shattered around them.

"Wow." She released a shaky breath, her fingers still trembling as she swiped a stray lock of hair from her sweat-drenched forehead. She'd never imagined such a primal mating from someone as practiced—as controlled—as Hayes.

Drawing her against him, he swept his lips along her shoulder, her neck, her jawline, whispering soft endearments as he stroked across her damp skin. The devastatingly tender gesture undid her. Scared her. Yet she couldn't bring herself to move away.

Pulling the covers over them both, he curved a possessive hand around her breast and knocked out.

But when she slept, Ryder troubled her dreams. Wielding a blood-stained scalpel, he chased her through a shadowy maze littered with her dead goldfish.

Clawing her way out of the nightmare, she took a deep breath as she processed her surroundings. Safe, away from Ryder, still on the floor next to her bed at the Blairs' farm—Hayes curled around her.

Maybe it was good their deal centered on never seeing each other again after Scotland, because how could she ever face him without remembering *this*?

It's not like their lives could ever mesh, anyway.

Hayes was nomadic, restless, too driven by whatever it was that haunted him to settle down in one place or to one business, much less with one woman.

Unlike him, she enjoyed her steady life—and never intended to change it.

They'd part ways soon, but she'd enjoy every drop of the quickly escaping time they had left together.

She could walk away when the time came.
She could and she would.

***

He never wanted morning to come.

After years of restlessness, of chasing the next venture, the next project, the next frontier, he finally found himself—for the first time—happy to be exactly where he was.

He gazed down at the woman asleep in his arms, her soft breath teasing his chest as they lay amid the crumpled remnants of his once-immaculate bedding. They never made it to the actual bed. Not that either one of them had noticed.

Careful not to disturb her, he studied her peaceful form nestled against him. Her still-flushed cheeks couldn't hide the shadows beneath her eyes. Was he responsible for them?

To get her to cooperate, he'd threatened her career.

It's not like he'd actually have gone through with it. Joy had to have known that… right?

Not that it mattered now. After Wednesday, he'd live up to his end of the bargain, and never see her again.

What had seemed such an easy decision just a few days ago now suffocated him with panic.

Before the gala, he'd tried to keep his distance. Joy was his sister-in-law's baby sister, after all. Even when he took her out on a few dates ahead of the hospital fundraiser, he didn't attempt to get to know her.

Now he had.

And the prospect of returning to his life without her sliced through him like the blistering blade of an uncapping knife.

Reluctantly extricating himself from under her, he slid out of the rumpled sheets and padded to the shower.

He'd survived being left for dead on the side of the road. He'd survive this gnawing emptiness too.

Running the water, he stepped under the stream, hoping it would pound at least some sense into him. Reaching for the soap, he scoured it over himself, scrubbing away the heady scent of her, the heavenly taste, the feel of her in his arms. He rinsed away the memory of her muscles clasping him deep inside her as she laughed.

As though his thoughts had summoned her, the curtain opened and Joy stood naked in front of him. Her eyes lowered over him in slow, appreciative perusal.

"Where was my invitation?" She stepped inside the tub.

His arms wound around her instinctively, and he brought her against his slippery chest. When she lifted her mouth to his, he took it, understanding it for the gift it was. He'd hurt her before, betrayed her. Even if she never trusted him again, she gave him her body, and he'd ensure it was a decision she'd never regret.

The desire between them was raw, rare. In moments of weakness, he might even allow for precious. It was there, a gravitational pull he didn't want to escape—yet.

Although he'd had her several times in the night, he needed her again, to sink deep and feel her heartbeats pulse around him. Cupping her breasts, he lifted them to his greedy mouth.

On a sharp inhale, she arched into him in eager encouragement, her nails sinking into his scalp.

She was perfect.

Slipping her hands down his lathered abdominals, she swept the soap to his cock and wrapped her fingers around him.

"Yes," he murmured as his dick throbbed against her palm. He pumped into her tight, slick fist, lost to the moment, lost to her.

He pulled away while he still could, grasping her wrist and tugging until she released him.

"I need you." He spun her around until she faced away from him.

Pressed against him, she giggled. "That's one way of getting me."

He glided his hand over her toned back. "Put your hands on the edge of the tub."

She obeyed, but not without protest. "It's slippery—hard to hold on to."

"I'll give you slippery." Remembering protection, he released his hold on her hips. "You're going to stay just like this and wait for me."

God, she was beautiful—her taut ass out on display, the sleek muscles of her back flexing as she readjusted her grip.

"Hayes…" His name faltered on her tongue, as though she couldn't decide whether to listen or kill him.

Intrigued, he doubled down. "I mean it. If you want to come, you'll wait here like a good girl."

She groaned, but didn't move. "Hurry."

He did. When he returned, he found her in the same position, bent over, waiting for him exactly as instructed.

The surprise of it froze him. The Joy he knew would have scratched his eyes out at the mere suggestion. Yet she'd heeded his orders.

Captivated by this side of her so new to him, he stepped into the steamy tub behind her, cutting between her and the hot water that hammered her back.

Sweeping a possessive hand across the perfect globe

of her ass, he slid through the slick arousal that coated her inner thighs. She wanted this—wanted *him* like this.

Testing his theory, he parted her with his fingers, probed her tight channel. The low moan of desire called to the primitive core of him, to the untamed side he rarely allowed free rein.

The last vestiges of rational thought fled as the urge to take her, to sink deep, to mark her as his clamored through him.

Rolling on protection, he fitted himself to her entrance and pushed one slow inch inside.

The burn of need urged him to press deeper, but he gritted his teeth and held to a measured, shallow pace until she moved against him in restless demand for more.

"Deeper," she groaned. "Harder."

Readjusting his grip on her hips, he gave in to her hoarse plea, sinking in another gradual inch before withdrawing, then deliberately another until he took her in long, smooth strokes.

The rapidly cooling water pummeling his back contrasted with Joy's feverish warmth, and he surged into her wet heat again and again until she tightened around him with a sharp cry, her inner muscles strangling his cock.

She'd remember this night for the rest of her life, he promised, continuing his relentless rhythm, drawing out her orgasm and launching her into another.

His vision blurred as he sank the entirety of his length into her and held there. "I love feeling you around me. So hot, so tight, milking me."

"Th—that was…"

The hitch in her voice made him feel triumphant.

"You don't think we are done yet, do you?" He flexed his hips, reveling in the corresponding flutter of muscles as she melted around him.

Buried to the hilt, he withdrew an inch before returning deep.

"*Hayes*," she moaned, her inner muscles quivering.

Pleased, he repeated the move.

She went wild in his arms, slurring words he could hardly decipher, clamping around him over and over as one climax melded into another.

When her legs began to shake, he yielded to his own need, holding her to him as he came in powerful spasms.

They both sank to the basin, barely fitting inside the small tub. The cold water he'd been able to block from her earlier now pounded both their heads. Reaching over, he shut off the stream.

"Hmmm," she purred, giving him her full weight as she rested against him.

Sliding a wet tress away from her face, he traced one velvety shoulder. "You feel okay?"

She didn't bother to lift her head, but he felt her slow smile against him. "Can we do that again?"

"Not in here. The next time, I want you on the big bed, so I can watch your eyes go all soft and misty and I know you're lost to the feel of me inside you."

"Smooth talker," she mumbled, but kept her eyes closed. "I need a little nap first."

He'd worn her out, he realized with primal satisfaction.

A shiver worked its way through her, and her skin began to cool.

"Let's get you under the covers." Gripping the edge of the tub, he rose to his feet, drawing her up with him. "We've still got a couple hours until breakfast."

# Chapter 26

Joy slept twined around him like honeysuckle. She smelled of summer, of warmth and the ocean. Nuzzling her hair, he let that unique Joy scent fill him.

Liselle was his first and last real relationship. Everyone since had been hookups and one-night stands—beautiful women who tolerated his idiosyncrasies, hoping to snag him. He rarely saw the same woman twice—he'd never be idiotic enough to get attached to someone who didn't share his feelings again.

People couldn't be trusted in general. His net worth was plastered all over the internet. How could he ever know if someone liked him for him, or for the dollar signs?

Joy was different.

She was killing herself to pay off her self-imagined debt to Evie, and yet she refused his money to wipe the slate clean. Anyone else would have jumped at the chance, but she'd only agreed to his offer when he brought up the Delices. Saving a life had meant more to her than having all that cash for herself.

He swallowed against the sudden lump in his throat. On Wednesday, he'd accepted her terms, but now the idea of never seeing her again needled.

Maybe he could convince her to change her mind.

After all, what they just shared had been better than good.

Clearly, she liked when he led in the bedroom. She'd rip his balls off if he tried anything similar outside of it, but here, she exulted in it.

They had a strong physical connection. Why not continue it after they left Scotland, and have some fun exploring their new dynamic?

Maybe they could work out some sort of arrangement.

It's not like either one sought anything serious. She was fresh out of a relationship, and he never wanted one again.

Sweeping his palm along her spine, he smiled.

This might actually work.

# Chapter 27

Holy smokes, what had she done?

She'd had sex with Hayes.

Not once—once was a fluke. Not twice—twice was forgivable. But five times in *one night*.

Sure, the first time had been her idea. And the second… and fourth.

She'd believed she would be just fine, but she'd underestimated how attracted she was to him, how vulnerable. If she wasn't careful, he could really hurt her.

He'd brought her untold pain and embarrassment before.

She'd assumed she was smarter now. What if that assumption was wrong?

The sun had risen long ago. At this rate, it'd be lunchtime before they made their way downstairs.

At the armoire, Joy chose items at random—a pair of jeans, a long-sleeved shirt—before stepping back so Hayes could access his clothes.

Everyone would be downstairs for breakfast by now. Her cheeks burned as she realized they *all* must have heard them last night—

*Don't think about that.*

Watching Hayes slide the shirt over his sculpted torso made her hanker to tear the cotton away, to push him across the flower-patterned bedspread, and make love to him again.

*Control yourself, Joy.* It's not like she was a teen-ager.

At her obvious, thirsty gawking, he lifted his head. The slow curve of his smile told her he liked her staring. Great. As if his ego needed a boost.

A spark of invitation danced in his eyes. "Should we stay in today?"

Quite the tempting offer. She nearly grabbed a fistful of his shirt and pulled him down for a kiss when unmistakable sounds of fighting reached them through the closed door.

Their heads whipped toward the yelling.

She knew those voices…

*Not again.*

"Whoa." She winced. "I didn't think Kenna and Benjamin fought so much."

Hayes gave her a superior look. "Told you they were sketchy."

As the couple stopped at the top of the stairs—that is, right by their door—the fighting grew louder, and the words clearer.

"I never want to see you again!" Kenna's voice broke into a sob halfway through the statement.

"Fine by me—get your own arse home!"

The heavy retreating footsteps down the stairs must have belonged to Benjamin. The lighter footsteps in the other direction were accompanied by a door slam— Kenna returning to her room, Joy surmised.

She hurried to finish dressing. "What do you think happened?"

Hayes buckled his belt. "Fuck if I know."

The harsh sobs from the bedroom reached them then. Kenna was weeping—and loudly.

"I should go talk to her."

But when she turned for the door, Hayes's tone pulled her back. "Are you kidding? Let her cry."

The man didn't do emotions, but she couldn't let Kenna sob it out alone. "She may want to talk. I'll see you later."

Crossing to her, Hayes gripped her shoulders. "Don't get involved, Joy."

Unable to resist, she traced the contours of his sculpted biceps. "I won't. I'm just going to see if she's okay."

His voice held a note of caution. "Whatever happened is their business, not yours. Don't get wrapped up in it."

Lifting to her toes, she planted a kiss to his lips. "I'll see you in a bit."

His hands skimmed to her hips, and he held her to him for a fraction longer.

When he finally released her, she steeled herself against the urge to crawl back into his arms.

*Don't get attached to him. The man is a user.*

They only had a few more days left together, and the end couldn't come soon enough. After all, she intended to leave Scotland with souvenirs, not a broken heart.

Pushing aside her unwelcome affection for Hayes, she went to see whether Kenna was all right.

***

Unlike Joy, Hayes refused to get caught up in another couple's problems. He crept down the stairs, determined to avoid Benjamin. The man seemed like a crier. Hayes didn't do tears.

213

He'd been on the farm since Friday, and he barely spent any time with Cal or Maisie. Today, he'd remedy that. Cal was usually out doing outdoor chores about now. He'd go help him.

Liselle and Gene's distinct voices reached him from the kitchen. Avoiding them like a roach nest, he exited the house in search of Cal.

A man's sobbing interrupted his trek to the barn.

*Fuck.*

Benjamin sat on the soggy ground next to the parked cars and wept.

*Can't catch a break.*

Hayes looked back at the house. Was it too late to backtrack inside?

But Benjamin had seen him. Realizing he'd been caught, the lovelorn fool jumped to his feet and rubbed at his eyes.

"You okay, man?" Hayes had no choice but to ask.

"No. Kenna and I broke up."

"Well… plenty of fish in the sea." He turned to go.

"I love her."

"Good for you, bud. You'll make it work." He took another step away.

"She broke it off."

Fuck. He should have never gone outside.

He flipped to face Benjamin, not making contact with his red-rimmed eyes. "Go talk to her."

"I can't."

"Why the fuck not?"

Benjamin ran his knuckles across his eyes. "We're not really engaged."

*What the hell?* "What do you mean you're not engaged?"

Benjamin's lip began to quiver.

"Good God, don't cry. Just spit it out."

Benjamin sank back to the ground.

Did he not realize he was squatting in mud? Apparently not.

His shoulders trembled. "Kenna's fond of this farm. She grew up just next door and doesn't want it to go to some stranger. You know how Cal and Maisie are set on selling to a proper couple. Kenna and I've been seeing each other, but we weren't at that stage yet—not enough for me to pop the question."

Hayes couldn't believe this.

Was everyone misleading the Blairs? Not that he should be one to talk.

Benjamin's distraught face morphed into pure dejection. "But being here, pretending to be engaged, it's doing my head in. We feel awful lying to the Blairs. Kenna wanted to come clean today, and I told her we can't because our relationship is a sham. I didn't mean it like that. I made a mess of it. She took it all wrong. We fought. She called it quits. I love Kenna, I want to marry her, I want to make our proposal the real deal."

This was it. His key to the farm.

Kenna and Benjamin were strong contenders. Kenna had history with the Blairs, with the farm, and she seemed so damn likeable.

The information—freely offered by Benjamin— would toss their hat right out of the race. One word to Maisie, to Cal, and they'd be stunned, offended. Hurt. The woman they treated like a niece had lied to them— had gotten her boyfriend to lie to them. If Hayes went to them, the farm would be his.

*Just back up… go find Cal or Maisie…*

The victory was so close, satisfaction began to tingle in the tips of his fingers. He could hear Cal and Maisie's voices somewhere in the near distance. It would be so easy to go and seal his win—that is, once Liselle and Gene were rejected.

Benjamin nestled deeper into the mud. Slumped over, he rested his face in his palms.

*Fuck.*

He couldn't do it. He couldn't capitalize on Benjamin's misery. As much as he hated to admit it, he didn't mind the guy. Didn't mind Kenna, either.

When Benjamin looked at Kenna, Hayes understood the emotion in his young, expressive eyes…

The kid was hurting. The love of his life was slipping away. For Benjamin, the world was ending.

He couldn't weaponize the younger man's confession into claiming Highlander Honey as his. It wasn't right. And it might end things between Benjamin and Kenna forever.

Stifling a groan, he knew what he had to do.

Rolling his eyes skyward, he mumbled, "Then why don't you?"

Benjamin stilled. His head lifted. The eyes that met Hayes's were flooded with despair, but a tenuous, tentative thread of hope surfaced too. Benjamin blinked, and hope obliterated anguish.

"You're right," he said, face shining. "Why don't I? I'll go find her right now."

Breathing hard, Benjamin leaped to his feet.

Invested now, Hayes asked, "What are you going to tell her?"

"That I love her, that I want us to get married, to make this real. She can tell the Blairs that we lied, if she wants, but we'll be engaged proper now. I can't imagine my life without her."

Puppy love. Hayes himself had been that foolish once. Liselle had taught him a valuable lesson. But Benjamin wasn't him, and Kenna certainly wasn't Liselle. Although he'd never let himself love anyone again, he recognized the sentiment between Benjamin and his soon-to-be-fiancée.

"Well, then do it right. Get her a ring."

"A ring…" Benjamin repeated. "Yes! I'll get her a ring. Shite. Nearest town's a good half hour away."

"Come on," said Hayes, surprising himself. "I'll drive you."

"You will? Cheers, mate. Let's get a move on, then. Before Kenna walks out of my life for good."

"Go change your pants first. You're not tracking wet mud into my McLaren."

***

Kenna had been inconsolable when Joy found her on the bed in the room she shared with Benjamin.

The sobs were so intense, Joy could barely understand her. Through the hiccups, she gleaned that Kenna and Benjamin had broken up, and Kenna didn't want to talk about it.

Close to hyperventilating, Kenna had hugged Joy to herself and, through the sniffles, stuttered that she wanted to go see her parents. Tears streaming down her freckled cheeks, she released Joy and slipped out of the room.

Joy hadn't seen her since.

Nor did she see Benjamin. Or Hayes, for that matter.

Nor did Hayes respond to any of her text messages.

She checked her phone one more time.

Nope. Not even an emoji.

Maybe last night had been too much for him—and now he was avoiding her. She should have expected that. After last time, one would assume she'd have learned.

Shoving thoughts of Hayes from her brain, she focused on making the most of her day on the bee farm. She ate a late breakfast with Cal and Maisie, which was delightful. Then Gene and Liselle joined them in the kitchen, which was less so.

Although Liselle and Gene tried to ferret out why Kenna and Benjamin had been screaming all morning, Maisie shut them down with a stern look. "Just a lovers' tiff. We'll say nothing more about it."

After breakfast, with Kenna, Benjamin, and Hayes still MIA, Cal and Maisie suggested a hike. With nothing better to do other than sit in her room and dwell on Hayes's unresponsiveness, Joy jumped at the chance to explore the local wilderness. Liselle and Gene agreed to join much less enthusiastically.

The weather cooperated and, two hours of beautiful trails later, they returned to the farm.

In a much better mood after the hike, Joy, intrigued by the honey harvesting despite herself, asked Cal and Maisie to walk her through the apiaries. Cal and Maisie were happy to oblige.

Gene and Liselle opted out of the additional beekeeping education. They didn't join her and the Blairs for lunch either, which was just fine by her.

After the hive tour and lunch, she and the Blairs sat in the kitchen, lingering over tea, when Kenna returned from her parents' farm, only a little worse for wear.

"Is Benjamin here?" she asked in a hoarse voice. "He and I need to talk."

Everyone pretended not to notice her red, puffy eyes.

Maisie smiled a bit too brightly. "I'm sure he'll be back soon. I haven't seen him or Hayes at all today. Would you like some tea? Or a chat?"

Cal pushed away from the table. "I better be off. Got some work to get done. I'll catch you later."

The poor man didn't escape far. He was almost out of the kitchen when he staggered back a step. "That's not good."

Joy twisted her head to see. *Oh, definitely not good.*

Gene lurched through the doorway, his normally bronzed face drained of color. "A fuckin' bee got me."

Gene's arm had ballooned to quadruple its size, the skin turning a crimson purple as it stretched taut over the overinflated flesh. Liselle hovered just behind him.

"You're allergic to bees?" Joy rushed to Gene.

"Since when?" Maisie exclaimed at her elbow. "Why didn't you tell us?"

"Where did you even find a bee in this weather?" Cal demanded.

Joy settled her hand on his shoulder. "Can you breathe?"

His panicked eyes met hers. "I… I… I don't know."

"Come this way. Sit." She eased him into a nearby armchair.

"Does he need adrenaline?" asked Maisie. "We have the auto injector."

Joy assessed his symptoms. He appeared to breathe fine, in which case epinephrine would do more harm than good. "It looks like it's a localized reaction, so we won't need it. Gene, look at me. It's going to be all right. Tell me what happened."

Her no-nonsense tone—and the comment about not needing an injection—seemed to calm him. "I was out and about, wandering around the hives just now. I was curious after all your questions earlier. Felt a tingle, tried to scratch it… but realized it was a fuckin' bee. The bastard got me before I even knew what was happening. I've had reactions to bee stings before, but never this mental."

"Allergic reactions to bees can get worse with each subsequent sting," said Joy. "Maisie, do you have antihistamines here of any kind?"

"Of course." Maisie ran to one of the kitchen cabinets.

"You knew he was allergic and you brought him to a bee farm?" Kenna accused Liselle.

"It's never been this bad before," Liselle said, her gaze fixed on Gene's swollen arm. "Never like this."

"But you knew he was allergic," repeated Kenna.

Liselle didn't respond.

"I don't think I can breathe…" gasped Gene. "I… I…"

Joy recognized the beginning of a panic attack. Leaning over him, she spoke in a calm manner. "Gene, look at me. It's okay. Maisie has the right medicine. You'll take it, it'll make you a little sleepy, and Liselle will take nice care of you today. Maybe you can even convince Cal to break out more of that mead of his later tonight."

Gene smiled. "I do like his mead."

"You'll have to convince Cal to share with me too, okay?"

Breathing better now, Gene nodded. "Deal. All the mead you want. If Cal says so."

Cal, clearly relieved, clasped his hands together. "I think the occasion calls for whiskey, but if it's mead you want, who am I to argue?"

"I want the whiskey," said Liselle, arms crossed. "What were you doing outside anyway, Gene? And next to the hives? Why didn't you bring your own Benadryl? You know you're allergic and we were going to a bee farm. It's like babysitting a child."

"Liselle." Kenna shooed her away from Gene. "Why don't you go get that whiskey and have a seat in the sunroom, and let Joy treat your husband?"

Liselle clearly didn't appreciate being dismissed. "Gene wants me here."

"Go take a minute, love. I know you're stressed out. Thanks for caring, but I'm all good with the doctor here."

When Liselle said, "Fine, but I'll be back soon," a wave of relief swept over the room. Now they could focus on Gene without his wife's histrionics.

Maisie returned with a selection of antihistamines. Searching through the options, Joy selected one and popped out the right dosage. "Here, take this."

Maisie, who'd had the foresight to bring a glass of water, thrust it into Gene's hand.

"Your arm might continue to swell or turn redder," said Joy. "Get me if that happens. If you can't breathe, or your throat feels scratchy or tight, get me immediately. But for now, we'll keep an eye on it here."

"Want a cold compress, Gene?" asked Maisie. "It might help."

When Gene nodded, Maisie bustled off to bring it. Meanwhile, Cal returned with his mead.

Joy pinned Gene with a look. "That's for later tonight. The antihistamines will make you sleepy enough."

Gene gave his swollen arm a rueful look. "Not even a wee sip?"

Joy sighed. Better a taste than another panic attack. "One sip."

Cal poured the mead for everyone.

Joy accepted a glass too, but set it aside after a mouthful. Gene's swelling didn't appear life-threatening, but she needed her wits about her in case it got worse.

"*Kenna, where are you?*" Benjamin's voice reached them before the sound of his footsteps did.

Kenna leaped to her feet, setting her mead aside. "Benjamin? I'm in here."

Benjamin burst into the room, sweat-soaked and panic-stricken. Even then, he had eyes only for Kenna.

Hayes strolled in after him. Before Joy could ask where they'd been all day, Benjamin sprinted to Kenna and dropped to one knee.

With trembling hands, he presented an open ring-box to Kenna.

Surprise colored Kenna's voice. "Benjamin, what is this?"

Joy had the same question. Weren't the two of them already engaged?

"Kenna… will you marry me?"

The younger woman's eyes didn't just fill with tears—they overflowed with them. Violent streams ran down her freckled cheeks as she kneeled next to her fiancé and nodded. "Yes, yes, I'll marry you!"

Both their hands shook so much, Benjamin only managed to slide the ring on her finger on the fourth try. Rising to his feet, he swooped his fiancée into a kiss, spinning her around until Hayes ordered him to put the girl down.

He was never one for romance, was he?

Liselle joined from the sunroom at the commotion.

"Should I bring out more mead?" asked Cal. "Weren't you two already engaged?"

As Benjamin and Kenna exchanged a look, Joy edged closer to Hayes. "What's going on?"

Leaning in so only she could hear, he filled in the missing pieces. "When they heard that Maisie and Cal are only considering offers from married couples, they panicked and said they were engaged. Benjamin decided to remedy the problem."

*Was no one in the house honest with the Blairs?*

The thought made Joy feel even more guilt-ridden.

"What's all this about then?" Maisie asked.

"I'm sorry, Maisie, Cal. See, Benjamin and I weren't actually engaged. I love this place, and we didn't want the developer to buy it and turn it into some fancy resort. We were drowning in guilt lying to you… and… and then…"

"I love Kenna, and it felt daft not to make it proper," Benjamin supplied.

Maisie and Cal didn't seem offended by the disclosure—only a little surprised. Maisie ran off to get more glasses to celebrate, and Cal sprinted for another bottle of mead.

Gene, the antihistamines having hit his system, sat on the couch with a sleepy smile.

Why his wife wanted a bee farm when he had such a bad allergy was beyond Joy.

She turned to Hayes. "Where were *you*?"

He grinned down at her. "Went with him to a couple of jewelers. Our boy needed a ring."

Tilting her head, she considered him. "You went with him?"

Hayes shrugged. "Didn't trust him to drive, the way his hands were shaking."

She'd have expected Hayes to out Benjamin and Kenna. Instead, he'd helped them get officially engaged. An unexpected move for a man who claimed not to believe in love. Maybe there was more to him than she gave him credit for.

A soft snore reached them from the couch. Gene, curled into the pillow, snoozed, oblivious to the commotion around him.

# Chapter 28

Because Hayes had to work after dinner, he sequestered himself in the small upstairs office.

Not in a mood to join the others for a movie and pretend like she wasn't still lying to the Blairs, Joy snuck up to her room to read.

Nestling in the middle of the bed, she opened the Walter Scott novel she'd borrowed from the bookshelf in the sunroom, but only managed to get through the first chapter when the door opened and Hayes stepped inside.

"What do you have there?" she asked, noting the roguish twinkle in his eyes and the deliberate way he held both hands behind his back.

Right now, with his shoulders relaxed and his lips curved into a crooked smile, he looked younger than his thirty-six.

She savored this rare carefree glimpse of him. Hayes was perpetually wound tight, consumed by whichever business venture commanded his attention. Maybe this place was good for him, after all. Somehow, after just a few days here, it had made him more… human. And very likeable.

Nope, she couldn't let herself see him that way. He'd brought her here, had used her—*again.* Finding him likeable wasn't an option.

Hot, she'd allow. That was a clinical observation—pure fact. But likeable was a no-no. It would do her no good to fall under his newfound charm. She'd never dig herself out from under it.

They were trapped on the farm until Cal's birthday. Until then, she'd work through her fixation with him. But she wouldn't dupe herself into thinking there was more between them than sex.

He prowled toward her until he stood at the foot of the bed, his hands still hidden. "Close your eyes and put out your hand."

Joy rolled her eyes. "If I had a penny for every time a guy said that."

His chuckle shot unexpected affection through her. She refused to like him, but this playful, relaxed Hayes was so different from the one she thought she knew, and the change in him caused all sorts of fluttery, unwelcome feelings.

Curious now, she tried to sneak a peek, but he eluded her attempt.

She released a dramatic sigh. "Let's see what you've got."

"It's a surprise. You have to close your eyes."

"What if I don't like surprises?"

He angled his head in blatant challenge. "You love surprises."

It was true: she did love surprises.

With another eye roll for good measure, she squeezed her lids tight.

His voice dropped to a silky command as he came around to her side of the bed. "Keep them closed."

She indulged him with a shrug. "Fine."

As he drew the covers from her lap, cool air swirled across her exposed skin.

Her eyes were sealed, but she could visualize the image she presented. In an effort to save her last remaining pjs set from being torn to shreds too, she'd left them in the dresser. Instead, she chose a body-hugging tank and tiny panties in his favorite color—sapphire blue. She hated that she knew that about him, or that she'd selected her nightwear with him in mind.

His low, appreciative groan made it all worth it.

"No bottoms, Ms. Campbell?"

Eyes still closed, she grinned. "That's Mrs. Icefall to you."

"Oh yes," he murmured. "How could I forget?"

His movements paused. What was he doing? Just standing there, looking at her?

Impatient now, she wiggled. "Well?"

The bed dipped as he bracketed her with his arms and lowered his mouth to hers, stealing a kiss. Expertly, he released the straps of her tank top and pulled it down her body. The panties went with it.

Curious about this surprise, she slitted one eye open.

"Eyes. Closed," he reminded her, and emphasized the command with a peck to the top of one breast.

Lying naked, with her eyes closed while he hovered just above her, zinged a dangerous little thrill through her. Her nipples tightened in anticipation of what he'd do next.

The mattress dipped deeper as he sat next to her.

"Are *you* going to get naked for this?" she asked, curious.

She felt his low chuckle deep in her belly. "Eventually."

As she waited for his next move, she had to remind herself to breathe.

His voice was gruff when he spoke. "You're so

beautiful. I can look at you for hours—days—and never get tired."

Swallowing, she squirmed against the brushed-cotton sheets.

"Sometimes," he continued thickly, "I think about tying you up, putting my mouth on you, and making you come, over and over, until you scream my name."

Something cold and syrupy touched her hip bone. The surprising sensation almost sprung her eyes wide, but she squeezed her lids tighter and waited. He spread the gooey substance across the sensitive ridge before swiping his warm, raspy tongue across it. Cool air nipped where he'd licked.

"Oh." She inhaled, arching into him even as he maneuvered away.

He trickled the nectar in zigzags across her belly, making each individual muscle jump and tremble as the thick ribbons coated her skin.

The sweet scent of flowers and pollen washed over her, confirming what she'd suspected. Honey. He was dribbling honey across her skin.

"You're sweeter than any honey." He nibbled along the trail he'd marked.

When the startling coolness touched her tender nipples, she yelped, but his hot mouth was already soothing away the sensation.

Why was he so thorough? Didn't he know she was impatient by nature, and lying here, spread out for him like a buffet, was driving her nuts?

He painted her lips with the fragrant nectar, licking it off with measured flicks of his tongue. Lifting her head, she sought his mouth, let the honey dissolve in the melting heat of their kiss.

The taste of him, mixed with the heady sweetness, spun through her.

She loved the way he kissed—that trace of possessiveness in every stroke of his tongue, the way he smiled against her lips just before pulling back, as though he couldn't believe that she was in his arms.

Slipping her hand between them, she found him through the soft material of his joggers. He was heavy and hard in her hand, and all hers. She knew by now how he liked to be touched, and she teased him with one long, firm stroke.

With a sound between a laugh and a groan, he pulled away. She lifted her heavy eyelids to watch him dip a small silver spoon into a glass jar of golden honey.

"Enough," she pleaded. "I want you."

"Patience, my love," he said. "Just a little while longer."

Holding her gaze with his hooded one, he spread her thighs wider—and trickled the honey over her bared sex. The coolness of it arched her off the bed, and she balanced on her forearms to watch him.

With a wicked grin, he slammed the jar and spoon on the nightstand and dipped his head. The scorching slide of his tongue that followed the cold, sticky honey twisted her gasp into a broken moan.

"I can savor you all day and die a happy man," he said against her in a soft rumble that ignited her nerve endings.

He lapped up the sweetness until she pleaded and begged. Bracing her feet on the bed, she lifted into him, needing him to end the torture, but Hayes was in a teasing mood, and he'd come to play.

"I wanted you since the day I saw you. You looked

so damned happy, I wanted to taste all that joy on your skin," he continued, dipping his tongue inside her.

Greedy now, she fixed his head against her and ground into him, the exploding pleasure bowing her clear off the sheets.

Boneless, gasping, she allowed herself less than half a minute before maneuvering up. Taking his mouth, she tasted herself on his lips—her musk and all that sweet honey. Pushing him to his back, she straddled him.

He gazed up at her with unmistakable male approval—and mild surprise.

"Your turn." Divesting him of his joggers and zip hoodie, she stretched over him and took those gorgeous lips.

His fingers tangled in her hair as he kissed her deeper, and she gave it back to him in full force before pulling away.

Extricating the silver spoon from the jar, she trailed the honey along the thick ridge of his erection and over the broad crown.

He gasped, jerked—the coolness of the liquid, she knew, would feel shocking against the hot length.

"Killing me," he said, fisting the sheets.

"You'll die a happy man." She smiled, and lapped up the sweetness with one long swipe of her tongue.

Wrapping her fingers around him, she took the swollen head of him into her mouth. His salty bead of need mixed with the sweetness of the honey, creating an erotic cocktail as she licked, sucked, took him deeper.

Hayes never gave up control, always so rigid and perfectly postured, his hair razored to a strict length. But here, now, with her, lost to this connection only the two of them shared, the veneer of detachment lifted, and she glimpsed Hayes without the armor.

It would be so easy to love this Hayes, who whispered fragmented love and sex words as she swallowed him deeper.

When she glanced up, needing to catalog his every response, he watched her with dark, heavy-lidded eyes. She recognized the want, the boundless hunger in his unguarded gaze, but there was something else there—fear.

The raw emotion tipped her off-balance, and she faltered.

He took advantage of her sudden discomposure, gripping her shoulders as he flipped her to her back.

Snatching a condom from the drawer, he sheathed himself and sank deep, moving before she could catch her breath. She wrapped herself around him, communicating to him with her body what she had failed to say with words: she'd never demand anything from him beyond this, wouldn't use what he said or did against him.

But it wasn't enough. Hayes didn't always understand subtlety. Bringing her mouth to his ear, she whispered the words. "It's okay. With me, you're safe."

Was it his control that snapped or hers?

He took her with a blind frenzy, fueled by his own secret demons. Ravenous for him, frantic, she met each stroke, giving as much as taking. Lost to the presence of anything around them, they tumbled together into the unknown.

***

Joy wiggled out from under his arm, and sat up against the headboard. "I'll never think of honey the same way again."

Still barely able to move, he squeezed her thigh. "I knew you liked surprises."

She ran her nails through the short crop of his hair, setting off pleasurable tingles along his spine. "I guess I do."

The shadows beneath her eyes had disappeared, and she looked rested and well-pleasured. He wished he could keep that look on her face forever, but he had no claim on her.

Languidly, she looked around them. "Not a drop of honey on the bedding."

"I dutifully lapped up every drop straight from the source."

"That, you did." And she fused her mouth to his.

Would he ever get used to her touching him so willingly? Touching him because she wanted to, and not because he had coerced her into playing the role of devoted wife? The kiss warmed, then heated, and he pulled her down next to him to deepen it further.

"Do you still have to work tonight?" she asked against his mouth.

"It can wait."

Sliding her hands to his shoulders, she kneaded his muscles. "Perfect."

Yes, this was. Yes, *she* was. Searching out the pulse in her neck, he let it beat against his lips and remind him that she was real, and here with him. Until Wednesday.

Just a couple more days of having her close, of kissing her whenever he wanted, of holding and touching her and hearing her laugh. Their time together would soon come to an end. Until then, he could pretend just for a little longer that she was really his.

Why did he have to pretend?

He thought he wanted Joy for a booty call—or as a friend with benefits to keep around.

But it wouldn't suffice.

He wanted more.

The realization hit him like a brick.

He must have looked it, because her perfect nose crinkled. "What?"

Understanding that he was staring, he shook his head, but the idea took root.

"You know," she said, stretching out on top of him. "Sometimes I find your silences mysterious and sexy. Other times, they're very annoying. All I want to do is tickle you until you're all giggly."

He tucked the hair that fell around her face behind her ear, used the opportunity to stroke along the soft curve of her cheek.

Yes, he wanted her.

The need to claim Joy Campbell as his—without pretense or coercion—surged through him. He'd settle for nothing less.

# Chapter 29

The whisper of lips along her chin, her temple, the slant of her forehead coaxed her from restless dreams.

"Time to wake up, sweetheart… I'm taking you out for the day." Hayes's deep voice rumbled through her, drawing her the rest of the way into consciousness. She reached for him next to her, but found nothing but cold sheets.

Confused, she pried open one eye.

Fully dressed, he leaned over her in the morning sun-drenched room.

When his lips traced a path along her jaw, she turned toward him, offering her mouth in invitation. His kiss was soft and tender and full of promises, and much too short.

When he pulled back, she sat up and blinked the rest of the sleep away. "Taking me where?"

Suspicion colored her tone, but he didn't seem fazed. "It's a surprise."

Remembering another recent surprise, she gave him a playful look. "Like the honey?"

When his eyes glazed over, she suspected he was remembering that particular surprise in equally vivid detail. Leaning over her once more, he skimmed his lips against hers. "Not as good as the honey."

She stole another kiss. "Then again, what could ever compare?"

Intrigued now, she let him pull her up.

On the table by the window, two plates held eggs, tattie scones, tomatoes, and baked beans, with his square sausage set separately on a smaller dish. A mug of tea steamed next to a half-full cup of coffee. He brought her breakfast to their room?

She tore her gaze away from the laid-out meal. "We're eating in private?"

Leading her to the table, he pulled out her chair. "Yep."

This *was* a nice surprise. The constant fibbing to the rest of the group was activating an ulcer.

Refusing to eat naked, she grabbed a robe from the armoire and shrugged into it before sitting.

Taking a restorative sip of tea, she surveyed the spread. "Did you make this? Or Maisie?"

He slid into the chair across from her. "I came downstairs when she was finishing up the tattie scones and sausages. The tea, I take full credit for."

Savoring another swallow, she set the cup aside to dig into the Scottish breakfast in front of her. Maisie was an excellent cook, and she knew that the food would be, as always, delicious.

"You sure you want to be away from the farm today?" She sliced into the tattie scone. "And leave Liselle here with the Blairs again?"

Hayes slid the sausage to his plate. "She and Gene are heading to meet friends in Inverness today."

That little fact dampened her excitement about the spontaneous outing. How asinine of her to presume Hayes would prioritize a romantic getaway with her over the farm.

Pushing away her disappointment, she bit into the

tomato. Surprises weren't his style anyway. Not unless they involved sex.

After breakfast, as she rose from the table, he caught her hand and laid a flirty kiss over her knuckles.

That wasn't like him either. Sure, when they were with the others, Hayes found countless excuses to touch her—playing the role of attentive husband for their audience. But now, alone in their bedroom, the display of affection set off warning bells. Was he angling for more sex or did he need another favor?

On guard, she tugged her hand away. "What do you want, Hayes?"

His playful gaze sobered. "Why do you think I want something?"

"You always want something."

"You're right," he conceded. "I do want something. Right now, I want you—in the shower, clawing my back while I pump into you."

How could she refuse *that* invitation?

After running the water to let it heat, he stepped into the tub and pulled her in with him, drawing her into his naked—and aroused—body.

She traced his tattoo with her lips. "I thought we had plans."

His hands slid over her with comfortable familiarity. "We do, and this is how we kick them off."

After they finally dressed, they made their way downstairs. The others gathered in the kitchen, but Hayes pulled her in the opposite direction. They stole through the mudroom and looped around the house to the back where his car was parked.

Slinking through the still-damp soil felt oddly exhilarating. Like she imagined sneaking around as a teen would have felt if she'd ever tried it. Hayes waited for her to get settled in the passenger seat before sliding behind the wheel.

"Are you going to tell me where we're going?" she asked as they passed through the farm gates.

"No," he said in an indignant voice. "Then it wouldn't be a surprise."

The sky cleared as they drove, its brilliant blue amplifying the autumn colors of the surrounding trees.

The drive took just over an hour. Joy got lost in the scenery, barely noticing that he'd turned onto a gravel drive and pulled into a half-filled parking lot.

Up ahead, the ancient castle walls looked exactly as she'd remembered from childhood.

"*Hayes*," she gasped. "This is Doune Castle."

"Yes. One of two remaining sites from your list."

"This is really special. It means a lot for me to see it on this trip."

Leaning over the center console, she pressed a soft kiss against his lips, conveying her appreciation for the unexpected gift. When he deepened the kiss, she lingered, basking in the taste and texture of him.

Finally, she pulled away. "We should go explore before we get arrested in here."

Hayes proved to be a treasure trove of knowledge about the medieval castle, not only painting a vivid picture of its history but also sharing fascinating facts about its appearance in popular movies and television shows.

"How do you know all this?" She threaded her arm through his as they made their way through the fortress.

"A good memory."

***

To his infinite relief, they completed their circuit of the castle just in time to dodge two large incoming tour groups. As they dropped off the audio guides and stepped away from the stone walls, the wind picked up around them.

Stopping on the paved path, Joy gave him a concerned look from beneath her lashes. "Are you cold?"

When she cupped his cheek to punctuate the question, her soft touch unleashed the longing he'd fought to contain since they'd left the farm.

"Not anymore." Settling his hands on her hips, he hauled her close and kissed her.

Her laughter vibrated through him.

By the time he pulled back, something molten burned uncomfortably in his chest, amplified by each unsteady heartbeat.

Lifting her hand, Joy tucked a stray curl behind her ear. As sunlight glanced off her sham wedding band, irrational possessiveness surged through him. *Mine.*

Not letting her catch her breath, he grasped her hand and pulled her away from the stone path and onto a stretch of still-green lawn that surrounded the castle, moving in the direction of the bordering forest.

"Where are we going?" she asked on a laugh when he towed her into the woodlands and along a narrow, leaves-strewn path.

He wove through the trees until he saw a small clearing, protected from prying eyes by a dense thicket that enclosed it. A brook babbled just out of sight and birds chirped above, but no voices reached them here. Unless someone walked directly into their hidden pocket, they were on their own private island.

She surveyed their surroundings with a mixture of anticipation and apprehension. "Here?"

He traced the pulse beating at the base of her throat. "I need you."

"Here?" she repeated, as though to double-check.

But she seemed game. Her smile widened, and she reached for the lapels of his coat.

Pulling off her jacket, he saw—and felt—her shiver. Why she chose a skirt, thin tights, and a flimsy sweater on a freezing day like today was beyond him. Refusing to let her feel a moment of discomfort, he pulled her against the furnace of his body.

When he traced the swell of her breast over the soft wool, feeling its warm weight against his palm, he went rock hard with realization. She'd planned a surprise of her own.

He tsked. "No bra today, Mrs. Icefall?"

Bringing her mouth to his, she nipped his lower lip. "Check if I'm wearing panties."

"Fuck, you're made for me."

Slipping under her skirt, he tugged down her tights, soothing the goose bumps the cold air raised across her bared skin.

"You're all I think about," he murmured, tracing her slick folds until her gasps broke against his ear.

She shifted against him, silently asking for more. He gave her what she wanted, sinking a thick finger into her tight, wet channel.

"Bending you over in the shower yesterday, watching you take all of me, that's my picture of heaven—"

Clamping her hands on either side of his face, she dragged his mouth to hers for an open-mouthed kiss that left him swaying.

He pulled away to drag her tights the rest of the way off. When he reached for his own belt, she brushed his hands away and released him with efficient movements, her wind-chilled hand closing around his hard length. The pants dropped around his ankles as she palmed his erection, stroking until he groaned.

"Protection," he managed, stepping away long enough to find and roll on a condom before he hooked her knee with his forearm and sank home. She gasped and squirmed against him as he filled her.

Engulfed by her, he lost the perception of time, of space. Only she was real.

As he lifted her other leg, she yielded completely, a rare and precious gift he'd never take for granted.

Every instinct in him sought to claim her, to protect her. She was his, and he'd never let her go.

He loved her. The realization didn't rock him. It felt right.

She was home.

***

Okay… that was a first. She'd never had sex outside before. Much less sex outside in *Scotland*. What had she been thinking?

But she wasn't thinking.

Not with Hayes.

As he slipped out of her, she struggled to find footing on legs that turned to jelly.

In one swift move, he caught her, drawing her firmly against him. The protectiveness of the gesture didn't escape her, though she feared she was reading too much into it.

When their breathing slowed, he brushed a leaf from her hair.

Joy looked up at the heavy branches above them, the fiery foliage glowing against the autumn sky. "I think we dislodged a few leaves today. Was this part of your surprise too?"

Rather than responding, Hayes searched her eyes.

Feeling naked and vulnerable under his probing gaze, she hesitated.

What did he want from her? To reassure him that she wasn't reading more into this? That it meant nothing to her?

She couldn't offer him that.

It would be lying.

***

Once dressed, they left the hidden glade as fog rolled over the castle and surrounding territory. She appeared as reluctant to go as him.

"That was the craziest place I've ever had sex," she confessed as they made their way back to the parking lot.

Pulling her into his side as they walked, he glanced down at her upturned face. "Me too."

Her brows lifted. "*Really?* Are we talking… woodlands near an ancient castle, or outside in general?"

"Both."

She looked intrigued. "I'd have thought this was small potatoes for you, just another boring weekday."

He laughed. "I've never had a single boring day with you."

She snuggled closer. "It was really hot. We managed to keep most of our clothes on."

The awareness that even now she wore no underwear thickened his voice. "Don't think I'll ever forget that."

"*Oh crap.*" Lurching away from him, she ran her hand along the thick nap of his wool outer layer. "Did we get mud on your coat?"

"If we did, it was worth it." Taking her hand, he led the way to the parking lot, dodging a busload of just-unleashed tourists. "You made Scotland bearable again."

"Good. Since you might own a bee farm here soon."

Her easy smile made his heart thump.

Unable to resist, he pulled her into another kiss, ignoring the whistle of some passerby.

As they continued on to the McLaren, hand in hand, he asked her, "Would you visit? The farm, I mean, if I buy it?"

A distracted teen—woefully underdressed for the weather and absorbed in her phone—nearly barreled into them. Hayes whisked Joy out of the way before they collided.

Joy responded when the teen was out of earshot. "I really like Highlander Honey Farm, Hayes. I see that it makes you happy."

"It's the only place that ever felt like home."

*Until you.*

Her lips twisted in a wry smile. "I know your parents, so I believe it. But it would make no sense for me to visit. Once I go back to California, there's no reason for me to return, is there?"

He stared. "I guess not."

Something flickered across her face. Relief? Disappointment? He wished to hell he could decipher which.

They stopped at the car, but he didn't reach for her door. "What if I bribe you with honey?"

Her eyes flashed. He'd said something wrong. "I'm

sure you can find someone else for a booty call. No need to drag me all the way from California."

"That's not what I meant."

"What did you mean?" she asked, her breathing shallow.

"You're not a booty call."

She held his gaze for an uncomfortably long stretch before speaking. "But you want me to fly over for sex with you once in a while?"

"No. I mean, yes, but not like that. You like the farm. Why not visit it?"

Drawing her jacket closer around herself, she blew out a long breath. "Because it will always be a place that we lied to good people to get."

"I'm doing this to protect them," he reminded her.

"You're doing this to spite Liselle. Kenna and Benjamin would make great owners."

Shoving his hands in his pockets, he glared. "He's besotted with Kenna now, but that won't last. You don't think they'll sell it after the divorce?"

"That's real pessimistic."

"Besides, he's applying to MBA programs as far away as London. You don't think they'll sell it when he gets in?"

She took a step away from him. "You had them investigated?"

"Of course."

Her eyes delved into his. "Did you know they weren't really engaged?"

"Not until he told me."

"And you didn't tell the Blairs."

The gathering realization in her features made him want to look anywhere else.

"Never got the chance," he clipped out, shifting his weight.

She pushed a lock of hair loosened by the wind behind her ear as she continued to study him. "I don't think you would have."

Intent on ending the conversation, he opened her car door. "Now we'll never know."

# Chapter 30

They didn't speak much on the drive back.

She'd clearly hit a nerve by refusing to visit the farm, but what did he expect? That he'd text her an eggplant emoji and she'd hop on the first flight to Scotland? She never took him for delusional… but maybe she missed the signs.

They only had until tomorrow. As agreed, they'd never see each other after that.

She wasn't about to let him mess with their deal.

Because foolish girl that she was, she could fall in love with him if she wasn't careful.

After Wednesday, she'd stay away from him for good, and make sure he did the same. He made her yearn for things she couldn't have, things he'd never be able to give her. Allowing herself to daydream otherwise would only crush her.

When Hayes turned onto the familiar road leading to the Blairs' farm, she considered the twilight unfurling beyond the windows. "The sun sets so early here. It's barely four. Think everyone is back by now?"

His eyes swept over her in sensual promise. "I hope not yet."

Anticipation zinged through her. When he looked at her with such uncontained heat, she was ready to have him pull the car over and—

"Hayes—watch out!"

He braked instantly. The seat belt stopped her forward momentum.

A large, shiny, wrapped giftbox had been left in the middle of the path to the farm, just at the turn of the road—and they'd almost barreled straight into it.

He shifted into park. "What the fuck is that?"

Joy leaped out before he could catch her.

With a curse, Hayes jumped out too, joining her at the velvet ribbon-tied package.

Her name had been scribbled across the immaculate wrapping in gold permanent marker.

*No. It couldn't be.*

"It's addressed to me," she whispered, forcing out the words through her dry throat.

He threw her a cool glance. "Your boyfriend won't take no for an answer."

"*Don't* call him that."

"He's not as stupid as I thought he was. Someone might have seen him from the house—he knew not to come closer."

Nausea burned the base of her throat. "Are you saying he scoped out the farm?"

"It makes sense. After almost getting caught on Friday."

When he reached for the box lid, panic gripped her. "What are you doing?"

"Opening it."

"Shouldn't we call the cops or something?"

But it was too late. He'd already shredded the red bow and the reflective, pink wrapping. When he lifted the top, she stumbled back, recognizing the contents.

"It's my nightgown. I packed in such a hurry in

London, I accidentally left it in the hotel." Leaning over the box, she lifted the green silk, relieved to have it back, even under these circumstances. Seeing what had dried across it, she dropped it immediately. "Eww. Is that…?"

Hayes made a face. "Charming."

Joy wanted to scream. He'd ruined her favorite nightie. "Why can't he leave me alone? I thought I'd never see it again. And now I can't ever wear it."

Hayes rose to his feet. "I'll buy you a hundred others."

"All I'll ever see now is his dried"—because she couldn't say the word, she opted for a more neutral term—"*stuff* on it. He has a weird hang-up on me. Do you think I should talk to him?"

His head whipped to her. "Don't go near him."

Even knowing that Hayes would never hurt her, the anger in his face had her backing up a step. "He won't harm me."

He towered over her in a clear attempt to intimidate. "Give me your phone. I'll explain what's what to him."

Crossing her arms, she refused to cower. "Stay out of it, Hayes."

"He comes to *my* farm to terrorize *my woman*?"

"First of all, it's not your farm yet. And I'm not your woman. So put your dick away. Ryder is my problem."

He didn't like that, she could tell. His nostrils flared.

How easy it would be to rage and rail at him and work all the fear out of her system.

She tried to call up the bitterness that she had once felt toward Hayes, but found none. She looked again. Nope. Somehow, these last few days of getting to know him had cleared her resentment. She'd thought him a selfish user, but Hayes protected those he cared about, and he wouldn't step aside and let her handle someone he deemed a threat.

A muscle in his jaw twitched. "I'll get his number."

She didn't doubt it.

Before she could insist he leave it alone, he tilted up her chin with a gentle finger. "I'll put a stop to it."

The possessiveness that hardened his features sent a funny flutter deep in her stomach. Did she like it when he got all… primal?

She shouldn't. She wasn't his to protect.

Knowing him, he wouldn't stop until he found Ryder. And she didn't need her ex in a body cast and Hayes in jail.

But the rigid set of his jaw spoke of his intent. That wouldn't do. She had to nip his feral behavior in the bud.

"Don't do anything rash, okay? Let's think this out."

Attempting to distract him, she drew his lips to hers. He stiffened under her touch, and for a heartbeat it felt like necking with a slab of granite.

But when she stopped, something in him gave way and he kissed her with a hunger that left her reeling.

Pulling back, he searched her eyes. "Are we on the same page here?"

Dizzy, disoriented, she drew in an unsteady breath. Did he just agree to not pursue Ryder?

"Yes?" she mumbled, unsure of what exactly he asked her.

On a satisfied growl, he seized her mouth again, and the blazing heat of the kiss burned away the last of her rational thoughts.

When he released her, she locked her knees and tried to appear unaffected. The last thing she needed was to feed his boundless ego.

But darn it, she was beginning to like him too much. It would make their goodbye so much harder.

Hayes disposed of the box—and its contents—before they returned to the farmhouse.

Immediately, he disappeared to their room without an explanation, leaving Joy all alone in the empty downstairs.

Trying not to feel rejected, she wandered to the kitchen. She hadn't seen the Blairs' car when they'd pulled up, so they must be out running errands. Liselle and Gene were probably still in Inverness, and Benjamin and Kenna at her parents' farm next door.

Filling the electric teakettle with water, she turned it on just as the outside door to the sunroom opened and Liselle jogged into the kitchen.

*Guess she and Gene are back after all.*

Wearing her signature branded athleisure, with a cropped white puffer jacket over it, she appeared just as surprised to see Joy. "Oh. You're here."

Joy glanced behind Liselle. "Where's Gene?"

"Upstairs taking a nap. We got back a bit ago. I went for a run."

"Ah."

*Well, this is awkward.*

The teakettle beeped.

"Want tea?" asked Joy, because her parents raised her to be polite.

Liselle stalked to the cabinet and pulled out a glass jar of instant coffee. "Hate tea. Hate instant coffee, too, but there's nothing else around here."

Cutting in front of Joy, she poured hot water into her cup, and added a spoonful of coffee granules.

How was the woman not out of breath after a run? How often did she exercise?

Joy splashed the remaining hot water into her cup, and dropped in a tea bag. Not wishing to chat more, she took her tea to the farthest spot from Liselle—the love seat in the sunroom.

Malik, napping in the corner, padded to her. She slid her fingers through his soft fur. The sweet boy purred and relaxed fully across her lap.

To her annoyance, Liselle followed her into the glassed-in space, sitting in the armchair next to her and giving her a bright smile.

Liselle didn't do bright. And she certainly didn't seek Joy out to chat.

"What do you want now, Liselle?"

Malik lifted his head. Giving Liselle a suspicious look through narrowed blue eyes, he leaped free of Joy's lap and disappeared into the kitchen. Even the cat couldn't stand the woman. Must be a good judge of character.

Liselle took a delicate sip of coffee. "Hayes's antagonism is rubbing off on you."

"Not really. You did hit on my husband on Sunday. Am I supposed to forget that little portion of the weekend?"

Liselle tilted her head in a practiced way Joy would never be able to emulate. "I wasn't hitting on your husband. I was just reminding him how things used to be."

"I'm sure he's blocked that part out of his memory."

"You seem so certain about that."

Joy glanced through the glass walls at the dusk that submerged the farm. "It's been a long day. Why don't we retire to our own corners until dinnertime?"

"You know he's buying this farm for a reason," said Liselle.

"I do."

"He's buying it for me."

Joy raised a skeptical brow. "You do live in your own little world."

Liselle rolled her eyes into her lash extensions. "Not as a gift. Though if I wasn't crazy in love with Gene, he might attempt it. Don't feel bad. You never forget your first love. I meant as a peace offering. Gene owns a chain of restaurants in New York that the Auclair-Icefall Hospitality Group wants. Gene will sign them over for a fair price—but I've put my foot down. I'll let him sign if Hayes gives Highlander Honey to me as a way to mend bridges." Joy's face must have spoken for her, because Liselle considered her. "You don't believe me."

How ridiculous. Hayes would never tangle himself up with her again. "No, I don't."

"He likes the farm fine, but it's nothing but a bargaining chip for him. Look." Pulling out her phone, she flipped it to face Joy, several email exchanges between Hayes and Gene discussing the restaurant chain at the ready.

"See? He is playing hardball. Auclair-Icefall Hospitality Group needs Gene's restaurants to expand in Manhattan. Hayes only showed interest in the farm once he knew Gene and I were angling to buy it—so he can use it in the negotiation for the restaurants."

"That's not why he wants the farm, Liselle, and we both know it." However, deep inside, doubts started to simmer.

It sounded like something Hayes *could* do. Give up something he loved in order to have something new and shiny. I mean, come on, was he really going to move to Scotland, even part-time?

Was that the deal that Liselle had brought up in the

hallway on Sunday night? The one she wouldn't let go through?

Liselle's comment had slipped her mind until now, and she never got around to asking Hayes about it.

Refusing to show Liselle that her words had gotten to her, Joy smiled with her teeth and stood. "Well, enjoy your coffee, Liselle."

"I have to admit," she said before Joy succeeded in escaping. "I was surprised when I heard Hayes got married."

Joy, done with the conversation, tried for a dismissive tone. "Were you?"

"Yes. I'd known him when he was young and romantic once. And then I knew him when he was less young and romantic. Even then, he suggested naming Poinsettia after me at first."

# Chapter 31

*He did what?*

Liselle was lying. Hayes would *never…* would he? Blood pounded against her eardrums, and she had to focus to hear Liselle's words.

*He wanted to name his company after the woman who'd abandoned him near-to-dead in a Scottish hospital?* That kind of love doesn't just go away.

Hayes's ex-girlfriend continued as though Joy's world hadn't just tilted off its axis. "I told him I didn't want him to name it Liselle, but he insisted. We actually had a fight about it." She lifted a shoulder. "I won. Instead, he let me name it Poinsettia, after my favorite flower. After all that, I just never thought he'd get hitched."

*The same flower he has tattooed across his heart.* He'd told her he'd gotten it as a reminder that people couldn't be trusted. All along, it was a love letter to Liselle.

But she wasn't about to show Liselle how much she'd stunned her. Clearing her throat, she grasped for an even tone. "Well, people can surprise you."

Liselle crossed one lithe leg over the other. "What's it like being married to him?"

Surprisingly great, Joy had to admit—not that she'd tell Liselle that. Hayes was charming and fun and considerate. Apparently, it was all for show. An act he performed for the Blairs or, worse, for Liselle.

Was he trying to show his ex what she'd missed out on? If he really was as tired of her circling as he said, why would he buy her husband's restaurants?

Was he playing the long game? Oh God, did he want Liselle back after all? Was she the one who got away?

"Joy?" Liselle prodded when she hadn't spoken.

Crap, did she ask a question? Joy couldn't recall which one. "I have to go."

"Wait." Liselle held out her hand. "Don't leave. I wanted to ask you something. I know you and Hayes eloped, but where?"

Oh, this one was sly. Was she looking into their nonexistent marriage license? Though Joy wasn't so sure Hayes by now wouldn't have found a way to take care of it—he had weird connections that spread to seemingly random corners of the internet and world.

"Does it matter?"

Liselle pursed her full lips. "Guess not. With me, he wanted a big, showy wedding. I'm just surprised he settled for a secretive little ceremony with you."

Unexpected rain lashed against the windows, matching Joy's thunderous mood.

*Time to go.* Irritated that she let Liselle get under her skin, Joy turned for the exit. Before she could make her escape, Hayes stepped into the sunroom.

His eyes hardened when he saw Liselle, but his voice remained casual as he approached them. "Having a nice chat?"

"I'm getting to know your bride a little better," purred Liselle, and sipped her coffee.

Hayes stopped next to Joy and pulled her into his side.

*Was* he pretending, hoping to get Liselle back?

The uncertainty made her want to shuffle away from him, but he held tight.

"Where's Gene?" he asked in a neutral tone.

"Napping," Joy responded before Liselle could. "I'll leave you two alone. I should probably call my sister."

Without giving him a chance to question her, she stepped out of his hold and hurried out of the sunroom. She couldn't spend any more time in Liselle's presence or she'd rip the woman's fake lashes right out.

Liselle still had a hold on Hayes, and Joy wasn't so sure he wanted her to let him go.

What would the two do with all their free time if they weren't plotting how to make the other miserable?

Joy was halfway to the stairs when she realized she'd left her tea. The thought ramped up her anger. All she had wanted was a damn cup of tea before everyone else returned to the house.

Hayes caught up to her just before she hit the stairs.

"Here." He handed her tea to her.

The thoughtful gesture made her livid.

She kept her voice low and far out of reach of Liselle's ears. "Go away, Hayes. Stop circling. We both know you want Liselle."

Now it was his turn to look livid. His voice took on a low, dangerous chill. "You think I want her?"

Joy refused to back down. "Yes."

"You're very sure about that, are you?"

"I call it as I see it. I'm still not convinced you're not here to get her back."

Fury flared in his features. Startled at a show of emotion from someone as measured as Hayes, she almost backed up a step, but held steady. He opened his mouth to speak—

The front door flew open, and Cal and Maisie bounded into the mudroom, shaking off the wet droplets from their coats.

"Got caught out in the rain!" Maisie explained, balancing several pink pastry boxes.

Cal, behind her, had his hands full of bags.

"We'll help you." Hayes strode forward, taking the soggy boxes from Maisie.

Setting her tea on a nearby table, Joy rushed to take the bags from Cal. In one smooth move, Hayes handed her the lighter boxes and lifted Cal's bags himself.

"We picked up groceries for tomorrow and some yummy tarts for this evening," Maisie singsonged. "But I'm chilled to the bone."

"Come into the kitchen. I'll make you some tea," Hayes said, already ushering them in that direction like a concerned parent.

Balancing the rain-splattered pastry boxes, Joy followed, relieved when Liselle—most likely evading grocery sorting—slipped past them with a fake smile and slithered away.

Just last week, she'd have believed that Hayes would give up a small farm in the middle of nowhere to acquire a New York City restaurant chain. But as she watched him kid around with the Blairs, she couldn't see it. He loved the Blairs—and this farm—and he'd never do anything to jeopardize the bond they shared.

After putting away the groceries, Joy stayed in the kitchen, having tea and catching up with Cal and Maisie. Hayes lingered too, until a phone call drew him away.

Ten minutes later, she found him in their bedroom, working from his iPad at the table. He looked up as she entered, and set the iPad aside.

"Would you rather live in La Jolla or Del Mar in San Diego? Del Mar is closer to Evie, but La Jolla is next to your residency—"

Was the man looking for a new apartment for her? She'd find that herself, thank you very much. But she had more pressing matters to discuss with him first.

Seeing the expression on her face, he rose instantly.

"You know," she said before he could speak, "if I hadn't gotten to know you the last few days, I'd be really pissed off right now."

He cocked his head. "But you're not?"

"Just before you interrupted, Liselle said that Gene is offering you a group of restaurants if you give her the farm. For a beat, I thought, would Hayes screw over the Blairs to get his hand on a prime investment deal?"

Stepping toward him, she planted her hands on his shoulders and guided him back into the chair, settling on his lap. His hands came around her.

"What did you conclude?" he asked carefully.

She shook her head, watched his guard come down. "You love the Blairs. You wouldn't hurt them to get ahead in your business."

He drew proprietary circles across her ribs. "I wouldn't."

"And you're not here to get Liselle back."

After he finished laughing his head off, his dancing eyes met hers. "No. I thought I made that obvious before."

She made a face. "She's clearly trying to get in your pants."

"My pants are very securely zipped to anyone but you."

"Well, that's something I very much appreciate."

Lowering her hands to said pants, she found him, stroked through the fabric.

Cupping her cheek, he brought her gaze to his. "Thanks for not thinking the worst of me. You'd be right to, after everything."

"You protect the people you love. You'd never betray the Blairs like that." She had one question to ask him, but she feared the answer. Finally, she bit the bullet. "Your tattoo… did you get it because it's Liselle's favorite flower?"

"Fuck no," he spat out.

The vehemence of his response made her laugh. "Then why?"

"I got it after I sold Poinsettia. Long after everything had ended with Liselle. A permanent reminder so I never forget that…"

Recalling their earlier conversation, she completed his sentence. "That people can't be trusted."

He brushed a kiss across her shoulder. "I trust you."

The simple statement brought an unexpected burn to her eyeballs. She'd come to trust him too.

"And," Hayes continued, "Liselle twisted everything around as usual. I am hedging my bets, yes. But not how you think. Gene's broke. Liselle might not know that. The restaurants are drowning him. I offered to buy them out in exchange for him withdrawing his offer on the farm. If he backs away, I'll get him out of debt."

"You really did do your due diligence on everyone." The calculation of it stilled her. "Hayes, you and I hadn't spoken in three years. How did you know about the Delices?"

His black lashes lowered, concealing whatever she might be able to read in his features. "I kept an eye on you."

She scrambled from his lap. "*Why would you do that?*"

"Because… because I couldn't get you out of my head *for three fucking years*."

Leaping to his feet, he faced her across the yellow rug, their erratic breathing the only sounds in the charged silence.

"Why?" She managed to squeeze the word out through her constricted throat.

"I never meant to use you."

"So, it was guilt?" she asked as bitter cold spread to her extremities.

"Yes," he said too fast. "No."

"Well, which one is it, Hayes?"

Why was she pressing the issue? What answer would make her happy?

The muscles around his eyes softened as he considered her. Too soon, the defenses slammed back in place. "I did feel guilty."

Disappointment crashed over her like an avalanche of quarry rocks.

I mean, what did she expect? For him to fall to his knees and confess his undying love for her?

Hayes didn't do love.

She shouldn't do love either. It's not like she had a great track record with it. She'd managed to pick not one but *two* wrong guys, and hadn't caught the red flags in either… and here she was, now mooning over one of them.

Annoyed with herself, she twisted away from him, but he caught her wrist.

"Wait."

When she turned to him, his gaze remained shuttered. He was as emotionless as the Hayes who'd walked away from her three years ago.

Good. That's exactly the reminder she needed.

They meant nothing to each other. He hadn't spent three years pining for her. He *maybe* suffered a bout or two of guilt, that's all.

Grasping onto the pain that swamped her, she pulled down his head and kissed him.

He drew back, his brow furrowing with surprise.

"No more talking," she said, drawing his shirt over his head. "We have an hour before dinner, tops. I leave tomorrow. Let's purge this attraction."

"What a sweet talker," he mumbled, swooping her into his arms and setting her on the bed.

Her phone in her skirt pocket vibrated once. Then again and again, in rapid succession. Who was texting her this much?

Intending to throw the cell phone across the room and get back down to business, she reached for it—but when she saw her sister's name, her intentions fled.

She unlocked the screen. "It's Evie."

Why was Evie sending her so many links? They kept popping up one after the other.

"Tell her we're busy," Hayes grumbled next to her.

Clicking open one of the articles her sister shared, she jumped off the bed. "*What the hell!*"

# Chapter 32

Instantly alert, Hayes stood too, pulling her into the protective shelter of his body. "What's wrong?"

She thrust the phone into his hands. "*Look.*"

He did. "Shit."

Hayes opened the next link, and the next. They were all iterations of the same story. The tabloids had found them—capturing them making out in the parking lot of Doune Castle in disturbing detail.

Evie's barrage of texts continued. This time, media snippets of influencers dissecting Hayes's new love interest: Dr. Joy Campbell.

*Who had recognized him in all that fog?*

Someone clearly did. The video of them making out at Doune Castle had gone viral. Two *million* views? *How?* This just happened a few hours ago.

She squeezed her eyes shut. "Please, *please* tell me they didn't film… what we did right *before* this—you know, in the woods. I don't think I can survive being known as a porn star."

Muttering a string of expletives, he scanned through the links. Clearly, he too remembered their forest tryst. "If any snippet of *that* is anywhere on the web, I'll hunt down the filmmaker and make it a personal goal to destroy them and anything they hold dear."

Dejected, she flung herself on the bed. "Ugh. If the Blairs see this…"

Mid-scroll, he threw her an annoyed look. "Married couples are allowed to make out."

She sprang back to her feet. "But we are not married. And with all the online snoops out there, they will know we lied. And that's not even the point. My work will see this. What if it affects my job prospects when I'm done with residency? Us kissing made the *news*, Hayes. That's crazy. All because you're some eligible rich bachelor! How did someone even recognize you? Aren't you supposed to be a recluse? How does this happen? Why are people interested in this? Oh God, what if Ryder sees this and goes even more berserk? This is a *disaster*."

Hayes extended her phone back to her. "Your sister is calling."

Joy didn't reach for it. "I didn't tell her anything about our… deal. She's going to flip out."

"Then don't answer."

"I can't not answer. She's my sister." Swallowing against the rising panic, she took the phone from him and accepted the video call.

If Evie's eyes grew any rounder, they wouldn't have fit into the screen frame. "*You and Hayes?*"

The squeal was so loud, Hayes winced.

Joy turned down the volume. "It's not what you think."

Evie's voice dropped an octave. "Are you guys hooking up?"

Maybe it *was* what Evie thought. "Well… yes. But… well… no, no, I guess, yes."

Her sister's brows nearly touched her hairline. "Which is it?"

"Evie, now isn't a good time," Hayes growled next to Joy.

Evie clasped a hand over her mouth to hide a scandalized grin. "Are you two… together *right this second*? Did I interrupt something?"

Joy pinned Hayes with a warning look before refocusing on her sister. "We're together right now, yes—"

Evie squealed again. "You and Hayes were making out by Doune Castle!"

Joy ground her teeth together. "I know. I was there."

Her sister stared expectantly at her. "Well, what does this mean?"

"Can we talk about this later?"

As if only now realizing that this wasn't the right time for prying questions, Evie nodded. "I'm in shock. I don't know what to even ask right now."

Hayes leaned into the phone frame. "Can this wait until next week? Where's Jackson?"

"Downstairs. Want me to go get him so you can share all the details?"

Joy detected the teasing notes in Evie's voice; Hayes didn't.

"Hell no."

Evie laughed. "All right, all right. I'll stop with the questions. But, Joy, I'm going to need a full-on play-by-play when you're back."

"You'll… er… get it," Joy replied, though she wasn't so sure what exactly she could disclose. Where would she even begin? With the strange deal she and Hayes had made? Hayes's coercion? The fake marriage? The lying to Maisie and Cal?

"Also, if Mom and Dad see this, they'll call with *a lot of* questions," said Evie. "But I'll try to head that off."

Crap. Her mother—and Hayes's mother, for that matter—were all over social media. It was a very real possibility they *had* already seen the media frenzy. All this insanity over nothing but a kiss…

Finally gathering her courage, Joy cleared her throat. "Evie… the photos… they're only of us kissing, right? I haven't clicked through all the links yet. There's nothing more out there, is there?"

Evie gaped. "Why? What else were you two doing at the castle?"

The rush of heat to her cheeks must have been answer enough.

Her sister grinned. "*Oh.*"

"Will you just tell me?" demanded Joy, her voice harsher than she intended.

"All I saw is you guys making out," Evie assured her. "I don't think anything more was captured."

Relieved, Joy sank onto the bed. "Okay. Good."

"I'm so going to need a play-by-play," Evie repeated.

Hayes crossed the room to his own cell phone.

"What are you doing?" Joy asked when he started tapping on the screen.

He didn't bother to look up. "I'm calling my attorneys. Taking all that shit down. I fought hard for my privacy. I won't let it be ruined by this."

"Think they can do something?" she asked, too afraid to hope.

"I pay them to do something."

Joy redirected her attention to her older sister. "Evie, I'll call you later." After she hung up, she joined Hayes at the table. "I'm mortified someone *filmed us*. Can you believe if people actually think we are together?"

He recoiled as though she'd slapped him. When he

spoke, the ice in his tone cut deeper than a Scottish winter. "Wouldn't want anyone to think you're slumming it with me."

"That's not what I meant." She reached for him, but her fingers only swiped his skin before he jerked away.

He clasped his phone so tightly she was afraid it would implode. "At least Liselle faked it better."

*Liselle.* If she never heard her name again it would be too soon.

"Are you going to punish every woman for what she did to you?"

His lips twisted in disdain. "I'm long over that."

Was he, though? Because he had loved Liselle enough to propose to her, to take her back after she'd done the unspeakable. He'd offered Liselle the life Joy longed to have with him—instead, all he'd ever proffered her was a phony relationship and an invitation to fly back to see him for sex.

Irrationally angry now, the words spilled out— words she didn't mean. "Yeah? I bet if they took a video of you kissing *her*, you'd be broadcasting it from the rooftops, not calling up your attorneys to have it be taken down. Liselle told me you wanted to name Poinsettia after her—and that was *after* she left you for dead!"

The reminder struck a nerve—a flush of color spread outward from his pecs. "I was young and stupid then."

"And you're still hung up on her."

"*I'm hung up on* you*!*"

The bellow thundered through the room, vibrating the floral curtains and rattling the picture frames.

It was her turn to stumble back.

His voice softened. "I wanted the social media posts taken down because they upset you. Not because I wish they'd caught me kissing Liselle."

Joy felt like crap. Why had she let Liselle get under her skin? Where had all the jealousy come from? She hadn't meant a word she'd thrown in his face.

She took a step toward him. "And I was upset because they captured a very private, very special moment between us. Not because I didn't want people to know we're together. That is, we're not together…"

Drawing her to him the rest of the way, he slanted a gentle kiss across her lips. "For all intents and purposes, until tomorrow, you're my wife."

How would she ever say goodbye?

Opening her mouth under his, she melted deeper into the kiss—

Benjamin's screech reached them from somewhere outside.

*"Cal! Maisie! Phone the police! I've nabbed the shitbag!"*

# Chapter 33

Releasing her, Hayes bolted out of the room—Joy scrambled to follow, almost colliding with Liselle and Gene at the base of the steps.

By the time she caught up to Hayes, he'd burst through the sunroom's glass doors and merged with the dark evening.

Joy had always considered herself fit, but she struggled to keep up with Hayes's powerful strides. Arms pumping, she pushed to keep pace through the muddy soil. At least the rain had stopped.

Gene fell in behind her, his labored breathing growing heavier with each step.

Kenna appeared first, racing up to them from the darkness like a darting faerie, her red hair whipping wildly around her. "The creep—the one on the motorbike! We've just clocked him again."

"Where?" Hayes demanded, scanning the surroundings.

"On my parents' farm earlier today—and now—when we got back—he was by the bee hives. Benjamin caught him, but the guy tried to deck him. Took a swing for his face!" She swung her own fist wildly in the air. "Benjamin knocked him right out. It's the tosser trying to buy up all this land."

Cal and Maisie joined them just as Benjamin appeared, dragging a silver fox of a trespasser. Blood ran from the older man's swelling nose and dripped down to his designer suede biker jacket.

Wow. Who'd have thought Benjamin had enough force in those skinny arms to make a nose bleed?

"It's the same shitbag from Friday night. It's his motorbike," said Benjamin. "He somehow got through the locked gates."

Shaking off Benjamin's grip, the trespasser touched the crimson stream coursing down his face. "Can't believe you punched me. I'll sue you, you fucker. Lissy, tell them there's no need for cops."

*Lissy?* That bitch.

Everyone swiveled to glare at Liselle.

"Explain," Hayes clipped out.

"I don't know this man!" Liselle exclaimed, backing herself into Gene's arms.

"What the fuck are you talking about, Lissy?" demanded the American. "You texted me the gate code." Reaching into his pocket, he pulled out his phone. "Here. Look."

Hayes seized the cell from him.

Joy peeked over his shoulder.

Whoa, she didn't just text him the gate code. The text thread went back days... and they didn't just include words.

*Ewwww...*

She shut her eyes and turned her head away for good measure. That was more of Liselle than she *ever* cared to see.

Hayes handed the device back to the trespasser. "May not want to show that to her husband."

"Why?" asked Gene. "Did she text him the code?"

"And a few… visuals," said Hayes.

Kenna, understanding, shuddered.

"Why'd you take a swing at me then?" Benjamin asked. "You couldn't just explain yourself earlier? Would have spared me some busted knuckles."

"You came at me from the dark," accused the American. "How was I supposed to know you live here? I thought you were crazy."

"But you were the one trespassing," Kenna pointed out.

The man's nose didn't look broken, but he'd need at least an icepack. Joy suspected that the others wouldn't appreciate her inviting him in for one, though she should offer to assess him for a head injury and any breathing problems.

"Are you okay to ride your bike like that?" she asked. "You may need an x-ray. Maybe you should have someone pick you up. What's your name?"

Hayes glared at her. "His injuries are what you're concerned about?" He turned to the lurker. "You're the developer."

He didn't look the least bit contrite. "Family business. My name's Thurston."

"Well, you can't have my parents' sheep farm and you can't have this place either, Thurston." Kenna flicked a glance at Liselle. "You can probably have her, though."

"Liselle…" Gene's arms dropped to his sides as he stepped away from his wife. "What possessed you to give him the gate code?"

She gave her husband a long stare. "Remember, how I wanted to expand this place, offer spa treatments, bee venom facials—"

"You never mentioned selling it for scraps to a developer," Gene ground out. "Or your *boyfriend*."

"Listen," Thurston reached into his pocket for a business card and extended it to Cal, "this sounds like a family situation, but my company wants this place. How about you think about it and give me a call when you're ready to talk numbers?"

Cal shredded the card in two quick moves before wrapping his arm around Maisie. "We're not interested. Get yourself off our property."

Thurston didn't have to be told twice. "I'll call you later, Lissy."

With that, he trotted away. Soon enough, his motorcycle kicked to life and its rumble faded into the distance.

"If you don't mind," Gene told the group, looking much older than his twenty-five years of age, "my wife and I need to have a word."

Without giving Liselle time to respond, he grabbed her elbow and towed her into the house.

"Hope he's got himself a decent divorce lawyer," said Kenna.

"Maybe they can still sort it out," said Benjamin. The outraged looks everyone gave him had him backtracking. He raised his hands, palms out. "Don't look at me. She's the one shagging the developer."

Cal waved everyone on ahead of him into the house with a promise of a stiff beverage.

As Joy started to follow the others inside, Hayes caught her hand.

She glanced up at him, knowing he'd come to the same conclusion as her. "It wasn't Ryder at the barn on Friday."

Threading their fingers together, his palm solid and warm against hers, he touched her lips with his. "Nope. Just Liselle's lover."

"Do you think they met up for a… you know? While Gene napped upstairs?"

"Wouldn't be surprised," Hayes said just as they stepped back into the sunroom and, from there, the kitchen.

Cal broke out the whiskey and Maisie the pastries. While everyone made awkward small talk, Cal and Maisie sat, shoulders drooped, and stared into their glasses. Their nephew's collapsing marriage would be a lot to process.

The sharp, angry clicks of high heels taking one stair down at a time warned of Liselle's approach.

"I'm not staying with people who don't believe me," she hissed.

Did others find her voice just as grating?

Gene's heavy footfall followed. "You cheated on me, Liselle!"

The heel clicks stopped when she reached the base of the steps. "You believe some stranger over me?"

"Stop. Lying. He had your fucking *photos*."

Liselle's voice dropped to a plaintive mewl. "Baby, you have to believe me. I don't know how he got those."

Back in the kitchen, Joy exchanged a look with Kenna.

"Aye, sure she doesn't," muttered Kenna.

"I thought you loved me." Gene's voice wavered. The man was clearly fighting tears. "How daft I've been. How blind."

"Gene, don't do this. Don't take some stranger's word over mine."

"Get out. We're done."

*Good for you, Gene. Don't backslide now.*

Liselle didn't seem to enjoy his brusque dismissal. "*You don't get to end this!*" Her shout was loud enough to make the whiskey in Joy's glass quake. "*I* fucking end this. And no, Gene, I never loved you. I could barely stand you slobbering all over me. I'm glad to be rid of you. Just like I was glad to be rid of Hayes! You know he proposed to me once? Wanted to name one of his companies after me?"

As four jaws dropped to the polished wood table and four pairs of shocked eyes looked at Hayes, Joy took a sip of her beverage. "Oh, that spiel again."

"Hayes, what's she on about?" demanded Maisie.

The wall clock ticked out fifteen seconds before Hayes spoke. "The woman who turned my proposal down before Cal found me—the one who refused to come to the hospital? It was Liselle."

Cal's face creased with pain. He laid a hand on Hayes's shoulder. "Hayes, we didn't know. Whyever would you not tell us?"

"She'd already married Gene," Hayes explained, swirling his drink in the glass. "What was there to say? I couldn't turn you against your new niece-in-law."

"I'm speechless," murmured Maisie. "We let her into our *house*."

"I'd have never let her have your farm," Hayes vowed.

"Next time, just be honest." The snap of irritation was uncharacteristic of Maisie, and spoke to how hurt she must be. The man she considered a son had kept something important from her.

The pain in her words stabbed deep into Joy's heart.

She and Hayes hadn't been honest with the Blairs

from the very beginning. Now that Liselle was out of the picture, they had to tell them the truth. But when? Just this second—when they were heartbroken for their nephew—didn't seem like the best time.

"Fuck you, Gene." Liselle's voice from the entryway brought Joy out of her spiraling thoughts. "I don't need you. You'll be hearing from my lawyers."

The front door slammed shut.

A half minute of stiff silence later, Gene stumbled into the kitchen, his pale face stunned.

"You okay, Gene?" Joy rose. "Want to sit? Or a pastry? Maybe a whiskey?"

He shook his head. "She took my car."

"Small price to pay for freedom, bud," said Hayes.

Gene made an unintelligible sound and sank into the nearest armchair, dropping his head into his hands.

Maisie returned her attention to Hayes. "I can't believe you didn't tell us that's who you proposed to all those years ago."

"We'd have never entertained the idea of selling our farm to her," added Cal.

"What happened between you and Liselle, Hayes?" asked Kenna.

Maisie looked to Hayes for permission. When he nodded, she explained how Cal found Hayes near-to-dead and his long journey to recuperation on the farm.

Hayes jerked with every exposed detail. Aching for him, Joy laid her head on his shoulder. Hayes relaxed in her hold, pulling her snug against him.

"That bitch. I reckon she married you *after* she met Thurston." Kenna turned to Gene. "A way to guarantee that Cal and Maisie would choose her as the new owner, and she could sell to the developer."

Gene, too deflated to shrug, grunted.

"You have a prenup?" asked Hayes.

"No," Gene said into his palms. "She said she didn't believe in them."

"Of course she didn't," Kenna muttered.

"I should ring my parents." Rising from the table, Gene disappeared upstairs.

"She took advantage of a kid," muttered Cal, pouring himself another whiskey.

Maisie took a healthy swallow of her own drink. "I'm stunned. This has been quite the evening."

Joy lifted her head from Hayes's shoulder. They still had their social media mess to sort out. "Let's go upstairs."

Releasing his hold on her, he lifted to his feet. "Good night, everyone." Coming around the table, he crouched next to Cal and Maisie. "I'm sorry for not telling you."

Maisie's lips curved in proffered understanding as she wrapped Hayes in a hug. Pulling back, she cupped his cheek. "She traumatized you. Hard to open that old wound again. And she'd already married Gene. I probably wouldn't have said anything either."

Cal waited for Maisie to release Hayes. When she did, he slapped him on the back. "I know you'd never have let the farm go to her. You love this place as much as we do."

The relief, the love that flitted across Hayes's face almost made Joy cry.

Blinking fast, he cleared his throat before tipping his head in the direction of Gene upstairs. "We'll assess the damage tomorrow morning."

Cal waved him on upstairs. "Go on up with your woman. You found a good one, lucky lad."

Hayes met the older man's gaze. "I know."

# Chapter 34

As soon as Joy stepped inside their bedroom, the reality of her new media fame came crashing back.

The phone she'd left on the table continued to vibrate with each incoming text. Hayes jolted with each vibration.

"I'll set it to silent." Hurrying to her phone, she switched it to soundless and scrolled through the dozens of messages. Her friends and coworkers had seen the news—and they wanted details. "Did everyone see the video? I'm getting texts from high school friends now."

Hayes cursed. "I'll check in with the attorneys."

Thankfully, her only social media account was private, but she had a hundred friend requests. Great. Who were these people?

All but two were strangers. Easy enough to delete.

The two she knew, she'd lost touch with years ago. One was a high school friend, with dozens of mutuals. Clicking into her profile, she scrolled through it. Yep, definitely Noelle. She accepted the request. The other was an old med school friend she hadn't kept up with since Aurora realized med school wasn't for her and left to pursue other interests.

They hadn't spoken in a while, but at one point they had been close. Clicking into her profile, she scrolled through her photos. Aw, she and Greg got engaged after all. Watching a few of Aurora's recent videos, she smiled—girl had moved to Montreal? Her adventurous friend hadn't changed a bit. She accepted the request.

A chat notification popped up.

Aurora:

*I couldn't believe it was you when I saw the video! Hi! Are you in Scotland? Greg and I are in Glasgow— but only until tomorrow. Are you near here? Should we have coffee?*

While Hayes spoke to—Joy assumed—his gaggle of attorneys, she checked the map on her phone. Aurora was too far away.

Joy:

*I'm actually on a bee farm in the Highlands, so I won't be able to see you. FaceTime sometime?*

Aurora:

*Where in the Highlands?!*

Joy:

*On Highlander Honey Farm.*

Aurora:

*That's not that terrible a drive from Glasgow. I miss you. I want to see you. I want to know all about this guy you're with! How about an early coffee? I'll come to you—we have a car rental. But it has to be early (maybe 7:30?) so I can be back in time.*

It was a no-brainer. She missed her friend, and an early morning catch-up would leave plenty of time for Cal's birthday celebration later in the day.

Joy:

*Yes! We can do as early as you want, if you don't mind the drive! Come have coffee on the farm here—I'll introduce you, and I'll show you the honey production. It's really cool.*

Aurora:
*Sounds good. See you tomorrow.*

Joy sent the exact address just as Hayes hung up his call.

"They'll get the stories down soon."

"Good. But something good did come from it. I reconnected with a couple of friends from my past. One is actually in Glasgow. I haven't seen her in years—we were in med school the first year together, and she now lives in Montreal. I invited her to have coffee here tomorrow morning. Do you think Cal and Maisie will mind?"

"They won't mind at all." He stopped close enough to settle his hands on her waist and pull her against him. "And I'd like to meet her."

Unable to help herself, she wrapped her arms around his neck and pressed a kiss to his lips. "You want to meet Aurora?"

"Sure. Don't worry. I won't hover."

What was the harm? "All right. She'll be here tomorrow morning at seven thirty."

"But don't leave the farm with her." He cupped her butt with a possessiveness she'd miss. "Until I find Ryder, you're to be an arm's reach away."

For once, his territorialism didn't bother her. Ryder had been unstable before. What if the media circus made him worse? Until the frenzy settled down, and that video went away, she wouldn't make herself a target—even on the off chance that he saw the footage.

The news very well might send him over the edge, and Joy didn't intend to put herself in that path. "That's just fine by me."

Pulling back, he gave her a perplexed look. "Huh."

"What?" she asked, instantly alert.

"You're never this agreeable."

"I'm never in the news," she pointed out, relaxing against him. How could this—simply standing in a room, holding each other—feel so damn good?

"Fair point. By tomorrow, hopefully you won't be."

They stayed like that, swaying in the middle of the cheerful space, his heartbeat steady under her ear.

She'd miss this when they said goodbye.

"I'm going to tell the Blairs the truth tomorrow." He skated his hands along her back. "You were right. I should have told them about my connection to Liselle from the beginning. I can't keep lying to them."

She nuzzled closer to him. "Good. I hate the lying."

"I'm sorry I roped you into it."

Lifting her head, she met his serious gaze. "Whoa. A rare Hayes Icefall apology?"

"I do admit when I'm wrong, you know," he grumbled.

She smiled into his chest. "Not often."

"I wish you could have met me years ago. Before Liselle. I wasn't like this then."

Confused, she held on tighter. "Like what?"

"Heartless."

The gruff word tore at her. Did he really believe that of himself?

If she were honest, last week, she'd have agreed with his observation. Yet the last few days had shown her that he was categorically wrong.

Tipping her head back, she waited until he met her gaze. "You're not heartless. Hayes, you have a beautiful heart. You wanted to protect the Blairs."

"I've been lying to them this whole time."

"Yeah, and that's not cool. But they'll understand now that they know the truth about Liselle."

Liselle…

The woman who continued to plague her man.

Her man? Where had that thought come from?

Hayes was *not* her man.

The first time she'd let herself fall in love with him had left her bitter and sad.

The second time would devastate her completely.

Discombobulated, she stepped away. "Should we get ready for bed?"

Before she could back up another step, Hayes caught her. The world tilted as he scooped her up and set her on the flowery comforter.

"We most definitely should get ready for bed," he murmured, and his hard, aroused body covered hers.

***

*I'm a lucky son of a bitch*, Hayes thought hours later.

Night inched painfully into morning, but the anticipation buzzing through his veins made it impossible to sleep.

He glanced at Joy, relaxed in his arms, on the farm he considered home. Over the last week, he'd been able to share this special place with her.

Even if Cal and Maisie chose Benjamin and Kenna as the new owners, he'd be fine with their decision.

He and Joy could always visit. Besides, Cal and Maisie would live closer to them now, and he'd ensure that he and Joy visited them often in New York.

What had he done to deserve her?

He'd judged Jackson when he married the woman

who'd driven him crazy. He'd pitied Nate for marrying Francesca—and taking on all her siblings.

*What idiots,* he'd thought. *Didn't they know love never lasted?*

Now, he understood what drove his brothers. Loving Joy should have scared him, but when he hunted for that twitch of doubt, it wasn't there.

While his love for Liselle had made him insecure and anxious, his feelings for Joy left nothing but a sense of deep rightness. Of excitement for the future that lay ahead.

Unlike Liselle, Joy didn't play games. The woman was honest to a fault. She couldn't even lie without blushing—or breaking out in hives.

And she loved him. For once, he knew he wasn't misreading the signals. She herself had agreed they were on the same page about this after they'd found her destroyed nightie.

Her job was in San Diego, so that's where his Realtor was looking for their new home. He'd lived next to Jackson before. Looked like they'd be neighbors again in San Diego.

The Realtor should have sent him listings to review by now. He'd check on that first thing in the morning.

Joy loved surprises—no surprise would top a house next to her sister.

Her left hand rested, trusting and warm, across his heart. As he traced the Celtic knots across her wedding band, a swell of contentment washed over him. That feeling of rightness he only felt with her.

Curling himself around her, he let sleep claim him.

# Chapter 35

For the first time, Joy managed to wake up before Hayes. Careful not to disturb him, she wiggled out of bed and hurried to the shower. Aurora would be arriving soon, and she still had to let the Blairs know she'd invited a visitor.

After the fastest shower on record, she brushed through her hair and gathered the tresses at the nape of her neck. It would have to do. Pulling on jeans and a blush pink sweater, she lifted her phone from the table and opened the social media app.

She ignored the news feed and the new friend requests, and went directly to her messages.

Aurora:

*Looks like I'll be a little early. See you at 7!*

Joy:

*I'll open the gates for you and show you where to park.*

Catching the glint of her wedding rings, she hesitated. How would she ever explain the situation to Aurora?

But the thought of taking them off and leaving them in the bedroom drew an instinctive reluctance. Besides, Aurora only reached out because of the video of her kissing Hayes. Might as well run with the whole marriage thing.

She found Maisie in the kitchen, the breakfast halfway prepared—Malik at her feet.

Looking up from the frying tatties, the older woman smiled. "You're up early."

"I hope it's okay, but I invited a friend from medical school to the farm for a coffee this morning."

"Certainly! Does she want to have breakfast with us?"

Maisie was too generous. Hayes better tell her the truth today.

"I think she'd like that." Joy checked the time on her phone. "She's almost here. I should go open the gate."

"You'd best put on a jacket—we're expecting a blizzard this morning. The gate clicker is by the door."

She'd seen more snow in the last week than she had in the last few years.

In the mudroom, she grabbed her puffer, stuffed the gate opener in her pocket, and stepped into the crisp early morning blue hour.

Aurora's car pulled up just as she reached the gate. Through the beam of headlights, she could make out her friend's blonde hair.

Lifting her hand off the steering wheel, Aurora waved.

Joy pushed the correct button on the access remote, and the gates slid open.

***

Hayes snapped awake, immediately aware of Joy's absence. Reaching for his watch on the nightstand, he checked the time. Her friend wouldn't be here for another half hour.

Who was this person anyway?

He never even got her last name.

Striding to his iPad, he began to hunt.

The woman was easy enough to find based on her medical school and current city of residence alone. Her extensive online presence didn't keep much private—she was active on every social media platform imaginable, just like Joy's mother.

Aurora's move to Canada, her engagement, her wedding planning, had been shared with her followers in cringing detail. Her trip to Puerto Rico played out minute by minute—

What the fuck?

If Aurora Leavenworth was currently in Puerto Rico, who the hell was Joy meeting for coffee this morning?

Pulling on his sweatpants and T-shirt, he scrambled down the stairs until he reached Maisie in the kitchen.

"Where's Joy?" he demanded.

Maisie waved in the general direction of the farm entrance. "Letting her friend in at the gate."

The words dried the breath in his lungs. "When did she leave?"

Maisie scooped fried tattie scones onto a serving platter. "A few minutes ago."

Hayes sprang outside through the sunroom door.

The fear that had strangled his heart lessened when he saw her through the morning twilight—waving someone inside the open gates and rushing toward the car.

"Joy!" he bellowed. "*Wait.*"

Although he was too far to read her expression, she stopped and turned in his direction.

Good.

He wasn't too late.

But as he sprinted toward her, the passenger door of the car opened and Ryder shot out.

Hayes surged forward, eating the distance that seemed to multiply before him.

Whatever Ryder did caused Joy to jerk as though electrocuted. Her body arched and she fell to the ground.

The scream caught in Hayes's throat.

Ryder threw Joy into the front seat of the car and slammed the door.

Darting to the driver's side, Ryder threw a blonde woman to the ground and disappeared behind the wheel. As he reversed the car, the tires squealed, shooting gravel in every direction.

Hayes reached the gates as the car disappeared from sight. "*Fuck.*"

The unstable junkie took his wife. Yawning hopelessness blurred his vision. He refused to give in.

Joy knew how to take care of herself.

*She'll be fine.* His hands shook regardless.

Once he found Ryder, he'd teach the bastard never to go after what was his.

He kneeled next to the bawling blonde on the ground. "Who the hell are you?"

The woman fisted his T-shirt and sobbed harder.

Hell no. He didn't have time for this. Ryder was taking Joy farther away with every minute the woman cried.

"Where'd he take her?" he demanded.

The woman kept wailing.

"Will you stop for a minute? Where's he taking my wife?"

"I-I-I don't know."

"You know him?"

She nodded.

"How?"

"He's staying at my Airbnb unit next door to me." Sobs cut between the words, but he made them out.

He gave her a shake. "Can you take me there?"

"Don't make me go back!"

"I won't let him hurt you. But he has my *wife*."

"He's mental. He…"

The words garbled into gibberish. Hayes didn't have time for this.

*Joy's location.* He could track her on his phone. Reaching into his pants pocket, he pulled her up on his cell. His heart plunged. She'd ended location sharing.

Maisie ran up to them from the house. "Hayes, what happened?"

"Joy's ex took her. I'm trying to get this one to talk." Grasping the sobbing woman's shoulders, he gave her a tooth-rattling jerk. "Tell me where your Airbnb is."

"Okay!" she agreed. "I'll tell you. But don't make me go there with you."

"The address will do."

"The Airbnb rental is separate from my house, but it's on my land." She rattled off the address.

Plugging it into his phone, he realized it was less than fifteen minutes away. "Was that his car?"

"Yes. I knew he was off from the moment he arrived on Saturday. He only left the cottage to skulk around my property. Gave me the creeps. He found me in my kitchen this morning, all crazed, waving the taser about, saying I had to pass for Aurora. Said he'd hurt me if I didn't drive him, if I didn't act like I was her friend until she got close enough to the car."

"Take care of her, will you?" Handing the crying woman to Maisie, Hayes sprinted to his McLaren.

Thick globs of snow began to fall as he merged onto the main road. Fuck. A snowstorm was the last thing he needed. He drove faster.

Fourteen minutes until he had his wife back. It might as well have been a century.

A fold of Highland cattle darted out of nowhere, cutting in front of his car.

Not given a choice, he braked, coming to a screeching halt. Slamming his fist against the wheel, he screamed every foul word he knew. The cows didn't care.

One after the other, the shaggy, horned beasts trotted by, their auburn hair swaying with each step as they crossed right in front of his vehicle, wasting precious time.

He laid on the horn.

It didn't make a difference.

Everything he held dear had been hurt and kidnapped by a fucking asshole, and fucking cows blocked his way.

If something happened to Joy, he'd hunt each one down and turn them into ground meat.

When the last of the animals crossed, he gunned it.

At the turn, the tires hit an invisible patch of ice, sending him skidding.

"Fuck." Gripping the wheel, he turned into the drift, righted himself, and raced onward.

The McLaren shaved off a precious chunk of time from the remainder of the drive, and he pulled up to the blonde's tree-lined property as the sun broke the horizon.

A snow-covered herb garden separated the stand-alone, single-room Airbnb unit from her main house.

Kicking in the door of the rental property, he searched for signs of Ryder or Joy, but found nothing.

If they were here, the car would be too.

Where the hell could he have taken her?

The icy wind whipped at him as he prowled to the main house. He wished he'd brought his coat, but there hadn't been time. Not that it mattered. No number of layers would have insulated him from the panic that chilled him from deep within.

The door had been left unlocked. He combed through the two stories, but found no trace of Ryder or Joy.

He stepped back into the snowstorm.

He'd promised to protect Joy, and he'd failed her.

Ryder had grabbed her while he all but slept. He should have tried harder to find the bastard earlier. Instead, he'd been too preoccupied with the farm—with Joy.

If anything happened to her—

The blonde mentioned he'd stalked her land. How far did her property stretch? Who were her neighbors? If Ryder had driven through here, his tracks had been long covered by the snow.

Bracing himself for the cold, he started away from the main driveway. Joy had to be close. Ryder wouldn't get far in a snowstorm. He'd bring her here. Hayes was certain of it.

Huddling against the wind, he followed a snow-dusted footpath to the other end of the blonde's parcel. The path took him through a thick outcropping of trees before spitting him out at the edge of a clearing.

His heart vaulted.

*Ryder's car.*

Parked next to a crumbling structure.

The remnants of the abandoned, two-story home

looked at least two hundred years old. Its bare stone façade appeared sturdy, but its windows had been knocked out an unspecified time ago. The decrepit door hung crookedly on its rusted hinges, and the second-floor balcony jutted out without intact railings.

Profound relief swamped Hayes, warming him more effectively than any down jacket.

He'd found Joy.

It was time to get his wife back.

# Chapter 36

The asshole had tased her.

The pain had been sharp and disorienting, and Joy had blacked out before she could fight back.

Even now, sprawled on the dirty wood floor, her muscles had yet to recover.

Fighting nausea, she forced herself to sit up.

*Okay. Not bad. Just shake it off.*

Using the cold stone wall for purchase, she rose on unsteady feet, balancing near the rectangular opening that had once been a window.

The blizzard Maisie predicted howled outside, and occasional gusts of wind snaked through the abandoned home to dust snow along the crumbling wooden boards.

Joy judged the distance to the ground below. Much too far to jump. She'd break both legs, and no number of horses and men would put Humpty Dumpty—in this case, her—back together again. No, a leap down was out of the question.

Moving her attention back indoors, she studied the filthy, abandoned space.

Bare stone walls, vacant openings that had once served as windows, and a balcony—its rails eaten away by time—just across from her.

In the far corner, a gap… not just a gap—a stairway down.

*My way out.*

Fighting her shaking muscles, she stumbled to the stairs—backing up immediately as Ryder appeared at the base of the rickety steps.

She didn't know what exactly he'd taken, but he was clearly on some kind of stimulants. His pupils stretched across his irises, making his brown eyes appear black against his bloodshot sclerae.

His gaze couldn't seem to focus, darting to his feet, then to the stone wall, then up above him, before he settled on her.

He rushed the steps, stopping a foot away from her. His shearling-lined jacket hung from his gaunt frame. "You're awake."

"Ryder, what is this?" She backed away.

He followed. "What's what? I finally got you alone so we can talk."

"You pretended to be Aurora?"

His smug laugh bounced off the stone walls. "I remembered you mentioning her. She's a social media whore—creating a copycat account from her photos didn't take much time. I sent off friend requests to all your mutual friends, and they accepted—without a second thought. Kind of proud of myself for all that. Lucked out that Alba's blonde. From a distance, they looked alike enough—didn't have to find anyone else. All that work because you left me no choice. You blocked me on *everything.*"

"You set up a tracker on my phone. *You killed my pets, Ryder.*" The pain of finding their floating bodies sliced through her as though it had just happened.

"You got me fired." He leaned closer, his rancid breath washing over her.

"I didn't get you fired. You stole drugs from the hospital. I didn't know anything until after."

"*You're lying!* You ruined my life. Destroyed it. One day, I was helping people. The next, my life was over."

She took a discreet step away. "Ryder, why do you think it was me?"

Like a wasp, he followed. "Because I know you. Miss Goody Two-Shoes. *Of course* you blabbed once you found out."

"But I didn't find out! I didn't know until later."

If she charged past him, could she skirt far enough around him to reach the stairs? And where would she go from there? Her gaze flicked to the vacant windows. Where had he brought her?

They couldn't be far from the Blairs. The view from here was achingly similar.

Maybe if she made it to the main road, she could find her way back to Highlander Honey Farm?

Did Hayes know she was gone? She'd left him asleep in their warm, cozy bed. She'd give anything to be back in that bed with him curled like a safety blanket around her.

Ryder snapped his fingers in front of her face. "Don't even think about it. You get me fired, then start dating some millionaire? I saw the video—it's fucking everywhere, like it's actual news. You got me fired to get rid of me so you can be with your lover."

Contradicting him would only make him angrier, she knew.

"I know you're hurting right now," she said instead, tapping into how she might feel if she were him. "They fired you so suddenly. I'd be so hurt if I were you. Did they give you a warning, explain what happened?"

"No," he scoffed, his eyes zooming around the room.

"What if we call them together right now? Find out what happened?"

"*Fuck them*. I don't want an explanation. I want you to get my job back. Tell them you lied."

"Is this really about the job? Or is there more bothering you?"

"You ended us! Ended us when my world was falling apart."

*You were stealing drugs from the hospital!* she wanted to scream. *You're an addict, and I didn't know. I never even realized.*

"I should have talked to you about it, Ryder. I was in shock too. It was a surprise to me as well. It's so early, and I'm so hungry. Are you hungry? Maybe we can go somewhere warm? Sit and talk? Have some tea and breakfast?"

"I haven't eaten yet today," he admitted.

"Maybe there's a place near here that makes vanilla lattes. You love a nice latte."

His shoulders sagged. "I thought you and I had something."

The words hurt because she had thought so too. "Me too."

Spinning away from her, he marched to the balcony.

"Careful," she cautioned as he stepped onto the sagging deck. In his state, he could easily tumble.

"Do you even care?" he shot back. "You ended it like we were nothing."

"You meant a lot to me, Ryder. What we had meant a lot. How long have you been—"

"I was fine! Do you know how much pressure I'm under? How long the hours are? I just needed something to take the edge off. *That's all*. I could have stopped any time. Then they fire me. Like that? After the *years* I've given them? Like I'm nothing? That job—and you—were my entire life. *And in one day, I lost both!*"

He paced the length of the dilapidated balcony. When he careened too close to the edge on his return, Joy bit her lip to stop from yelling out. Did he not see that no guardrails would stand between him and the drop below if he so much as tripped? Apparently not, because he continued on as though he hadn't just escaped a broken neck.

He'd terrorized her for weeks, but she couldn't watch him fall to his death because he was high and hurting.

Maybe she could get him to agree to seek some help.

"Ryder, I still care for you." She shifted closer to the balcony. "I'm worried about you. Maybe, with everything that's happened at work and... between us, this could be a fresh start for you. Why don't you come inside, and we can talk. Maybe we can find some treatment options together that might help you?"

He stomped back to the far edge of the crumbling balcony. "I'm not an addict, Joy. I'm hurt because my girlfriend got me fired—and then ran off with her own sister's brother-in-law. Or did you think I'd never find out? You wouldn't let me kiss you in public, but you had no problem with his tongue down your throat for the whole world to see and record!"

***

Hayes was halfway to the broken front door when Ryder stumbled onto the balcony, if one could call it that. The crumbling skeleton clung to the side of the house by two rusty nails, tops.

293

Changing course before Ryder caught sight of him in the middle of the clearing, Hayes ducked behind his car. If Ryder spotted him now, he could take it out on Joy.

Ryder muttered to someone as he paced, agitated and uneven on his feet.

Was he rambling at Joy?

The fucker had tased her.

Was she hurt? In pain? He couldn't even recall whether she'd worn a jacket. Exposed to the elements in the abandoned home, she must be freezing.

The wind flayed his own unprotected skin, the snowflakes cutting like microscopic blades. He couldn't remember the last time he could feel his fingers or toes.

Violent tremors rolled through his body, his muscles jumping uncontrollably no matter how hard he fought them. He could have blamed the gusts of wind, but he knew better. It was the crippling fear for Joy's well-being that made him tremble. Though the cold didn't help.

He ground his chattering teeth together until his jaw ached, and strained to hear. The vehement wind and churning snow swallowed most of Ryder's words.

Despite the snowstorm, darting across the open clearing would still leave him too visible.

If only Ryder would go inside.

Hayes would need ten seconds—tops—to clear the door.

That's when Ryder started to jump.

***

"*Stop it*," Joy commanded.

The bark worked, because Ryder halted his crazy leaping and turned toward her.

"It's snowing hard out there," she continued, keeping her voice as calm and reasonable as she could manage. "Maybe you want to join me in here? Easier to talk that way."

He shot his hands out wide into the air like a starfish. "Why don't you join me *out here*?"

"Ryder, come inside. Let's talk. You're a great doctor—you've done so much good. You were a great boyfriend—you have so much love to give. Come here, let's see what we can do together. Maybe we can call someone. Do you want to speak to your sister? Your mom?"

He spat at the ground next to his feet. "They shunned me like you did."

"They're worried about you. We care about you—we want the Ryder we know back."

"No. One. Cares. About. Me." He punctuated each shouted word with a stomach-twisting jump—like he was on some possessed, invisible pogo stick. "No. One. Believes. Me. You! All! Walked! Away!"

That balcony wasn't going to hold. This *house* might not even hold that much action.

At this rate, he'd plummet to death.

She had to bring him inside.

# Chapter 37

Ryder continued his erratic leaping, rock and wood chunks and stray, rusted nails raining from the creaking balcony.

Did the man have a death wish, or no common sense?

At least the hurtling around kept him distracted as he spoke to someone just out of sight.

As long as he didn't turn, Hayes could make it to the door.

It was his only chance. He launched forward. Reaching the entryway before Ryder could spot him, he glanced at the balcony.

That was when he saw her… *Joy*.

Wide-eyed and shivering, she stepped out onto the balcony with Ryder.

What the hell was she doing getting that close to a drugged-out psycho on a ledge two breaths away from collapsing?

*Fucking go inside*, he willed her.

Ryder continued his frenzied hopping across the decaying surface.

The last resisting pieces of wood and nails gave out.

A nauseating crunch split the morning air.

The balcony gave way. Tearing free of the stone wall, it crashed to the ground with an earsplitting thud, launching snow and debris into the air. The flurries-covered soil beneath his feet jolted with the impact.

"Joy!" Her name tore from the deepest reaches of his soul.

He hurtled to the remnants of the balcony.

Dropping to his knees, he clawed through the rubble.

The jagged wood shredded his hands, the rusted metal sliced them, but he didn't care. Blood gushed as he flung planks and debris aside to get to her.

He couldn't think about the impact of the fall or the wreckage that now crushed her. She'd be okay—she had to be.

"Hayes!"

Had he imagined it? His name on Joy's beautiful tongue, called from somewhere above him.

Too afraid to hope, he glanced up.

Joy stood—hale and whole—at the threshold to where the balcony had once been.

"We're okay. I pulled Ryder inside in time!"

The rest of her words dissipated as he sprinted into the house. When he leaped onto the second floor, Joy sat on the ground—paralyzingly close to the opening left by the collapsed balcony—while Ryder sobbed, his face in her lap.

Closing the distance to her, Hayes hauled the sniveling addict away from his wife and punched him square in the face. The shock of it dropped Ryder to the ground.

"Hayes—" Joy began.

"That's for choking her." Lifting the fucker to his feet, he swung again. "And that's for scaring her."

Despite the impact of Hayes's second punch, Ryder succeeded in staying upright, launching at his attacker with a high-pitched howl. Hayes swung again, connecting with muscle and bone. "And that's for her goldfish."

Ryder stumbled back several steps, and fell to his ass on the ground.

"*Stop it!*" demanded Joy, cutting in front of Hayes. "I had it under control."

"You were out on the balcony with him!"

"When I heard it give, I managed to get us both inside."

"You have superhuman strength or what?"

Ryder curled himself into a ball on the ground.

Picking him up by the scruff of his neck, Hayes shook him. "Apologize to the lady."

Ryder spat.

Hayes's hand grasped his shoulder. Joy didn't know what exactly he pressed, but Ryder fell to his knees in pain. "Ow."

"I said… apologize to the lady."

Ryder squeezed his eyes tight. "I'm sorry."

"What for?" Hayes prodded.

Ryder didn't say anything.

Hayes's hand on his shoulder flexed again.

Ryder yelped. "Okay! For everything!"

"You sorry for killing her pets?" Hayes snarled.

"Yes! I'm sorry!"

"She ever gonna see your face again?"

"No."

"I'll make sure of it, either way."

"We should call the ambulance," said Joy before Hayes could inflict any more damage.

Hayes's hands shook as he reached for her, pulling her into his quaking body, his mouth claiming hers, his hands roving brazenly.

"I'm okay. I'm okay," she assured him between kisses, but it wasn't enough. "I swear I'm okay."

***

He clutched her tighter. "I thought you fell—the balcony—you stepped out—"

"Shh." She rubbed soothing circles across his back. "It's all over now."

Tilting up her chin, he brushed her hair away from her face. "He hurt you?"

"No." Rising on her toes, she kissed him. "I took care of myself."

"I knew you'd be able to deal with him. You're the most capable person I know," he said, unwilling—no, unable—to release her.

God, he loved her. The heart-sinking crunch of the balcony coming off the wall would haunt him for the rest of his life.

Joy didn't seem that eager to leave his arms either, pulling him tighter against her as though she could fuse them together. "You're freezing. Hayes, you're in a T-shirt. Go inside your car before you get frostbite. I'll deal with Ryder."

She was joking. He opened his mouth to tell her so, but the wail of sirens cut him off.

Maisie must have called the police.

"You knew before I did that it wasn't Aurora," she said into his chest.

He nuzzled her hair, let that comforting Joy scent seep into him. "Your friend is in Puerto Rico. I realized it too late—Ryder rented the blonde's property. She gave me the address."

Easing back, she laid her warm hand on his cheek. "Let's go inside your car, blast the heat, warm up."

"Hayes? Joy?" Maisie's panicked voice reached them from the outside.

"We'll be right there," called Hayes, leading Joy away from Ryder and down the stairs.

The police and ambulance met them on the ground level.

Hayes jerked his finger upward in Ryder's direction. "We're fine. Deal with him. He kidnapped my wife."

Maisie and Cal hovered at the entrance. Maisie had brought Hayes's coat, which she wrapped around him as soon as she saw him.

"Are the two of you all right?" She enveloped both in one big hug.

Cal hugged them too. "What the bloody hell's going on?"

"Let's talk in someone's car," said Joy. "Hayes has been out in a blizzard in a T-shirt."

The blonde paced outside. Seeing Joy, she rushed forward and hugged her. "Hi, I'm Alba, and I'm sorry! He said he'd do me in if I didn't drive him to your farm," she cried. "He had that taser pointed at me and made me wave at you. You okay?"

"I'm fine," said Joy. "Believe it or not, I used to date him."

***

The local police took Ryder into custody. Joy hoped this would be enough of a wake-up call for him to seek help. As soon as they were back Stateside, she'd speak to his family and get him into rehab.

The snow stopped falling by the time they reached Cal's car parked alongside Hayes's. The Land Rover Defender was by far larger than the McLaren, so Joy marched straight to Cal's utility vehicle.

She wrenched open the front passenger door. "Hayes, you sit in the front, near the heater."

Setting his hand on her lower back, he gave her a gentle push into the seat she'd just indicated. "No, you sit there. You're barely dressed."

Like hell. She didn't even want to think about how long he'd been outside in nothing but a thin layer of cotton. "I'm in a sweater and a jacket. Stop arguing. Just sit."

Cal and Maisie exchanged a look next to them.

"You *both* sit in the front." Cal opened the back passenger door for Maisie.

Crap. The hectic morning made what today was slip her mind.

"Cal!" Turning to him, she closed her arms around him and hugged him tight. "With everything that's happened, I forgot. Happy birthday!"

Behind her, Hayes cursed, embracing Cal in turn. "I forgot too, Cal. Happy birthday."

Cal chuckled. "I forgot myself. We've all had an exciting morning."

"Let's go home to some hot breakfast for us all," said Maisie as everyone settled inside the pickup.

"Hayes could use a hot shower." Blasting the heater, she touched Hayes's ice-cold nose, cheek, forehead. "You're still freezing."

Turning his head, he swept a kiss into her palm. "I'm great, now that you're safe."

That's when she remembered—his injuries.

She grabbed his bloodied, torn-apart hands. "Hayes! *Look* at these."

"It's fine." He attempted to pull away.

She refused to let go. "These are really deep cuts, and your skin's covered in splinters. Did you scrape any rusty metal? Is your tetanus shot up to date? We should go get you a booster."

"I'm fine. Barely a couple scratches. And my shot's up to date."

"We need to get you home and disinfect your wounds. Then you better get into a hot shower. Think we should leave the McLaren? Will the police want to speak with us?"

Hayes lifted her hands to his mouth, his dry lips skimming across her knuckles. "I'm getting you home first. We can deal with the police later."

Cal leaned forward from the back seat. "Should I drive us back? I can give you a lift here later to get your car."

"I'm never returning to this place," said Hayes. "Joy and I will follow you back."

But he didn't release her hands, or make an attempt to move.

She didn't need to ask why; she knew. It was time to tell the Blairs the truth.

Hayes turned toward the Blairs. "Cal, Maisie… there's something I have to tell you."

"Is this where you come clean that you're not actually married?" asked Maisie.

Joy pulled her hands away from Hayes so she could turn her whole body toward Cal and Maisie. "*You knew?*"

Cal settled back against his seat. "At first, we just had our suspicions. Hayes never mentioned a bride. Then we tell him Gene got hitched, and out of the blue he says, *Me too*. Pulls up a photo of you—"

"On LinkedIn," put in Maisie. "That was our first clue."

*LinkedIn? Oh brother.*

"No wedding photos," Cal continued, "no pictures of you two together. He never once mentioned you before."

"Then the Doune Castle—"

Joy cringed. "You saw the video?"

"Who hasn't?" Maisie chuckled. "I went online. Not a single outlet mentioned a marriage. That was our second clue."

"And Alba was the third," said Cal. "She told us what Ryder told her. We put it all together."

How were they so calm about the whole thing? They should kick them out of the car—*out of the house.*

Her gut twisted with shame. "I'm so sorry we lied to you."

"It wasn't Joy's doing. It was mine. I panicked. If you can ever forgive—"

Cal cut Hayes off. "We get why you did it. We shouldn't have set such requirements for the new owners. Deep down, we were never keen on selling. It was our way of putting up boundaries."

"Still, it was wrong," said Hayes.

Maisie gave Hayes a kind look—much more understanding than Joy would have ever been. "Very much. But if you had to fake-marry someone, we are glad you fake-married Joy."

"Besides. We doubt it'll be *fake* for much longer." Cal flashed them a smile, which earned him a sharp elbow from Maisie.

"Don't butt in," she cautioned.

He quickly moved along. "We already told Kenna and Benjamin, and it's time you know too. Last night, we made our decision. We've decided to keep Highlander Honey Farm after all. We want to live closer to our grandchildren, but we will split our time between New York and the farm."

Joy looked at Hayes for his reaction. Was he angry? Disappointed?

Undeniable relief softened the strained muscles of his face. "I'm glad your farm will stay with you."

"Me too," said Joy.

Maisie laid a hand across Hayes's shoulder. "And it'll always be your home, Hayes. We think of you as a son, you know that. And, Joy, getting to know you this past week, we've come to think of you as our own as well. You're always welcome at the farm."

"I'm sorry I lied to you," Hayes repeated.

"You all just made us realize—we've got a special place, and lots of folks who want to cherish it as much as we do. We needed this weekend to see that. And you all helped us get there."

# Chapter 38

The police refused to let them leave without statements, but they let everyone stay in Cal's heated car for the process.

Once the questions wrapped up, Hayes and Joy switched to their own vehicle, and Hayes started the engine.

Cranking up the heat, he pulled in Joy for a kiss. "Let's take a hot bath as soon as we get home. I'll show you the house my real estate agent found for us in San Diego. It's close to Jackson and Evie's place—"

"Wait. What?" What was he going on about? Had she misheard? Pulling back, she waited for an explanation.

"Well, your apartment isn't large enough for us both. Our new house has a yard—and a pond, when you're ready to have goldfish again. It's close to the beach, so you can surf before work, and it's a relative straight shot to the freeway so I can get to the airport when I need to travel for work."

Had a stray chunk of lumber from the balcony hit his head?

"What are you talking about? Now we're moving in together?"

He looked genuinely confused. "Well… yes… I thought we were on the same page about us. You love me."

*Did he have to say it in such an accusatory tone?* "The same page about what?"

"About making this official. We talked about it. I've been looking at houses for us."

Had *she* hit her head? Each one of his words made sense separately, but the string of them together blended to gibberish.

"When did we have that conversation?"

"On our way home from Doune Castle. You said we were on the same page."

Oh. *That's* what he had meant? Maybe she should have asked a follow-up question between all that kissing.

Hayes leaned farther away from her. "I'm not wrong about this. I didn't misread you. You love me."

"Stop saying that!"

She hadn't even processed the emotion herself yet. Having him throw it in her face, along with the house he apparently was about to buy them, was too much for her still-addled brain.

She'd been electroshocked, shouted at, had almost plummeted to the iced-over ground with the rickety balcony—and now, somehow, he skipped through the dating part and went straight to playing house. Had he already named their children?

"Hayes… you're jumping the gun here. I don't know how to respond. Let's get back to the farm, take that bath, have something warm to drink. And talk about it later."

Tearing his gaze away from her, he swiveled toward the wheel and shifted the car into drive.

***

*I don't know how to respond.*

That was exactly what Liselle had said over a decade ago when he'd proposed to her at the Dome.

It happened again.

He'd fallen in love with someone who didn't share his feelings, who didn't want him in her life. This time, he thought it would be different because what he and Joy had was different.

Once again, he'd been wrong.

He'd thought she loved him as much as he loved her. It had been so clear. So obvious.

To him.

Had he misunderstood—misread—everything between them?

She knew how he felt about her. He'd thought she'd felt the same. How had he misinterpreted her feelings for him?

She said she wanted to talk later, but what would be the point?

If she intended to end it, why drag it out?

Except… he *couldn't* have misjudged what they meant to each other. He *knew* how she felt. She knew how he felt.

Unable to wait, he pulled over on the side of the road and shifted into park.

"Look me in the eye," he turned to her, "and tell me you don't love me."

She blinked at him. Once. Twice.

An emotion he couldn't name—alarm? pain?—creased the space between her brows, and she twisted away from him.

"I don't love you," she said casually, staring—too hard—at the snow-covered trees beyond her window.

But the flush of red that raced upward from her neck and bloomed brighter on her cheeks implied otherwise. Did she realize she always blushed when she lied? For once, he hadn't misread the cues.

The telltale sign kindled fledgling hope inside his aching heart.

"You love me," he insisted. He wasn't wrong about this.

She turned her head farther away, her red, splotchy neck straining. "What will it take for me to convince you that I don't?"

Refusing to give up, he laid his hand on her knee. "Say it without blushing. And to my face."

"I'm not blushing."

"Yes, you are."

She faced him, her cheeks a bright crimson. "It's… sunburn."

"Yes," he drawled. "This bright Scottish sun has been brutal."

"Windburn, then."

Taking her hand, he brought it against his chilled heart. "I go after what I want, Joy. I want you. You love me."

"It's been a really long day." She pulled away. "My ex shot an *electric current* through me. I'm exhausted. I'm not in the right mindset right now to discuss this. You have to understand. Liselle broke your heart once—well, you did that to me, too. I thought I knew Ryder well, and look… he's off his rocker. I missed the signs. It's not that I don't feel anything for you. It's that… I don't know if I can trust my gut here. I need to think."

Despair closed an icy fist around his heart and squeezed.

Like an idiot, he'd let himself fall in love against his better judgement.

Yet again, he hadn't been enough.

And he'd imagined the whole thing.

If he didn't move now, she'd see the tremors that rolled through his body.

Ignoring the gaping, painful wound where his heart had once been, he pulled back out onto the road. "All right. Let's go home."

***

*Protest. Argue. Tell me you love me.*

Joy waited for the words—even for a few syllables of explanation.

Only silence greeted her.

*What kind of person buys a house for someone and wants to make a fake marriage real with someone they* don't *love?*

Hayes, apparently.

Because the words she expected—the words she hoped for—never came.

Instead, he drove back to the farm in silence.

She glanced at him when they reached the Highlander Honey Farm gates.

His heart-wrenching scream before he dropped to his knees next to the destroyed balcony rang through her head. He'd tunneled through the remnants with his bare hands, searching for her, before she'd gotten enough air in her lungs to call out to him.

A man who felt nothing for her wouldn't do that… right?

If he loved her, why couldn't he say the words?

Had Liselle destroyed his ability to love?

Or had Joy made something of their relationship that wasn't there again?

She'd fallen in love with him, but she'd walk away if she had to. If he didn't return her feelings, every minute spent around him would dismantle her heart piece by piece.

They strode silently into the house. Maisie met them at the door, shuffling them into the kitchen, where everyone gathered around a hot breakfast.

"I have to take care of Hayes's hands first," said Joy, directing him to the couch.

She tweezed the splinters from Hayes's torn-up skin and disinfected and bandaged his cuts. Malik supervised from his spot on the couch arm.

Although Hayes suffered through the long process in silence, she'd caught him watching her with emotion that bordered on bitterness.

Maybe she *had* invented his feelings for her in her mind.

*Great*. Yet again, she allowed herself to live in a fantasy world.

Too soon, the house filled with people—Kenna's parents and several friends from neighboring homes battled the snowy conditions to celebrate Cal's birthday.

For the rest of the day, Hayes avoided her. Avoided everyone, really. He kept to the corners, not engaging much with anyone.

They needed to talk, but Cal's birthday party wasn't the place for it.

They had time. The snowstorm made it impossible for her to leave the farm today anyway.

After the sun set, several folks still lingered downstairs, but Joy started to droop.

Trying not to draw attention to herself, she tiptoed to their room. A scalding shower would help her think through today—and Hayes's unexpected house purchase announcement.

In their bedroom, she pulled off her rings, heart lurching as she set them down on the nightstand.

*Damn it, they're not really mine. Why am I getting mopey?*

With a deep breath, she turned away from them just as Hayes walked in.

Finally, they had some privacy.

"We should talk." She took a ginger step toward him.

His gaze drifted to the gold bands on the nightstand. "I'll drive you to Edinburgh."

What? Just like that?

"Now? It's getting late. I didn't even make a hotel reservation. Cal said he'll drive me tomorrow after the snow clears."

Damn it, why was he so hard to read? Was he upset? Relieved? She couldn't tell.

Sidestepping her, he strode to her rings on the nightstand.

She waited for what he'd do. Would he demand she put them back on? Tell her that life without her was meaningless?

Not Hayes. Wiggling off his own ring, he set it next to hers on the table.

Her heart plummeted. Was this his way of saying goodbye?

Guess it was over.

They were done.

Fake marriage and deal concluded.

It hurt to look at the gold bands on the nightstand, so she turned away from them—from him.

It was for the best anyway.

Better to part ways.

But in this manner?

She wasn't about to let him shut her out—if all he saw in her was a buddy with benefits, he better say it right now.

"There's nothing you want to tell me?" she demanded, cutting him off before he could leave the room.

"No. You held up your end of the bargain. You'll never see me again."

*What the hell? He went from "Let's move in together; you love me" to this?*

"Hayes—"

"It's been a long day. I'm tired."

"We should talk."

"I can't have another breakup in Scotland. Not at this place. We'll talk back in the States."

He was breaking up with her?

They weren't really together… but ending it *like this*?

She really hadn't seen it coming. Like she hadn't seen him leaving years earlier.

*Great, I bamboozled myself again.*

"You're serious," she said.

His tired gaze held hers. "Do you love me?"

This again? He wanted complete surrender—to leave her with no defenses while he hemmed and hawed and acted as if she meant nothing to him? Nothing but a convenient fuck he could walk away from? Like he'd walked away last time?

"You're right. We should talk later."

The hollow ache in the pit of her stomach expanded, radiating outward until tears scalded her eyes. She couldn't bear to be in the same small space with him. Better to leave while she still had the strength.

Clearing her throat to fight the despair, she reached for the door.

*Tell me you love me. Tell me this meant something to you.*

But he stayed quiet.

She had no choice.

This time, she walked away from him… walked away while she still could.

# Chapter 39

The next morning, Joy rolled her suitcase to the bedroom door just as the clock struck seven.

Time to say goodbye to Highlander Honey Farm and go home.

She surveyed the bedroom one last time. She'd miss this bright, warm space, with its florals and pastels.

She'd fallen in love with Hayes here—

Her cell phone lit up on the table, shooting a pang of anxiety through her gut. Who was it now? A reporter who wanted to run a story? Evie, telling her there were more videos of her and Hayes?

Seeing her coworker's name relaxed her twisted muscles. Nina was a NICU nurse she'd grown close with at the hospital.

"Nina? Is everything okay? It's late where you are."

Nina all but trilled. "I just got home. Guess what?"

"What?"

"Some anonymous do-gooder covered the Delices' hospital bills!"

Thinking of how relieved the Delices must be momentarily chased away her desolation. The tears came anyway. She blinked them away. "I'm so glad."

"Not only that. Mrs. Delice said that this individual—who asks to remain anonymous—offered her husband a job in his company, too—with healthcare for the whole family! Can you believe it? I wonder who it could be."

Hayes had done that? As her thoughts raced, she fought for a coherent response. "Yes, I wonder."

"Rumor has it, the same individual paid off all the other NICU hospital bills for families with bad or no health insurance."

Joy froze. "*What?*"

"Yes."

Hayes did that? *Unasked?* This, she hadn't anticipated.

"Can you believe it?" repeated Nina.

Suddenly lightheaded, Joy sank to the edge of the bed. "I can't believe it."

Hayes was a generous philanthropist, she knew, but she hadn't expected him to do something like this.

After catching up a bit more and hearing that the Delices' baby was on his way to full recovery, Joy hung up.

What had inspired Hayes to do that?

Should she tell him that she knew or let it slide?

Hearing him on the phone in the office next door, she marched inside without knocking. "Why'd you do it?"

Hayes sat behind the desk, his back rigid even in the comfortable-looking office chair.

He raised a brow in response. "Do what?"

"Pay off the NICU bills."

Telling whoever was on the phone that he'd call back, he disconnected the call and met her gaze with his serious one. "Ah. The hospital told you."

"Yes."

He shrugged. "It just didn't seem fair to me. And it's not like I can't afford it."

When he attempted to stride past her and out of the small room, she stepped into his path. "Wait. You also hired Mr. Delice."

"I did," he rapped out.

"Why?"

He gave her another shrug. "Had an opening with his exact skill set requirements."

On reflex, she laid her hand on his arm. "Hayes, you know that you just changed their lives, right?"

"Cal is waiting for you downstairs."

Slipping past her, he strode into their bedroom and grabbed her suitcase from the spot where she'd left it. Maybe he couldn't wait to be rid of her.

Clearly, he did not wish to discuss his good deed, but she couldn't help herself. "You pretend like you don't care about anyone, but you do. You have a good heart, Hayes."

He stopped before the stairs, spinning to face her. The sudden movement made her stumble back a step. Dropping the suitcase, he caught her before she fell flat on her butt, gripping her elbows as he pulled her into his body and planted his mouth on hers. Through the thin linen material of her long-sleeved shirt, she felt the outline of his bandages.

The kiss ended as abruptly as it began. When he released her, his hands lingered, holding her steady while she found her feet under her.

"Was that to distract me?" she asked, rueful.

Instead of responding, he took her suitcase downstairs.

# Chapter 40

Joy left.

Hayes hadn't stuck around to watch Cal's car disappear through the farm gates. He couldn't, or he'd chase her down like a codependent puppy.

He'd thought she loved him, but he'd misread the signals. What others could easily intuit was often difficult for him, but he'd never expected to be wrong about this. And yet, if Joy loved him, why wouldn't she say the words? Had he projected his feelings on her when she had felt nothing for him, just as he had with others before?

He was used to being alone. He liked the quiet and the solitude. Yet the idea of returning home without her hurt.

Worse than the mugging and the attack, worse than being left for dead in the cold, worse than the broken ribs and dislocated hip. He'd take that pain over this.

He'd offered her the world and she refused him.

What more could one do?

Maisie came to get him for breakfast, her gaze drowning in sympathy as she found him on the couch in the small office.

He refused the invitation, but she wouldn't take no for an answer, so he trudged after her.

In the kitchen, Kenna and Benjamin were setting the table. Why the fuck were they still there? The farm was no longer for sale. They should get on with their lives. Didn't they have coffee shops to run and stuttering kids to see?

"How you feeling?" asked Kenna.

He grunted.

Benjamin's follow-up question was just as stupid. "Joy leave for Edinburgh?"

Hayes grunted at him too.

Maisie hovered near him like a mama duck. "What's going to happen between the two of you?"

He shrugged. "She doesn't want anything to do with me. I tried."

Maisie squeezed his shoulder. "Did you tell her you love her?"

He hated the pity in Maisie's eyes. "She knows that."

The woman's face creased with concern. "But you didn't tell her?"

Had she dragged him down to be interrogated? Couldn't everyone just leave him alone and let him wallow in solitude? Even Malik gave him a look of compassion from his spot on the armchair.

"No, I didn't tell her. Wouldn't have mattered."

Kenna slammed the plate she was setting down on the table. "You didn't tell her you love her?

"*What?*" Benjamin exclaimed at the same time and let out a disapproving groan.

He scanned the three faces that stared at him in disbelief. Malik narrowed his eyes in judgment. What the hell kind of reaction was that from everyone?

"No. I told her she loves me."

Kenna's eyes bored into his. "You're an idiot."

What were they saying?

*Shit.* The misplaced pieces of the puzzle inched into place. He told her she loved him, but he never said the words to her.

"Wait. Do you *all* think it would have made a difference?"

"Yes!" All three shouted at once.

*Fuck.* "I—"

"How could you not tell her how you felt?" Maisie demanded, wide-eyed.

Out of nowhere, Kenna shoved him. "Hayes, what were you thinking?"

"Go fucking get her," said Benjamin.

Maisie already had her cell phone in hand. "I realized this morning that Cal forgot his phone, but I'll try Joy."

Saying the words over a telephone somehow felt wrong.

"You want me to tell her on the phone?" he clarified.

Kenna rolled her eyes. "Well, you didn't tell her in person."

"Darn, she's not picking up," said Maisie.

*Ah.* Hayes knew why. "She didn't hear your call. She set her phone on silent because I don't—I can't handle the phone buzzing."

The three exchanged a look again. It was starting to get annoying.

"You need to go to her hotel!" Maisie commanded. "Do you know where she is staying?"

No. He didn't know that. He doubted she'd return to the George.

Except… Joy had left much too early for a hotel.

Her flight back was tomorrow, and she had one place left to visit from her childhood trip.

After a brief stop upstairs, he grabbed his coat and ran to the McLaren. He knew exactly where to find her.

He drove fast, as fast as the winding roads would let him. He drove as it started to rain and drove when the sky cleared into a crisp blue.

She'd be at Culross.

There was no way she'd leave before taking a picture of the small town for Evie.

When he drove into the village, it really did feel like going back in time. He could only imagine what the experience had been like for Joy as a kid.

To his right, a stretch of green lawn gave way to the blue of Culross Harbor. To his left, behind a row of white-harled houses, he glimpsed the ochre walls of Culross Palace.

He didn't have time to admire the red-tiled roofs or the cobbled streets. He had his wife to find.

She'd be here. Somewhere.

Cal's car, parked just ahead, confirmed it.

Pulling up behind him, Hayes sprinted out, unsure which way to go.

Cal and Joy weren't seated in Cal's car, nor were they at the nearby playground. Maybe they were strolling the coastline. He sprinted across the lawn to the walking path that lined the harbor. Nope. Not here.

Where was the ice cream shop?

He hurtled back across the green in search of the ice cream parlor she'd mentioned.

That's when he saw them. They sat side by side on a bench outside a small store, ice creams in hand while Joy sobbed on Cal's shoulder.

He'd destroy whoever made her cry.

Hayes jogged across the street until he stood in front of them.

That's when they saw him.

Lifting her head from Cal's shoulder, Joy blinked as though she didn't believe he was there. "Hayes? What are you doing here?"

She'd asked him the same question when he had found her in her hotel room last Wednesday.

Discreetly, Cal rose. "I think I forgot something in the car."

When he slipped away, Hayes took his spot on the bench. "Who made you cry?"

She wiped at the tears trailing down her cheeks. "You did. You didn't mean it, but you did."

Fuck. He'd screwed this up bad. "Was it because I didn't tell you I love you?"

Her sad eyes held his. "Yes."

Pain sliced through him. "I fucked up. I assumed you knew."

"Well, I didn't. I suspected it. But then I thought maybe I misunderstood."

He'd made her doubt his feelings. If only he'd said the words yesterday…

Desperate to hold her, he laid his bandaged hand on her knee. "I love you, Joy. I'm an idiot for not saying it yesterday. I'm so hopelessly in love with you, I can't handle the pain. It hurts to know that I may wake up tomorrow in a world where you aren't my wife. Tell me what it'll take to make you happy, and I'll do it. You may have to spell it out for me sometimes—because I miss signals once in a while. But I swear to you on my life I love you and I'll do anything to make you happy."

Her hand covered his, the touch careful of his injuries. "You love me?"

"I do. It's like… you're this sinkhole in my heart, and I know it should terrify me but, instead, it makes me feel whole."

Her lips and eyebrows twisted. "Er… that's… romantic of you."

"Maybe that wasn't the best analogy. Let me try again. You're like… a flock of chickens that swooped in when I least expected to peck away at the straw walls of my—"

Hand clasped over her mouth, her sobs morphed into outright, hiccupping laughter. "Stop, I beg of you," she wheezed out.

"That didn't sound right. You're a river of honey and I'm standing in your sweet, sticky—"

He stopped when she doubled over, her shoulders shaking. When she straightened again, amusement danced in her eyes as she chortled. "You're killing me."

"Joy…" That vulnerability, that fear that he wasn't good enough to explain his feelings twisted at him. "You do know what I mean? I love you."

Her smile melted away all his doubts. "Yes, yes, I do. I love you too, Hayes. You're a… sinkhole in my heart too."

Juggling her cup of ice cream, she kissed him, her laughter reverberating through him.

Taking the ice cream from her, he set it to the ground at his feet. "I've planned out our whole future together. There was just one thing I forgot to do—to actually *tell* you about it."

"You did. Could you really move to San Diego? Uproot your life?"

"It's not uprooting. It's setting roots. I moved to Nevada when the nightclub needed oversight. It runs itself now. After what happened with Liselle, settling down terrified me. I'd look at Jackson, at Nate, and think—those fools. Fell for a pipe dream. It'll all fall apart soon enough. I felt sorry for them. But I was wrong. I want that with you. Only with you." He traced her tear-streaked cheek. "I didn't mean to make you cry."

"These are good tears," she assured him. Hesitation flooded her features. "My flight is tomorrow. I have to get back to work. Maybe, when you're—"

"I'll go with you. My trip here is done."

When she breathed out a sigh of relief, it warmed him from the inside out.

Her gaze drifted somewhere beyond him. "Should we go tell Cal? I think he's going to get a crick in his neck pretending not to be looking over here."

"Yes. But first…" From his pocket, he pulled out the rings he'd grabbed before his mad dash to Culross. "I can't imagine a world where you aren't my wife."

She stared. "Are you serious? Are you… proposing?"

"Yes. You can pick out our house, the city you want to live, but this is nonnegotiable. Joy Campbell, I love you. Will you make our sham marriage real?"

"Yes. This sounds crazy, but yes, I will."

Taking her trembling hand, he slipped the rings on her finger, where they belonged.

# Epilogue



*One year later*

Hail strafing the windows pulled Hayes from restful sleep. Dim morning light, diffused further by the layered storm clouds, struggled to fill the room. The perfect excuse to stay in bed.

Tightening his hold on his wife sleeping soundly in his arms, he threaded their fingers together, tracing the Celtic knots on her wedding band as he'd gotten used to doing the past year.

It had been a whirlwind twelve months. They held a small wedding ceremony on Highlander Honey Farm, at Cal and Maisie's insistence. After going back and forth on the neighborhood, they settled on a house close to Evie and Jackson, and right next to Joy's favorite surf spot. The beach-side home came with a yard, and he'd have her goldfish pond ready by springtime.

Both of them had demanding jobs—hers at the San Diego hospital, and his on the plane half the time, bouncing from Nevada to New York to Chicago. He hated the overnight trips, but returning home to her made the absences worth it.

It was Joy who surprised him with a last-minute trip to Highlander Honey Farm ahead of their one-year anniversary. The Blairs were in New York with their son and his family, and Joy and Hayes had the place all to themselves—with Malik there to supervise—for the next three weeks. They invited Evie and Jackson and their kids, Nate and Francesca and Francesca's siblings, Oliver, and Joy's parents to join them for the third week of their stay.

Hayes intended to make the most of their two weeks of privacy before the crowds descended.

They'd arrived last night, holing up in their old room even though they had free run of the entire house.

"Mmmm…" Joy murmured, snuggling closer as she stirred awake. "This is nice."

He sifted through the silk strands of her hair. "Have I told you how much I love you recently?"

Turning in his arms, she brought her smiling mouth to his. "Not since last night."

"How remiss of me, Mrs. Icefall." He rolled over her to kiss the spot under her ear that always made her shiver. "Good thing we have days and days of seclusion so I can show you exactly how much."

She arched her neck. "How do you want to start?"

"I have a few ideas." He nuzzled the pulse at the base of her throat.

Her beautiful eyes met his as she flashed him a brilliant smile. "I love your ideas."

Hayes reached for the jar of honey on the nightstand.

And kissed his wife.

# About the Author

Anya London resides in California. When she's not writing, she enjoys running, hiking, reading, and traveling.  Please contact her at www.anya-london.com.

# Also by Anya London

*A Very French Scandal*
*Once Upon a New York Summer*
*A Very Italian Scandal*
*A Very Scottish Scandal*